FIFTY-EIGHT MINUTES TO LONDON

BENNY GREEN

Fifty-Eight Minutes
to
London

MACGIBBON & KEE

First published 1969 by MacGibbon & Kee Ltd
3 Upper James Street Golden Square London W1
Copyright © Benny Green 1969
Printed in Great Britain by
Bristol Typesetting Co Ltd
Barton Manor, St Philips
Bristol

SBN 261 63160 8

CONTENTS

'Electric trains to London in 58 minutes'
Notice on Brighton Railway Station

PART ONE

The Syncopaters

1

Landau was working on the pier that summer. He sent me
a postcard the day he arrived, and a short note, more or
less indecipherable, later the same week, but on the morning
I caught the *Brighton Belle* there had been a silence of
more than a month. His address would have helped, but he
had forgotten to put it on either the card or the letter, and
I didn't feel inclined to write to him at the pier in case his
bosses had rules about that sort of thing. That was why
I planned to arrive around lunchtime. Landau always practised from eleven to two. I knew his routine better than he
did, an hour on the saxophone, an hour working on chords
at the piano, and then an hour improvising on the clarinet.
By the time I tracked him down he should be well into his
clarinet hour, which was a good thing. The clarinet always
put Landau in an expansive mood. When I reached the pier
I mentioned his name to the turnstile attendant, but he had
no idea what I was talking about.

'A tall boy with a slight stoop and no chin. You must
know him. He works in the band here.'

But he didn't, and it cost me threepence to pass. Although
it was early June the pier was deserted. The trippers had
slunk off in search of lunch, leaving behind the occasional
carcass sprawled in a deckchair, stunned by the heat. It
was the most oppressive day so far that summer. Under my
feet, through the wooden ribs of the deck, bottle-green water
slopped coolly against the piles.

Halfway along its own length, Landau's pier swells into
one of the most endearing architectural monstrosities in the
south of England, a bulbous growth which subsides back
into the normal lines of the pier as suddenly as it leaves
them. In those days it was the tea-room, fresh cream paint
outside, varnished walnut gloom inside. It was an octagonal
nightmare, and I remembered Landau's one and only letter,

with its surreal glimpses of the light music he played in there every afternoon. '. . . tea-dance . . . selections . . . Novello, I think . . . scrape away . . . no chicks . . . bad sound.' I peered through its windows. In its solitude the room looked grosser than ever, an imbecile set deserted by the players. For the moment it was hushed, but the high-domed wooden roof told me its acoustics would be impossible. Landau certainly wouldn't practise here if he could possibly help it.

I strolled on, practising breathing from the diaphragm as I went. One slow pace equals one crotchet, I told myself, and found that a lungful of air could be made to last at least four bars, which is as much as any sane orchestrator can ask. After nearly two choruses I reached the ballroom, which was about as far as you could go. Beyond were only the matted piles of the pier-end and a few amateur fishermen trying to tempt something on to their lines. In a disastrous attempt to enhance the ballroom's maritime flavour, the Corporation had broken out in a rash of crude impressionism. In the centre of the roofless dance floor, balanced against the sky by iron hawsers, loomed a huge inane ship's mast, festooned with a riot of nameless flags. All the windows masqueraded as portholes, and at intervals along the stunted wooden wall bordering the arena were clumsy murals of disproportionate sailors being gallant to watery young girls in flowing pre-war dresses. At the far end, segregated from the anglers only by a hardboard screen, was a small concrete bandstand with a tin roof. Its acoustics must have been worse than those of the tea-room.

I pushed through a white wicket gate leading on to the dance floor. There was no sign of Landau or anyone else. My heels clicked martially on the bleached timbers, underlining my role of intruder. But the bandstand itself looked familiar enough. I flicked through a pile of music lying on top of the piano. The paper was damp and beginning to rot from constant exposure to the sea air. Landau had told me that this band had been playing on the pier for the past twelve summers, and it seemed he wasn't exaggerating. Some of this music was twenty years old. The moment I felt the printed sheets under my fingers I could hear what this band sounded like. Landau thought it was a very good band, but then he had never been much of a judge. He was always inclined to be more than charitable towards anyone who employed him, although to be fair, his verdict had been announced in the first few days, before the novelty of working regularly had begun to wear off. I could tell where his place was on the bandstand. Right at the end of the line was a music desk strewn with soiled paper handkerchiefs, boxes of throat lozenges, empty matchboxes and blunt pencils. On the floor between the desk and his chair a dozen cigarette butts had been ground into the wood, leaving dark brown blotches on the honey-coloured planks. Landau could create a little slum of his own in almost no time at all, with what he referred to, quite seriously, as the little necessities of life.

I jumped back on to the ballroom floor and looked around. Either Landau had found a boarding house where they let you practise, or he had surrendered to the weather and gone off to acquire a tan. I knew he had to report for the afternoon session by four o'clock, so I decided to wait on the pier. I strolled back past the tea-room and selected a deckchair shaded by the overhanging eaves of some kind of roof-garden. On it someone had left a copy of the *Daily Telegraph*, but almost before I had started to read, a girl emerged from the door of a small white-painted kiosk and stood on the threshold smoking through a long mother-of-pearl cigarette holder. On the side of the kiosk, painted in ornate red lettering, were the words, 'Madame Vivienne, Occultiste'. It occurred to me that I had been wasting my time with the turnstile attendant. I should have looked for the nearest girl. This one looked vaguely Jewish, which was unpromising. Landau had a deep distaste for girls with the necessary religious qualifications for marriage. She was tall and slim, which was better. Landau fancied himself as a connoisseur of the female form. And she looked straight at me, which was excellent. Bold women fascinated him, the bolder the better. I nodded and called out, 'I'm trying to find a musician.'

'Aren't we all, darling,' and she disappeared inside the kiosk. Her voice was low and resonant. Landau would have called it sexy, but probably it was just part of her professional equipment. Soon she reappeared holding a large photograph. She sauntered across, sat next to me and stretched her legs with a sigh of relief. I took the photograph. It was identical to a thousand others, as much a prototype of its kind as the bandstand and the tattered bundles of music. Seven musicians in bow ties and white shirts pretending to play. Only the leader wore a jacket. Wine-coloured, probably. The photograph must have been taken on a hot day. Landau's employer stood leaning against the piano, pointing a trumpet at the camera with painful optimism. Next to him was a music stand with a purple drape announcing 'Van Rhodes and the Modernaires'. Landau sat at the extreme left, smiling an asinine smile, a clarinet across his lap, a saxophone to his lips. He looked the freshest of the bunch, the only one in the photo who didn't seem to be suffering from arthritis.

'That's him,' I pointed.

She laughed. 'It would be.'

'You know him?'

'He tried to make me the first day he was here.'

'Naturally.'

She drew in her legs and rattled the cigarette holder against her front teeth.

'After that, I tried to get him to let me read his palm, to see whether it was worth his while trying again.'

'You're Madame Vivienne?'

'Want your palm read? For you, seven and sixpence.'

'I already know my future. Use your powers and tell me where he is.'

'Well, when he first arrived, he used to come here about eleven every morning. Then when the hot weather came he stopped coming. I bet you he's down there somewhere,' and she waved the cigarette holder airily down at the beach.

There was a short silence while I considered the position. She glanced at me. Landau would have called it a lecherous look, but I think she was just curious.

'Was he expecting you?'

'I shouldn't think so. Landau never expects anything.'

I could feel her examining me, and stared up at the clouds, drifting past like floats in a pageant. I wondered whether Landau really had tried to make her. On the first day, perhaps, when everything still looked strange enough to be promising. If not then, probably not at all.

' You a musician?'

' Saxophone. Same as him.' I pointed at Landau's grinning face. Already I was beginning to get a discouraging sense of his new routine down here, a different address, a new sky-line, new girls, a novel routine in the salt air of an unfamiliar town. The last time I had seen him was in another world which knew nothing of Madame Vivienne, Occultiste, or Van Rhodes and his Modernaires. Victoria Station had been a confusion of milling bodies with the Brighton train the focus of the panic. When Landau extended his arm from the car-riage window and gripped my own, he had done it with the air of a great explorer poised on the brink of mysterious spiritual hinterlands. Down at the far end of the platform, where the station roof abruptly ended, the gloom of the giant shed was cut off by a thick slab of golden evening sunlight, as though the last remnants of the day were departing on Landau's train. Around us swirled animated commuter-Lon-don, fighting for seats, glancing apprehensively at the station clocks, shoving around the bookstalls, bundling into the bars for the last quick one of the day. When the train began to slip away, Landau had an afterthought. Sticking his head out of the carriage window he shouted what might have been, ' Don't worry. I'll put you in it.' I watched the train snake lazily towards the river and out of sight.

Only a month ago, but no doubt in that time Landau had discovered a whole universe of new people. He was always discovering new people wherever he went. The band would be full of geniuses. All the girls would be ravishing beauties. The meals he ate on seafront cafés would taste better than anything you could get at the Savoy Grill. I never knew whether it was a vice or a virtue, this tendency of his to mistake something unfamiliar for something wonder-ful. Once, after playing a dance at the Northumberland Hotel, where we had both drunk too much, Landau had staggered out into the empty streets at two o'clock in the morning and tried to take the credit for Landseer's avuncular parodies of Victorian lions. He was like that. It wasn't so much conceit as a naïve delight in the discovery that there were other people in the world besides himself. Everything

15

and everybody was a masterpiece till proven mediocre.

I had told him on the night of the lions, 'You're just like Arnold Bennett's hypothetical novelist. You see everything like a child or an imbecile.'

'And you only see them through books.'

The worst of it was that I, being an old acquaintance, was relegated to the commonplace. I thanked Madame Vivienne and rose from the deckchair.

'What shall I say if I see him?' she asked, not in the least interested.

'Don't bother. I'll probably find him long before you do.'

I left her sprawled in the chair. As I turned the corner of the pier deck I looked back and waved. She flopped a hand at me and grinned.

There was still more than an hour to go before the tea-dance began. There were no other musicians I knew in the town, the pubs were closed and it was too hot to eat, so I chose another deckchair a few yards from the exit turnstiles and began to read my newspaper. I must have fallen asleep almost immediately, drifting into a disturbing dream in which I mislaid my instrument a few moments before the start of an historic recording. I had the feeling that Landau knew where it was but for reasons best known to himself was unwilling to help. The recording began and sounded disastrous. The orchestra was out of tune and the internal balance appalling. It was almost impossible to distinguish the melody. And I, who might have saved the day, was unable to contribute so much as a single note. The band in my dream, aware of its own shortcomings, tried to cover up by playing progressively louder, until I felt I had to protest. I tried to shout something and awoke strained forward in the deckchair. The awful band was still playing. Its music blared out from a loudspeaker no more than two feet above my head. The entire pier had been wired for sound, so that whether you stood by the turnstiles at the start of the pier, or with the fishermen at the end of it, you were obliged to listen.

I sat back, wiped the sweat from my forehead and studied the noise that had awoken me. It was a transposition into actuality of those tired sheets of manuscript I had thumbed through earlier that day on the bandstand. The tunes were

relics from some forgotten pre-war hit parade, and the interpretation a kind of mincing parody of what the composers
had intended. So intrigued was I by the possibilities of this
monstrous band that it had played right through a 'White
Horse Inn' medley before I noticed that the clarinet voice
was missing. I waited for the next item in the recital to
make sure. A few bars of 'The Jolson Medley' told me that
the three-man saxophone section had indeed been reduced
for some reason to two and that it was almost certainly
Landau's voice that was missing.

I walked back to the tea-room, handed sixpence to a vine-
gary young girl seated at a small tin table just inside the
door, and passed among the tables towards the bandstand.
The room was clamorous with crockery and small-talk. The
chair on the extreme right of the bandstand was empty. At
the final chord of 'Toot-Toot Tootsie' there was a feeble
patter of applause. Van Rhodes smiled with professional
unction, bowed jerkily and laid his trumpet on the piano.
He leaned across to the drummer and said something, spin-
ning round obligingly when I spoke. He must have thought
it was a request, but once he sized me up the obsequious smile
died before establishing itself.

'Excuse me, but I'm looking for Landau. Does he work
here?'

I had been right about the wine-coloured jacket, but kicked
myself for not having also deduced the signet ring and the
clip-on bow tie.

He turned to the other musicians. 'Here boys, there's
another one who's looking for Landau.'

His employees dutifully laughed, and he turned back to me.

'You a friend of his?'

I nodded.

'So was I till this afternoon.'

He tore a sheet from a tiny notebook, scribbled hastily
and handed me the paper.

'This is where he's staying. If you manage to get him
out of bed, tell him he's on a week's notice.'

'Righto, captain.'

'And get yourself a better friend.'

He dismissed me with his back and began thumbing

through his music. I walked back among the tables. A few people watched me curiously as I passed them. Van Rhodes had a loud voice. Half the people there must have heard our conversation. I was tempted to go back to the bandstand to ask for directions, but while I was considering the point, more music began leaking out of the band. It sounded vaguely like Ivor Novello, but the bad intonation coupled with the missing voice created a virtually impenetrable disguise. The man at the turnstile examined my piece of paper and told me where to look.

Landau was living up in the cheap shopping district, in a boarding house that looked as though it had once known better days. I took it for the once spacious house of a family reduced by circumstances into letting. Hemmed in by a fish shop on one side and a threepenny library on the other, its only outward mark of distinction was the false front which concealed from the passer-by the fact that it lay back from the main road. Between the sham entrance and the real front door stretched a narrow stone courtyard open to the sky. The peeling walls were badly in need of a fresh coat of whitewash. I found myself ready to believe that things might happen in that courtyard far more sinister than anything on the shelves of the library beyond its left wall, far bloodier than the innocent dissections beyond its right. The courtyard was a suggestive *al fresco* interlude between the private and the communal quite belying the dull decrepitude of the house it linked with the street outside.

Before I rang the bell I tried to conjure up a portrait of the woman who would answer it. Surely Landau had found himself a landlady with sex appeal, somebody specialising in footloose gentleman boarders? But then I had vague recollections of a story Landau had told me about his mother insisting on coming to the coast with him and vetting each boarding house before granting her seal of approval. On recalling this fact, my imaginary landlady instantly aged thirty years, declined from an hourglass vision to a pinafored amorphous mass with a face like an old map. It wasn't very accurate, but it was a lot closer to home than my first attempt. The way I was received suggested that since his arrival here a month ago Landau had inspired a stream of wild eccentric callers. The woman who opened the door looked me up and down with tired eyes and at the mention of Landau's name ushered me in.

'You can wait in his room if you like. All the others do. Only I can't say when he'll be back. Doesn't he work in the afternoons?'

Landau's room was on the first floor at the back of the house. From the great bay window facing the door you could just catch a glimpse of the sea sparkling away beyond the vista of Edwardian façades. My hostess hovered with her hand on the doorknob for a moment, reassuring herself about me.

'It's my best room,' she said, and was gone.

Landau was never the man to bother with refinements. The room bore no indication that he ever intended doing anything more than pass through from time to time, and was obviously no more than a base from which to conduct operations. His hairbrush and shaving cream had the mantelpiece to themselves, and hanging over a chair at the open window, twitching in the sea breeze, was a turquoise windcheater he had evidently tried to wash all by himself. A packet of soap powder lay on its side at the foot of the chair, the white dust of its contents scattered like stardust on the carpet. On the table by the unmade bed lay a few magazines and newspapers, and on the dressing-table was a stick of sealing wax, a fourpenny bottle of ink, some cheap notepaper and an unopened tin of black shoe polish. Clipped on to the frame of the dressing-table mirror was a blurred snapshot of a tall brunette in a swimsuit. Only one snapshot in four weeks. Landau must be slipping. The only indication that the occupant of this room was, by his own definition, an artist, I found on the chest of drawers hiding behind the door. On its top lay a copy of the *Klose* Clarinet tutor, mint condition the neglected symbol of nameless aspirations that had come welling up in Landau's breast on the day he knew he had been engaged for his first professional season. It had been a great stroke of fortune, and the tutor had been his expansive gesture to show he meant to capitalise on his luck. In twenty weeks by the sea, he calculated, he could practise a minimum of 420 hours, by which time he could return home armed with a technique so infallible that never again would he have to worry about finding work. This season was to be the rock on which all his future fortunes would rest.

I stretched myself out on the bed and flicked through the magazines, wondering what it was that stopped me from taking Landau's schema seriously. All the facts were on his side. In twenty weeks he really could practise all those hours, and there was no doubt that if he did, he would come home a far finer musician. It was not his arithmetic that was faulty but his temperament. It was too much like mine not to run haywire the moment it was faced with the prospect of unlimited freedom. Why, for instance, had Landau absented himself from the tea-dance? Was that too part of the plan? A year ago, six months, three, Landau would have died rather than fail to fulfil an engagement. Still, perhaps, he felt that this kind of default was all part of being a true professional. Perhaps he was right?

My sleep, dreamless this time, was interrupted by the bells of a nearby church. I glanced round the room. Nobody had been there since my arrival. Advancing shadows had already reached the foot of the bed, and the church bells must have struck at least eight times. I rinsed my face in the sink in the corner next to the window, combed my hair and walked downstairs, shutting the door behind me as gently as possible. There seemed no point in leaving a note, because Landau evidently had no intention of coming back now until the end of the evening's work. He must have been waylaid somewhere and gone straight down to the ballroom. There was no sound of life in the house, so I slipped into the courtyard, closed the front door and walked back towards the pier.

By the time I arrived there the evening's dancing was well under way. Fifty couples shambled round under the deepening blue of the night sky, while Van Rhodes and the Modernaires innocently polluted the air with 'The Way You Look Tonight' at the regulation forty-eight bars to the minute. At first my view of the bandstand was obscured by the swirling mass grimly trying to get the holiday spirit, but as I edged round the rim of the ballroom I saw that the saxophone section was still one man short. It was now half past eight and still Landau had not arrived. I sat down on one of the worn wooden benches bordering the floor and decided to wait on events. It was not until twenty past nine that the clustered dancers dispersed to make way for a tall young man striding doggedly towards the bandstand with a hunted look in his eyes. I knew that expression well. It was Landau at his very extremities, back to the wall, fighting for his life. Under his left arm was tucked a black leather clarinet case, and as he walked he fumbled with the wings of his shirt collar, trying to adjust a drunken-looking bow tie. He walked to within a few paces of me without making any acknowledgement, but I doubt whether at that moment he could have seen anything but the looming bulk of the bandstand. Without slowing down he vaulted on to the tiny stage, marched to his place at the end of the line, and began burrowing under his music desk, assembling his instruments as fast as he could. He had just lifted the clarinet to his lips when Van Rhodes, who had been watching this performance with black hatred in his eyes, placed his trumpet on the piano, nodded to the pianist to take over the mangled remains of whatever it was that the band was in the process of murdering, and went over to Landau's chair. He stood over him, blanketing the defaulter from my view, waving his arms in a mad parody of his own conducting technique. Landau must then have said something to him, because the arms wilted, the stance melted into something less belligerent, and the head inclined forward as though it were intimacies and not insults the two men were exchanging. At the end of the song and a titter of applause, they went on talking for several minutes, before Rhodes actually put his arm round Landau's shoulders and shook him by the hand before returning to his place at the head of affairs.

This was obviously a kind of professionalism I had never dreamed of. How do you tame an angry employer as quickly as that? One and a half choruses of a regulation quickstep and Van Rhodes had been transformed from an outraged maestro to a father-figure. It seemed that there were after all more things to being a professional musician than just blowing an instrument. I tried to catch Landau's eye after that, but he was so intent on giving a good if belated performance that he hardly looked up once before the interval. I intercepted him on his way to the bar, and he seemed confused rather than pleased by my sudden apparition.

'Tom, what are you doing here?'

'Nothing special. I wanted to talk to you about something, but it can wait.'

'Come on, let's go get a drink. I need it, I can tell you.'

In his four weeks he had taken good care to establish diplomatic relations with the barmaids, and it was not long before we were sitting in the corner of the crowded bar sipping free beer. Landau drank half a pint in one gulp, banged his glass on the table and lit a cigarette.

'Phew, what a day.'

'What happened to you? I've been hanging around since lunchtime?'

'It's ridiculous really. I met this nurse, see. The hospital's about eight miles the other side of town. She gave me her word she'd drive me back here in time for the tea session. So what happens? The car breaks down, no garage, no phone for miles. So we just sit there on the downs for three hours trying to thumb a lift.'

'Is she with you?'

'Her? The last time I saw her she was still sitting on the downs. She can stay there for all I care. There was only room for one in the lorry.'

'Is that what you told Rhodes?'

Landau laughed and then said, in the tone he reserved for those occasions when he pretended to be appalled by his own ruthlessness, 'Here, you know what I told him? I said I got a wire saying my old man had a heart attack and was asking for me.'

'That's nice.'

'The way I look at it is this. My old man's always saying he's about to have a heart attack. Maybe he really will one day. And if he did, he'd be sure to ask for me, right? And how about all the attacks he has had that I've never said anything to Rhodes about? How about that one last Easter, answer me that?'

'But you didn't know Rhodes then.'

'Course I didn't. What's that got to do with it?'

He laughed again and finished his beer.

'I tell you, Tom, when you're dealing with these bastards you have to fight them with their own weapons.'

It occurred to him that I had still not accounted for my presence.

'How long you here for? Got anywhere to stay?'

'That depends on you.'

'How, Tom?'

'I'm six payments behind on my horn. I got seven days to raise some money, you're the only one I know who's working, so I thought . . .'

'Listen, Tom, I'm up to the ears in debt myself. I owe Rhodes, I owe my old lady the rent at the digs, and there's a tailor in this town who's given me a new dress suit on tick. It's out of the question, Tom. Sorry.'

'Well, in that case I might as well go back to town and see what I can do there.'

'Look, you need a job, not a loan.'

I said nothing. Landau was rising to the bait after all. I was counting on his resource, not for the first time.

'I tell you what,' he said, pondering deeply. 'You stick around for a bit and I'll see what I can do. You can bed down in my room. The old girl won't mind.'

'How long?'

'Give me twenty-four hours. There's a few bandleaders in this town who are bound to be stuck by now.'

'How do you mean, stuck?'

'One thing I've learned about this season business is that there's a big turnover. Fellows giving in their notice and switching jobs all the time. Hey, I wouldn't be surprised if the Arcadia's not the best bet. You leave it to me. Listen, wait for me by the bandstand when we finish tonight, will you? There might be a couple of chicks in.'

'What's mine like?'

'Actually, yours is the best looking one, only she doesn't want to know about me. You'll like her.'

Landau always delivered this little speech whenever the girl he had his eye on happened to be chaperoned by a particularly repulsive friend, but I let it ride. As it happened we went back to the boarding house at Kemptown alone that night. I slept in a camp bed under the window in Landau's room. The next evening, before he went to work, Landau took a walk down to the Arcadia, alone. Two days later I was playing the tenor saxophone there in Bertie Fields' Noveltones.

2

OVER THE front entrance of the Arcadia Ballroom hung a giant hoarding whose fraudulent contents gave it a neat congruity with everything else about the place. 'The South Coast's Most Unique Ballroom', the hoarding boasted, baldly ignoring the fact that not only was the Arcadia not unique, but that uniqueness was the very last thing its proprietors desired. Had the directors of Happiness Dancing Ltd really believed that there was anything different about the Arcadia, half of them would have shot themselves while the other half busied themselves in firing managers, suing architects and interior decorators, purging musicians and generally conducting themselves as entrepreneurs of mass entertainers usually do. For of all the crimes it was possible to commit while taking wages from Happiness Dancing Ltd, uniqueness was the most heinous. The Arcadia was one of fourteen company ballrooms dotted across the country like pimples on the face of the body politic, and the working rule for the administration of these lugubrious fun-palaces was simple to the point of imbecility and far beyond it. The aim was to make each of these establishments identical in every detail to all the others, so that no matter where the dedicated dancer might find himself, he could step across a Happiness threshold and find the reassurance of familiar surroundings.

The Arcadia at Brighton could have been the Paradise in Manchester, or the Dreamland Gardens in Birmingham or the Romantic at Bristol. Once inside it was all the same, from the plastic teacups and the gilt-painted wicker chairs to the unperforated paper in the gentleman's lavatory and the alternating crimson and yellow lights girdling the hall round the lower rim of the balcony. After many years of diligent research, Happiness had succeeded in doing what no architect or regional planner or statesman had ever done. It had contrived to make one town exactly like the next, right down to the musk on the band-room floor, which no connoisseur of domestic smells could ever have mistaken for anything but authentic Happiness musk.

But having changed the course of social history in this way, the directors of the company soon found that life was not quite as simple as all that. They may have achieved uniformity of shape, size, smell and light in selling music, but how were they to achieve its concomitant, uniformity of the men hired to play it? Although the shareholders found the proposition abhorrent, there was no doubt that at least for purposes of economic argument, musicians were human beings, and therefore prone to all the quirks of anarchic behaviour that the artist delights in when confronted by the monolith of a vast corporation. Every Happiness ballroom housed two bands, and every Happiness band was composed of anything from four to fourteen musicians. How to make this army of sullen discontents as characteristic as the lavatory paper and the teacups? The resource with which Happiness approached this frightful problem was wholly praiseworthy, unless of course you happened to be part of the army.

The Happiness System is best described as the Iron Fist in the Iron Glove. For one thing, there was no nonsense about musicians being treated as creative artists, a decadent view which went out with the Renaissance. In the early days of the company's life, when there were a mere seven ballrooms in the bag, Happiness was quick to realise that there were in Britain more aspiring musicians than there were jobs to keep them alive. And so Happiness rates of pay were adjusted accordingly and its musicians allotted an indeterminate status wavering uneasily between that of kitchen hand and cleaning staff. The company also broke new ground in another direction. Most corporations are in no hurry to reward their employees. Not so Happiness. Instead of being presented with a watch at the end of his time, the musician was presented with a book of rules at the beginning of it, and was well advised to cherish it, partly because it was the only thing Happiness was ever likely to give him for nothing, but mainly because of its elaborate system of fines for serious offences against the company code, such as talking to customers, failing to address the ballroom manager as 'Sir', and arriving on the bandstand with untied shoelaces.

Having thus created a dangerous unity of discontent among the serfs, the next problem facing Happiness was how to divide allegiances, and this was done simply by making each bandleader liable for half the fines his musicians incurred. There were further refinements. As Happiness owned several ballrooms it was possible for the grand masters at head office to move bandleaders around like pawns on a chessboard, with the promise of a London engagement shining golden over the heads of all. Working for the company for any length of time became an insane game of musical snakes and ladders, where the zealous bandleader working 130 miles from the capital found himself rewarded for five years of abject lickspittling by being transferred to a ballroom only 125 miles out. The fact that the Arcadia was only fifty miles from London placed it very high in the company league, and I might have been justified in expecting a bandleader who was a cross between an unbalanced martinet with his eyes on the hinterlands of Charing Cross Road and a gibbering wreck whose blood pressure soared ever higher with each waltz medley.

However, no system is foolproof, not even the Happiness System, and it was instructive to observe the way in which this curious method of promotion, so beautifully logical in theory, had collapsed totally in practice. In fact its failure was symbolic of the entire Happiness organisation. For all that company's meticulous plugging of holes through which manifestations of the artistic spirit might seep, for all the precautions so painstakingly evolved to induce humans to behave like robots, something had undeniably happened, or had not happened, to halt the rise of Happiness to the heights. That something was nebulous certainly. It was nothing you could put your finger on, nothing which showed in the annual balance sheets or the insane pirouettings of its patrons, but it surely existed. The Happiness family of ballrooms had ceased propagating once its number reached fourteen, and drifted along now like a marriage afflicted by impotence. While the larger, more powerful combines grew larger yet, Happiness lagged further and further behind, until by the time I came to work at the Arcadia it could hardly be said to be entered in the race at all.

The deadly flaw at the heart of the Happiness promotion system was that its planners in their provincialism had overlooked the fact that everybody might not want to come to London. The Arcadia's maestro, Bertie Fields, had lived on the coast all his life, and having over the years acquired ownership of several lucrative domestic properties by the simple expedient of marrying an ugly woman who was richer than he was, was the only leader on the entire circuit who had no desire to be moved further up the league table. This meant that the Noveltones were a cautious, unambitious bunch who never once captured the Quarterly Efficiency Cup, or ever won honourable mention in the Annual Attendance Competition. Fines were rarely invoked and the rule book almost never referred to, and had it not been for the giant fallacy lying at the heart of my position with them, life in the Noveltones would have been dull but safe.

The contradiction lay in the fact that Happiness wanted uniformity and yet from time to time could not help employing people like myself whose only interest was in jazz, the least predictable of all music. It was possible to get yourself thrown out of Happiness for life by playing just one improvised chorus, and but for the convenient fact that none of the Happiness ballroom managers knew what improvisation was, many more of my musician friends would have been out of work than actually were. Fields was philosophic about it.

'Your friend Landau tells me you're a talented jazz player, but I'm going to give you the job all the same. Only use your loaf. Crawford, he's the new manager here this season, he never comes in much before nine, so if you want to blow something, make sure you do it before then. Once he's in, you go faceless, understand?'

I assured him his words had been noted, but I doubt whether I had much idea what he was talking about. The truth was that I seemed to be suffering some kind of temporary brainstorm. Although less demonstrative about it than Landau, I was just as overwhelmed as he had been by the first brush with professionalism, and if Fields had told me that at nine o'clock each night all the patients turned into dromedaries, I would have given him the same glassy-eyed nod. The shock of working in a real ballroom had increased the emotional intensity of life so dramatically that I could only assume that everyone else must be aware of this change. These mysterious beings who came into the Arcadia every evening, where did they come from and what were they up to? Surely they did not belong to the same species as those I had been mixing with all my life? Surely they were not subject to the same physical laws as the customers at week-end dances in suburban municipal halls? Did they go to work in the day, this shadowy band of swirling sophisticates, or were they part of that vast conspiracy I had sensed the moment I stepped off the London train, of a whole town smirking complacently about a recent past which it knew I had played no part in? I found it impossible to believe that anyone who bought a ticket for the Arcadia actually went to work in the day or busied himself with the same mundane chores as the rest of us. I saw them as privileged people kept in cold storage by Terpsichore until it was time for them to dance each evening. I came to know the regular faces as intimately as my own mental portraits of Edmund Dantes, Artie Kipps, Mr Micawber, Sherlock Holmes and Rudolph Rassendyll, and built around them stories just as preposterous. The man who sat alone on the balcony each night without ever removing his snap-brim trilby; obviously he was bald and had an obscene birthmark on his skull. That middle-aged couple, primped and suntanned, who danced all the tangos, they might easily be using the imbecile intricacies of their home-made choreography to pass messages. That glamorous lady in black who sipped gin, smiled to herself and only accepted partners for the last two or three dances, looked to me very much like a private investigator. Then there was the boy with the broken nose who only showed up on rainy nights. A famous prizefighter perhaps, about to defend his title in the open air and who came in when the fight had been rained off. And surely the whole bunch of them were interlocking pieces in a vast super-plot which used music and dancing only as a camouflage?

It was this kind of morbid preoccupation with the customers that reduced me to mumbling idiocy for my first two or three weeks at the Arcadia. Fields told me I was morose and that it was worse than death to be morose in a profession where a smiling face counted for more than all the technical ability in the world. The girls who smiled at me as they swayed past found themselves rebuffed by what must have seemed to them like the suspicious stare of a professional spy. The blonde who worked in the restaurant next door tried night after night to catch my eye without success, and being a girl of some resource, found out that Landau was my running mate and went to him with the problem. Landau was most distressed.

I was reading the papers in bed one morning when he came in and with a martyr's sigh, sat himself on my feet.

'Listen, this chick came up to me last night. She reckons you're either queer or blind. What's the matter with you, Tom? You're getting yourself a bad name.'

'What's she look like?'

'Tall, slim, nice face, blonde, moves well. Very sexy, I should say. She reckons she's been showing out to you every night, and you just look straight through her. That true?'

'It's a funny thing,' I said, putting the paper down, 'it's something about that place. I don't seem to function properly in there . . . I don't know really . . . I think it must be the shock of working regularly or something. All those people. They seem like strangers.'

'Of course they seem like strangers, because that's what they are. You can't expect to know everybody.'

'No, not strangers exactly. It's just that they all seem strange.'

'Well, I don't know. This blonde looked normal enough. I don't get it.'

'Well, put it this way. When you first went to work down here, at the start of the season, didn't you feel there was something peculiar about the people down here? I mean, didn't they seem different from any other people you'd seen before?'

Landau gave me a long, stern look. 'Why should they be different?'

'I don't know why. It's just that I'm surprised that the audience should stay the same when we've changed so much.

There's professional musicians, so I keep getting this feeling that there must be professional audiences to dance to them.'

'Look, a blonde is a blonde, especially when she starts showing out.'

'I know. But I don't seem to be able to get adjusted yet. I mean, I bet you if I saw this girl you're telling me about, if I saw her in London or in the street or Tottenham Baths or something, it would all be different.'

'Sometimes,' said Landau, giving himself all the best of it, 'I just don't understand you.'

'And I'll tell you something else. It's affected my playing too. I can't do myself justice down there.'

'You're really in a bad way. You can't see chicks and you can't play the saxophone. What's left?'

'Maybe it's just a passing phase. It's bound to wear off soon.'

'All you have to do is behave as though the Arcadia is just another dump, which it is.'

'It's no good. It won't work. I tried pretending it was a town hall on a Saturday night, but the tans were a give-away.'

'Then I'll have to help you.'

'How?'

'I don't know, but there must be something I can do. I mean, I got you the job, so it shouldn't be hard for me to figure a way how you can hold on to it.'

'You mean break the spell?'

'Right. Shrink all these people down to size. This is very important to us, Tom. It's all part of being a real professional. Not just working regularly, but behaving as if we do, so that next time we get a job, we know how to carry it off. I ask you, what's the good of working if it makes chicks think you're a blind queer?'

From that moment Landau put his mind to the problem of how to bring the Arcadia down to reality for me. He treated me as an invalid who relied on him for a cure, but although I was grateful for his moral support, he was not entirely justified in regarding me as a man whose brain has snapped. What had happened was that, indulging in my old

31

habit of looking for method in everything, I had been simply unable to accept the awful truth that surface appearances at the Arcadia were an accurate indication of reality. The sheer inanity of the cycle of shuffle and stop, shuffle and stop, all conducted against the satanic background of those crimson and canary lights, numbed my senses, and in desperation I looked, and looked too hard, for more subtle justification of the charade in which I was being paid to play my part. It occurred to me that as an aspiring professional I was dooming myself for ever to this stale, witless environment, and almost before my career had begun I was subconsciously resolving to find a way to end it. In the meantime, I was diverted by the not entirely comforting thought that Landau intended to do something about it.

But while he was still considering the problem, something else happened which brought the Arcadia back with a jolt to the world of banalities and put paid for ever to my rash of ballroom romanticism. It was about half past ten on a Friday night. The hall was uncomfortably full. All my regulars were there except the man who came in when it rained, which told me I was cooped up in this cage while fine weather flattered the free souls outside. All the girls seemed deeply tanned and all the men deeply attractive to the girls who were deeply tanned. There was not a face I knew in that swirling mass, not one single scrap of evidence to refute my persistent conviction that I was virtually invisible. Like the postman in Father Brown I was reduced to the status of an insignificant piece of furniture. Even when it was time for our interval and we trooped over to our table by the snack bar for our nightly ration of watery coffee in plastic cups at the specially reduced rate of sixpence a cup, I found it impossible to identify with anything going on around me. I sat at the band table and sipped the coffee with a kind of detached disgust at the taste. Around me the other musicians were chatting amiably, but I heard nothing they said. And then, in one moment, the spell of mystery and romance was broken for ever. Through the knots of dancers clustered on the floor waiting for the relief band to start playing, there burst a small, scruffy young man who might have been in need of a shave but who might just as conceivably have embarked on the task of growing a beard. He wore a creased blue serge suit and brown shoes with thick crêpe soles. He waddled rather than walked with his feet splayed out, and on his childlike face was that expression he always wore when he was not quite sure whether he had overstepped the bounds of friendship. Landau had been puzzling for a mundane counter to the spell of the Arcadia, but as I glanced up and spotted the young man walking towards me, his bulbous nose reflecting the crimson and yellow lights like a beacon in the night, I knew that no further research was required on Landau's part or anyone else's. What more potent proof of the fact that nothing had changed than Emanuel Blitski?

It was some time before he spotted me, so I had the chance to retain my invisibility for one last sweet moment. Blitski was hopelessly out of place in a dance hall. As a matter of fact he was hopelessly out of place almost anywhere. That man had the greatest gift for sheer incongruity I have ever come across. Take him out of his mother's kitchen in that steamy flat behind Euston Station, and he looked like a lovable but unfortunate error. The day I caught the *Brighton Belle* I had told him where I was going and why. The fact that he had not heard from me since must have told him that somehow I had managed to find a job down here. There were only three main ballrooms in the town, and the other two had photographs of the band in the foyer. It must have been easy, even for Blitski's devious brain, to deduce where I must be. He bumped into a couple just about to launch themselves on a quickstep, apologised, stepped back and walked straight into another couple. One of my fellow-workers turned round and said, ' Hello, I think there's a punchup.'

' No it's not,' I told him. ' It's only Blitski.'

While he was tripping and stumbling out of the arena, filled now with sidling couples, he caught my eye. He nodded uncertainly and half-waved. Before I could stop him he had navigated the last few yards between us and taken his place at our table.

' Hi.'

' You've just cost me half a crown.'

He went white, as he always did whenever anyone mentioned money to him.

'Who, me?'

'It's against company rules for a musician to talk to a customer. I'm a musician, you're a customer. You just spoke to me, didn't you?'

'Well, yes . . .'

'There you go again. That's another half-crown.'

He looked so terrified that I could not help laughing.

'It's all right. Nothing is done properly in this hole, not even the enforcing of the rules. Talk as much as you want. What are you doing here anyway?'

'It was a coincidence. You being down here. I guessed you were working somewhere, and then there's this meeting here tomorrow . . .'

'What meeting is that?'

Even as I asked the question I had an acute attack of the horrors. Blitski was the one person I knew who could boast political commitment, although perhaps that is the wrong phrase to use in reference to his burning faith that one day, in our lifetime, the redistribution of wealth would have made life so equitable that new theatres would have to be built consisting entirely of front row stalls. Having observed his own refreshing lack of desire for money, Blitski had deduced that Man must therefore be fundamentally good, and that it was only the System which turned him into a monster. Change the System and you changed Man. Once the economics of Capitalism were converted into the economics of Mutual Love, existence would overnight resolve itself into a dilettante's idyll. According to Blitski, at the moment the world was a place where artists were treated like dustmen. When his Utopia was established, dustmen would be treated like artists, and as Blitski's knowledge of both these groups was inclined to be vague, none of us bothered to argue with him. He was perfectly harmless, and although his indomitable moral resolve stopped him from compromising with the System to the extent of getting a job, he had one of the most priceless of all the attributes of a really good man in that he had never been known to try borrowing money from friends. His one drawback was that from time to time he suffered attacks of acute political militancy. In the few years I had known him, he had drifted into the ranks of dozens of utopian societies perched on the lunatic fringe, and although he had always drifted out of them again with commendable speed, as soon as he had looked over the female membership and failed to fall in love, he sometimes stayed long enough to get himself involved in the machinery of committees, demonstrations, petitions and fund-raising campaigns.

'So you've done it again, eh? What's it all about this time?'

'It's just a meeting. The details wouldn't interest you.'

He flushed as he spoke, embarrassed as always when confronted by my unhealthy scepticism about almost everything.

'Where's this meeting being held?'

'Depends on the weather. If it's fine, as we hope, on the front.'

'Who's we?'

'The Committee for the Progagation of the Gospel of Economic Emancipation. Pigee for short.'

I glanced hastily round at the other members of the orchestra. The last thing I needed was to be known as a friend of an organisation with a name like Pigee. But the musicians sitting at the table seemed to have lost interest in my visitor, who kept glancing round the hall, trying without much apparent success to acclimatise himself.

'Well, as long as you don't start involving me.'

I had recollections of a dance I had once played at where Blitski had brought along the entire membership of a club called the New Lifers, whose thirty-one members had attempted to launch the new life by picketing the bar. Blitski looked at me in hurt surprise.

'Why should you be involved? You're such lousy revolutionary material anyway that it wouldn't be worth our trouble trying to recruit you.'

'That's one of the nicest things you've ever said to me. Now. This meeting. When is it?'

'Tomorrow night. The committee decided that our best chance of getting through to the proletariat would be on a Saturday night. I shall be speaking about nine o'clock. It ought to be getting dark by then, and research has shown that speakers are always more effective when they're in the dark.'

'You should do very well. Where you staying?'

'Well, that's one of the things I wanted to talk to you about.'

'I thought it might be.'

'It's like this. I'm only here for one night. Tomorrow, after the meeting, we all go back to town by coach. The party's got no funds to waste on hotel bills, so what's the chances of sleeping on the floor in your room tonight?'

'Well, I'm not sure that . . .'

'I've hardly got any luggage. And it would just be for tonight.'

I tried to think of some excuse for saying no. In the course of one night a man like Blitski could create complications which might linger for the whole season. The musicians at my back laughed in concert at a joke told to them by our trombonist, who augmented his wages by doing a milk round in the mornings. I half-looked round. They had forgotten about me. Blitski was searching my face in that uncertain, half-panicked way.

'Just for the one night then. Definitely no longer. And definitely nobody else. I don't want any daughters of the revolution shacking up with you in my room, understand?'

'Understood. Anyway, I couldn't stay longer even if I wanted to. We're doing Southend Sunday afternoon.'

It was only after the Noveltones remounted the treadmill that I wondered how Landau was likely to react to this new arrangement. Up till now I had succeeded in my policy of keeping the categories of my friendship strictly sealed off. Landau knew none of my non-musical friends, and Blitski had met none of the musicians I played with. Now that the pair of them were to be under the same roof, even for one night, all kinds of tensions might start to build up. Life might never be the same again.

3

At first my worst fears seemed to be justified. When Landau walked into the kitchen that night to see Blitski sitting there supping up tea he glanced at me in extreme distaste.

'Who's he?'

'This is Blitski. He's staying the night.'

Landau looked at Blitski's stubble, his outrageous houndstooth check shirt, his wild hair and his bulbous nose. Then he looked at me again and said, 'Why?'

Blitski glanced up from his cup and, not for the first time, waited for me to defend him.

'I don't know. Does he have to have a reason?'

'It helps,' Landau said, and then noticed a heap of packages propped up against the dresser.

'What's all this junk?'

'Nothing much. Just his soapbox and a few things.'

'What's he want with a soapbox? He looks like he never uses the stuff.' Until now Landau had been indulging his disconcerting habit of discussing inferior strangers in their own presence as though they were deaf, dumb and blind, but at this Blitski was stung into retaliation.

'Look, I'm only sixty-one inches tall. If I'm going to preach to the people I have to stand on something.'

In that moment the bonds were forged of the most unlikely friendship.

'Preach to the people? You're not a parson are you? No, you look too Jewish.'

'He means political preaching.'

'Hey,' Landau said, and smiled broadly as he sat down at the table opposite our guest and chummily offered him a cigarette.

'You never said anything about politics, Tom.' Then he refocused his beam on Blitski and said, 'You mean you're actually going to stand up and make a speech in front of people, in the street, in this town?'

I could see what was happening. Landau was in the process of discovering one of his new people. Blitski would now doubtless be added to his collection and mentally labelled 'Politician'. Before the week-end was over, Landau, who would by then have known Blitski for two days, would be describing his temperament to me, who had known him for two thousand. Blitski, beginning already to bask in the glow of this unexpected warmth, began expatiating on the difference between oratory and demagogy, but even while he was in mid-sentence Landau threw up a dramatic arm, jumped impulsively from his chair and, still smiling, dashed from the room. As we listened to the slow diminuendo of his footsteps galloping up the carpeted stairs leading to his bedroom, Blitski looked questioningly at me.

'His name is Landau,' I said. 'He's playing on the pier down here, and it was him who got me the job at the Arcadia. He won't understand a word you're talking about and he's as mad as a hatter.'

'He seems very sociable towards me.'

'That's because he senses you're as mad as he is.'

Before he could reply Landau returned holding six bottles of Nuits St Georges in his arms. A corkscrew protruded from his outbreast pocket. He planked the bottles down on the table with a generous gesture, took his seat and said, 'We must drink to this. This is important.'

For the next hour the two of them sat there exchanging idiotic banter and drinking wine out of chipped teacups while I sat on the creaking wicker chair in the corner watching two disparate strands of my social life weave themselves into a hopeless tangle. After all the trouble I had taken to present two entirely different versions of myself to these two, here they were, likely to compare notes at any moment and reduce me to size. As I sprawled there watching the wine swiftly melting Blitski's diffidence, I saw that the two of them had everything required for passionate mutual admiration. Blitski had always considered it miraculous for a man to take the stage with an instrument in his hands, while Landau found it equally miraculous for anyone to take it without one. Before long Landau was bawling into Blitski's flushed, smiling face his pet theory about public entertainers being the most important people on earth.

'. . . you see, that's why I say it's up to people like us to bring a bit of the old razzle-dazzle into the dull lives of the ordinary person.'

Blitski had never envisaged his socialist crusade in quite this light, but stimulated by the wine, was willing for the moment to accept broad concepts. He flourished his glass airily. A few drops slopped on to the floor.

'Exactly. We have to open their eyes, that's what we have to do. We . . .' The train of his thought arrived at an unexpected terminus, and his proclamation petered out in self-quotation.

'. . . well, just open their eyes.'

'And their ears. Don't forget the ears,' Landau added, springing to the defence of our glorious profession. 'The ears are very important. Do you speak from the diagram? I mean in public.'

'I never use any notes,' Blitski answered proudly.

'He means the diaphragm,' I explained.

'That's what I said. Do you speak from the diagram?'

'Not usually. I just breathe. The state the world's in there's no time for niceties. Here, open another bottle.'

Landau refilled Blitski's cup and then came over to perform the same service for me. Already his walk was unsteady.

'Do you realise,' I said, 'if I drink one more cup of this stuff, all this stuff you're talking will start to make sense.'

'You drinking the stuff or talking the stuff?' Landau said, bemused by his own question. Blitski started to shriek with laughter so violent that the china figure on the dresser reverberated for a few moments. The figure had annoyed me ever since I moved in. It showed a boy backing away from a harmless looking sheep and was called 'The Reluctant Shepherd.' It was, I gathered, the only *objet d'art* in the whole house for which Mrs Stewart, our landlady retained any affection, and in my fuddled brain the thought registered that Blitski's shrill falsetto might yet shatter it into fragments.

'Good old St George,' Landau said as he wobbled back to his chair.

'Tilting at the dragons of non-communication,' Blitski responded, dipping his nose into the brimming cup. Landau looked puzzled.

'Tilting what?'

'It's a figure of speech, that's all,' Blitski told him.

'Ah. Talking of figures. I knew there was something I wanted to ask you. How much do you get for a gig like tomorrow night? I mean, how much do they pay you for speaking?'

'Oh, you don't get any money for it. It's all for the Cause.'

This remark puzzled Landau even more, whose revolutionary spirit had never gone so far as to spurn the advantages of a fair day's pay for a fair night's work.

'In that case, how do you live?'

'From hand to mouth, and can you think of a better way to eat?'

Blitski exploded in riotous appreciation of his own wit. After watching him uncertainly for a moment Landau joined in. I drained my cup and went to the table for another refill, surprised to discover *en route* that the kitchen floor, until now perfectly reasonable, had begun undulating gently but disturbingly. Landau took a deep draught of his wine and stood, holding the edge of the table and swaying slightly. I made a note to reproach him the next time he claimed the ability to hold his liquor.

'In honour of this meeting of the Knights of St George, I think . . .'

'Nights,' I said. 'Not knights. Nights.'

'What?'

'Nights. St George. At night-time.'

'Here,' Landau said to Blitski, 'I think he's gone mad. Just sit down here, Tom, and don't panic.'

'Nights. You know. When it gets dark.'

'Dark? What are you talking about? Here, have some more wine. It'll clear your head.'

I watched him splash some wine into my cup and then drank some of it. It really was strange the way the floor had now induced the walls to move in tempo with its tremors. I decided to return to the sanctity of the wicker chair. Its bottom seemed to leap up to meet mine.

'Now, in honour of this occasion,' Landau resumed, ' I think that you, Blitski, are entitled to give a demonstration. Let's see how this soapbox really works.'

Blitski giggled.

' I can see you don't grasp the ethics of this business. I can't just stand up and preach to the converted. The environment has to be right. The atmosphere has to be conducive to . . .'

Once again he was defeated in his search for words. Instead of finishing the sentence he leaned back in his chair and expended a deep breath.

' You don't mean you're shy? Not a public speaker like you?'

' It's not a case of being shy. It's more . . . I tell you what. Give us a drop more wine.'

Landau splashed the dregs of the sixth bottle into Blitski's outstretched cup. He drained it, half-rose, fell back into his chair and with a heroic effort finally managed to stand up. But when he stooped down to gather the packages against the dresser doors he became giddy and sat down on the kitchen floor with a bump.

' Here,' he said, looking happily at me, ' I think your friend's slipped me a Mickey Finn. Maybe he's been sent by a rival party to nobble me. Them bloody Trotskyists, I shouldn't wonder.'

He pushed himself up on to all fours and crawled the rest of the distance to the parcels. While he rummaged about, Landau said to me, ' He's great, Tom. He's a great man. How about that, eh? A soapbox.'

' Just remember it was your idea, that's all.'

Blitski had now arranged his equipment to his own drunken satisfaction. Lifting up what looked like a bundle of firewood he began declaiming at the opposite wall, where a spotted mirror hung over the refrigerator. Blitski always spoke best with an audience, and never better when that audience was his own extraordinary reflection.

' Now, we have here an interesting manifestation of modern revolutionary methods. I refer, my friends, to the collapsible soapbox.'

He then tried to put the pieces together, spurning all help

and looking like a parody of an armless man wrestling with a deckchair. Landau stepped forward to offer his assistance, but Blitski pushed him away, half-falling over again in the process.

'No, please. We're all trained to construct our own platforms. It's part of the party programme. Not only does each member write his own platform, but he builds it also,' and he collapsed into a shaking heap on the carpet as he laughed at his own epigram. Finally he picked himself up, continued fiddling with the slats of wood, and finally succeeded in raising a rickety edifice which only remained upright because of the nearby dresser at its back. By now the whole house seemed mobile. The walls of the kitchen swung to and fro as though we were all suspended in a giant domestic bird cage, and the strange thing was that the movement only seemed to add depth to everything we said. The naked yellow bulb over the table was a bright promise spreading its own benign glow about the room. The crockery ranged on the dresser shelves winked in its light, apparently waiting as avidly as we were for the demonstration in the art of rabble-rousing. The Reluctant Shepherd alone of the room's occupants remained aloof, worried more than ever by that sheep. Under the circumstances it seemed the most natural thing in the world for Blitski to mount his home-made podium and we to applaud him for doing it. But then, even in my semi-stupor, it seemed clear to me that Blitski could not possibly succeed in doing what he was setting out to do.

'You're not going to climb up that thing? It'll cave in on you the moment you get near it.'

Blitski smiled a superior and very drunken smile.

'Friends of St George. Is it likely that a trained revolutionary would spurn the challenge of the platform? Anyway, I was specially chosen to use this soapbox. The party only uses it for speakers who weigh less than nine stone. It saves expense.'

Supporting himself on Landau's shoulder, and requesting me to hold the room still, he gingerly mounted the broad face of the dresser, and then carefully transferred his weight to the box. He wavered unsteadily for a moment, like a tightrope walker getting the feel of the atmosphere, and then stood erect. Landau stepped back and began to cheer. Blitski bowed in his direction, wobbled and just recovered himself. He smiled at his thousands of non-existent supporters, put on what he must fondly have believed to be a stern expression, and said in a hoarse voice, 'My friends, I come among you . . .'

Having come among his friends he then disappeared in a confusion of splintering wood and crashing crockery, shouting slogans as he went. The debris seemed to swallow him up, and I wondered seriously if I would ever see him again. Then he crawled out of the wreckage, his head festooned with pieces of wood and broken china. Landau cheered even more wildly, rose to his feet and screamed, 'To the barricades.' Then he went to help Blitski up. I noticed that suddenly he was as sober as I seemed to be. Probably it was the noise of the fall that had cleared our heads.

'End of meeting,' I said. 'Come on. Let's take him up to bed.'

We carried him unresisting to my bedroom, where Landau propped him up while I made as comfortable a bed as I could with heaps of old blankets, pillows and dirty underwear. While we were tucking him in for the night, Mrs Stewart came wavering along the passage.

'I thought I heard something. Did I hear something?'

Landau had the presence of mind to step quickly between her and Blitski.

'It's that window sash in the kitchen. Nearly frightened the life out of me.'

'Oh, well. Never mind. It'll wait till tomorrow. And wish your friend good night for me. Doesn't look too healthy to me.'

She shuffled back to her room. Landau closed the door, rubbing his hands.

'Tomorrow night then, Blitski. Nine o'clock, did you say?'

But Blitski was already fast asleep, the resonance of his snoring a grim preview of what lay before me for the next twelve hours. Before he retired Landau said, 'Why didn't you tell me about him before, Tom? He's great. Really great.'

'Have it your way.'

'You don't think he's great?'

'It's easy for you to appreciate him. He's not sleeping at the foot of your bed.'

'Oh, come on. Stop making all this fuss. If a revolutionary leader wanted to sleep on my bedroom floor, I'd be honoured.'

'In that case you won't mind if I sleep there. If I stay in here all night I won't get any sleep at all with that racket going on. Listen to him. It sounds like "Nola" on the trombone.'

My suggestion had wiped the smile from Landau's face.

'Listen, Tom. You know I can't sleep with anyone else in the room. Except a chick, of course. But you know what I mean. If I knew you were on the floor while I was in the bed, it would make me nervous.'

'All right. I tell you what. You go on the floor and I'll get in the bed. It won't worry me. My nerves must be better than yours.'

'Look, why don't you be serious for five minutes? He's your friend, so you share with him.'

'Now he's my friend all of a sudden. Just now you said you'd be honoured.'

'Did I say that? I suppose I did.'

That night I slept on the floor in Landau's room. The sound of his snoring kept me awake till past four o'clock.

4

WHEN I awoke the next morning Landau was still out to the world. He was lying on his back, arms outstretched, frowning as he concentrated on the subconscious task of maintaining a steady snoring tempo. The sight of him brought home to me the fact that my mouth was dry from last night's wine. Through the half-open curtains bright sunshine poured into the room, and from beyond the window drifted the murmurous presence of the Saturday morning traffic cruising along the promenade. I sat there for a few moments gathering myself while Landau snored blissfully on. Soon I came to the conclusion that last night had been a wasteful experience. I did not mind wasteful experiences at the moment I was living them, but when the dissipation splashed over into the next day, I began to get guilt-ridden. I leapt up, shook off the heap of old clothes and dirty sheets and tiptoed from the room, determined to pursue what was left of the morning like a clean-living boy. My watch said ten minutes to ten.

After I had washed and dressed I walked down to the café opposite Landau's pier and ate a good breakfast. Then I sauntered along to Hove and indulged a few sporting fantasies on the municipal putting green, almost but not quite managing to pick up two brunettes whose pallor told me they were trippers just arrived. Later I bought the newspapers and attempted the crosswords, doing so badly that I told myself I needed more refreshment. So I walked back to the pier, drank coffee on the roof-garden and tried to read the editorials. Having salved my conscience with all this industry I decided it was time to go back to the house and reproach the other two for being lazy. But when I got there they had both gone. By now it was half past eleven. What would Landau do on a morning like this? I glanced around his room, noticed that the *Klose* tutor was no longer on the dressing-table and congratulated myself on my powers of deduction.

I eventually found him alone in a long rectangular room broadside on to the sea. The pier's structure was too irregular for me to place our exact whereabouts, but we seemed to be somewhere under the ballroom and further in towards the shore. I found out later that Landau had come to regard this room as his by default. Stumbling on to it one morning after a last desperate attempt to reconcile himself to the acoustics of the tea-room, he had settled into the routine of morning practice here. The place was ideal for his purpose. Its remoteness from the main decks muffled any noise, and it was obvious from the room's general condition that nobody else intended using it this summer, least of all the Corporation, which seemed to have forgotten its existence. A pile of broken deckchairs had collapsed in a heap in one corner, and there were several deal tables standing on rusty trestles. On the short wall facing the door, but at a distance from it of at least thirty yards, were some old election posters and a mottled mirror in a gilt frame. But what gave the room its distinctive character was its seaward wall, nearly a hundred feet long, consisting of an unbroken series of dusty windows, a few of which Landau had wiped clean with crumpled balls of old newspaper.

Now the midsummer sun streamed into the room. Landau was at the far end seated at one of the tables, laboriously compiling lists of harmonic sequences from a great heap of sheet music stacked on the table before him. It was one of his contentions that whatever band you joined, no matter how bad it might be, the experience was worth it if you managed to secrete the piano book and sift it for songs which might be added to your own repertoire. His head was bowed over his task, and from the door it looked as though he was ducking to avoid the sharp swords of sunlight passing just over his head to strike the wall behind.

He stopped scribbling for a moment and without looking up, tossed one more sheet of manuscript paper on to the scattered pile strewn about his feet. This kind of excavation was his favourite pastime, as it was mine, and I felt no desire to disturb his evident absorption in the music. The motes of dust sailing through the rays of the sun seemed like a physical barrier between us, and for the moment it seemed sacrilegious to disturb either them or the student at the end of the room. Suddenly he sensed my presence. He threw down his pencil and looked up.

'Hello, Tom. Welcome to the Conservatoire.'

I joined him at the table and watched him light a cigarette.

'Find anything good?'

'Nothing much. See what you think.'

He pushed some sheets of paper across the table. They were covered in his private hieroglyphics. I sat there trying to hum one of the tunes he had notated. He watched me for a while, then reached under the table for a small black leather case rather slimmer than a doctor's bag but not unlike it in shape. From it he took the parts of a clarinet which he slowly assembled. He began to blow a few arpeggios, but the reed kept squeaking, and soon he laid the instrument on the table between us. We both contemplated its silver keys glinting in the sun.

'Not much here,' I said, nodding at the manuscript.

'I know.'

A pained expression wrinkled his face, beginning to show signs now of weeks in the sun. He took a long draw at his cigarette and peered at its lighted tip as he expelled the smoke from his lungs.

'These bands,' he said. 'They fill their libraries with all this crap, no wonder they sound like they do.'

'Ah, but they don't know it's crap.'

He grunted. 'No ambition. That's their trouble. What are they, that crowd I work with down here? They're not artists, course they're not. They're just looking for an easy time, that's all. I was talking to Charlie last night, he's the bass player. I asked him about working here every summer, and you know what he said? He said it was better than going to work. What an attitude, I ask you.'

I thought of his admiration for these same musicians when the season first began, but I said nothing. Landau was simply getting things into perspective once more. As the sun drifted behind sudden sombre clouds a great shadow swooped across the room, and Landau's mood seemed to modulate accordingly. He sat there smoking, staring out towards the distant shoreline, his feet propped on the table. Bathers were already scrambling out of the water, and the beach parties beginning to disintegrate into isolated blotches of colour crunching across the pebbles towards the sanctity of the promenade. Landau took one last drag on his cigarette and stubbed it out in an old cocoa tin lying at his feet. Then he leaned back with his hands locked behind his head and said, 'Look at them down there. Ants on parade.'

Even as I followed his gaze the first drops of rain began to streak the windows.

'Come on. Time to move.'

'Where to?'

He swung his feet off the table and began gathering his papers.

'This is the fair-weather room,' he explained. 'In times of emergency the caravan moves on. Take my clarinet case, will you?'

He tucked his instrument under his arm and made for the pile of deckchairs. For a moment I thought he was fooling, but then he turned and said with real impatience, 'Come on then.'

I stood up and watched him. When he reached the deck-chairs he kicked one or two aside and knelt down, his arms still full of instrument and sheet music. He nodded to me and said, 'Give us a hand. It's a bit stiff.'

'How did you find this?'

'The first time I came here I heard voices. They seemed to be coming from under the floor. It took me a whole week to figure it out.'

I pulled back the trapdoor and Landau gingerly descended the iron steps of a spiral staircase. I followed him down and pulled the trapdoor after me, shivering in the sudden chill air. The staircase led us down about twenty feet into a small windowless room lit by a single gas bracket set into the wall. Without looking round Landau went through a door into a small chamber with a battery of light switches against the far wall. We had arrived backstage at the pier theatre. Stepping over packing cases and broken music stands, he trotted up a small flight of wooden steps and stood in the orchestra pit waiting for me to follow.

Inside the theatre everything was dusty purple plush. After the naked glare of the room upstairs we peered like bats. Our only light came from a small skylight high in the roof. The steady monody of rain beat against its opaque face. Landau opened the lid of the piano. Soon he began playing the chords of ' Embraceable You '. It was one of the tunes he had put down on his list of things to master during the season. I walked half-way up the stalls and chose an aisle seat from which to watch Landau's hunched back as he gradually became immersed in his own solecisms. He still remembered enough of the rudiments of piano lessons taken in infancy to be able to struggle through a song, but he would never have passed anywhere for a real pianist, and knew it.

' Wrong chord,' I shouted.

' Where? Which one?' He turned his head and peered through the shadows at me, hands still on the piano keys.

' Where it goes " just one look at you ". It's augmented.'

' Really. Augmented? You sure?'

He turned back to the keyboard and fumbled for the right permutation.

Eventually he found it.

' That's it.'

He stopped playing again and spun round on the stool.

' Hey, what a beautiful sound. Who wrote it, Tom?'

' Gershwin, I think.'

' What a man, eh?'

He played the phrase over and over again, exulting in the sumptuousness of the sound as though it were his own creation.

' Hey, that's enough of that, play something else.'

' Like what?'

' Like " The Song is You ".'

' Don't know it,' all the time repeating that augmented chord.

' All right. What about " Yesterdays "?'

He began to play ' Yesterdays ' and started to become engrossed all over again.

' Great song, Tom. Who wrote it?'

' Kern, I think.'

'What a man, eh?'

Gradually he worked himself into an impossible harmonic predicament, crashed a few petulant discords and slammed down the piano lid. The bang resounded through the empty auditorium.

'You hear that? I actually know the tune and still I can't play it. It's a complete lack of talent.'

He left the stool and climbed over the seats towards me. I knew he was depressed by the knowledge that neither he nor I would ever write a tune like 'Yesterdays', and so assert in tangible terms our superiority over the musicians in the pier band, the ones with no ambition. I knew also that Landau would never admit any of this, and was perhaps not even aware of the true cause of his fit of self-disgust. He slumped into the seat next to me.

'My mother had to go and make me take piano lessons when I was a kid. Couldn't she see I was born to blow a saxophone?'

'I wish I could play piano as well as you. At least it's something.'

'It means nothing, Tom.'

'Go back and play some more for me. I was enjoying it.'

'No, it's a load of crap. How can you bear to sit there and listen to it?'

'Go on. Keep it to simple tunes.'

He hopped back into the pit, opened the piano lid and ran through the small repertoire of songs he knew really well. These were mostly the old Broadway standards. Without realising it, he and I were becoming connoisseurs of the popular song through our incessant burrowings through the files of the bands whose ranks we passed through. I sat there in the darkened theatre listening to Gershwin and Rodgers and Romberg and Kern floating up from the pit while through my mind's eye drifted the absurd phantasms of the dramas that had inspired them, the mysterious strangers, the mistaken identities, the anonymous legacies, identical twins, rich heroes and poor heroines, poor heroes and rich heroines, impoverished dukes and bogus duchesses, butlers posing as socialites and socialites as butlers, lawyers and chorus girls, comic cops and escaped cons. The weak rays from the fanlight played about Landau's head, forming a butter-coloured shifting aureole about him. The music wafted me away on a tide of old associations, and before long I was telling myself that in a few years time, after the jazz world had been conquered, it might be enjoyable to write a few musical comedies. Between novels, of course. I had almost succeeded in convincing myself that the jazz world already had been conquered and that we were already writing a few musical comedies, that the songs being thumped out down there in front of me were our songs and not George Gershwin's, when the sound of a falling body followed by the clatter of flying music stands disturbed my reverie. Landau stopped abruptly, looked up and then started laughing. A few moments later Blitski came into view, limping and holding his left ear.

'Go on, laugh. I might have killed myself.'

'You can't die yet,' I shouted. 'Not before tonight's meeting.'

I joined the two of them in the pit. Blitski seemed shaken by his fall, but Landau, the trite sadness of the music forgotten, looked eager and expectant once again.

'What a chance for you to practise your speech, in a real theatre. Go on, get up there and give it to us.'

But Blitski would not be persuaded. His invocations to the working classes were not meant for our decadent ears and he told us so.

'While I'm spouting tonight, you two will be dispensing cat noises to the masses, distracting them from the real business of life, which is listening to people like me.'

'Don't be so sure,' I said. 'If you're on at nine, I might be in the audience yet. We're off from eight forty-five to nine-fifteen, and it's not more than two minutes from the Arcadia to the seafront.'

He looked horrified.

'You stay away from me. If I see you standing there it'll ruin everything. You know how you always put me off when I'm trying to be serious.'

As it turned out, it was not me who put him off his revolutionary stroke that night.

At forty-six minutes to nine Bertie Fields and his Noveltones ground to the end of a particularly objectionable version of 'Change Partners'. The dancers, overcome by their own virtuosity, swirled on for a few moments before the fact seeped in that the music had stopped. Then they retired to the carpeted fringes of the floor, politely applauding themselves as they went. No more than ninety seconds later I was standing in the side street at the back of the hall, happy in the knowledge that in leaving the premises between sessions I had committed yet another breach of the labyrinthine Happiness code. As I hurried down to the front in search of utopian uplift my awareness of the crime gave a fine edge to my pleasure. Behind Landau's pier the sun was setting in a cheap, exhibitionist sort of way, and as I strode along, the corporation coloured lights flashed on as though giving a signal of the diversions to come. The gay reds and greens and yellows formed a looping necklace of light out to the pier and beyond it, and under the chromatic glow I saw that about half-way between the Arcadia and the pier a large crowd of idlers had gathered, leaning lazily over the promenade rails, gazing down at some kind of spectacle on the shingle below.

As I hurried towards the scene of the action I was vaguely conscious of the hum of self-indulgence about the whole town. You could just hear the faint squeaks of Van Rhodes and the Modernaires playing doggedly away four hundred yards out to sea. More music was coming from a still-operating pin-table emporium, a group of holidaymakers away behind to my left were singing against the swish of the open-top buses plying their trade to and from Rottingdean, and behind all was the soft insistent whisper of the surf mingling with the noise of those who had come that day from all over England to swim in it, and bathe in it, and frolic in it, and, if they were anything like Landau, occasionally to piss in it.

I pushed my way to the front of the crowd clustered round the railings. I saw immediately below me a group of youngish people holding banners around a much more substantial soapbox than the one that had so very nearly done for Blitski the night before. The banners looked enormous, disproportionately large among the small group sporting them. Their carriers were obliterated by the fluttering red dusters, so that each banner seemed to have a life of its own, moving about the beach on a pair of its own legs. On the soapbox a young redhead was shouting incoherently about the excesses of *laissez faire*. The coloured lights and the darkling sky flattered her features, and I surmised that it was probably she who had tempted Blitski into this pantomime. But of him there was no sign. The speaker's awesome threats about the wrath to come were punctuated at fairly regular intervals by the jeers of a crowd so complacent about its own immortality that the more dire the predictions about its own eventual fate, the more resonant the raspberries. Although I was surrounded by at least two hundred people, it looked as though not one was listening. After about five minutes of this depressing stuff, the stream of jeremiads from the soapbox ceased, and there followed a feverish consultation among the banners. Then one of the red flags dropped to reveal the flushed features of Blitski.

The redhead stepped down from the platform, shook his hand, patted him on the back and then made way for his ascent. The crowd, seeing the smallest public speaker any of them could remember, began shouting ribald encouragement. A man standing next to me wearing a paper hat with ' Hello Sexy ' printed on its peak, shouted out, ' Look, he's shrunk in the wash.' The crowd laughed. Blitski ascended his martyr's throne, glanced down at a small piece of paper in his right hand, looked up at the sea of laughing Saturday night faces, and began.

' I come among you tonight . . .'

A round of riotous cheering greeted this information and Blitski paused.

' I come among you tonight, not to destroy but to build, not to criticise but to advise . . .'

' Not to bury Caesar but to praise him,' shouted a wag behind me.

Blitski paused again and glanced at his notes before resuming.

' My Shakespearian friend has a point,' he said, smiling wanly, ' I come to bury nobody, but only to point out that unless society—and that means every one of you standing here tonight—unless society mends its ways very soon, there will be nobody left to bury anybody.'

The news that it was about to be obliterated apparently tickled the crowd to the point where the cheering rose to a crescendo so deafening that Landau told me later you could hear it on the pier.

'We talk of love of country,' said Blitski, 'but I ask you whose country? Not yours, not mine . . .'

Hello Sexy shouted out, 'Go back to your own country,' a remark followed by a concerted 'Hear, hear' from the rest of the audience.

'I am a man without a country, my friend,' Blitski said, 'I have no country and I have no . . .'

'No common sense either,' roared a bullnecked man a few paces from me.

'I tell you that the only possible salvation for us, for every one of us here tonight, you and you and you . . .'

At this point a scuffle seemed to develop somewhere at the back of the crowd. There were a few shouts and one scream. Then a small object flew through the air, looking ominously black and solid against the backdrop of coloured lights. It described a neat parabola over the heads of us all, swooped down on to the shingle and caught Blitski neatly on the left nostril. Two of the banners caught him as he fell. A third picked up the offending potato and bravely lobbed it back into the crowd. While Blitski disappeared threshing vainly in the folds of his own party banners, I slipped quickly through to the back of the crowd, walked along twenty yards and down the steps leading to the beach.

The Committee for the Propagation of the Gospel of Economic Emancipation appeared to have arrived at a crisis in its history. While the crowd expressed its wittiness by chanting 'Why are we waiting?' a knot of Blitski's supporters were doing their best to staunch the flow of blood from his nose. The scene was a confusion of scurrying figures, forsaken banners trampled into the pebbles, coloured lights and hoarse voices. Against the vast background of the sea and the night sky the remnants of the meeting looked very small beer. I had a sudden mental picture of how fairylike and unsubstantial this meeting must have seemed and sounded to anybody in a boat a couple of miles out to sea. When Blitski saw me he struggled out of the arms of his comrades and said, 'Did you see that? I hope you saw that.'

The redhead, tight-lipped and ashen, asked me if I was a friend.

'A friend but not, I'm afraid, a comrade.'

She glanced contemptuously at my bow tie and my dress suit, and then looked in silent reproach at her hero, who evidently enjoyed closer connections with the bourgeoisie than he had led the party to believe.

'Listen, I have to be back at the Arcadia in a few minutes. Why don't you come back to the house for a drink tonight before you go home?'

He waved weakly and put a grubby handkerchief to his nose.

'It depends. On when we start back. If I miss the coach I'll be stranded.'

'He has to speak at Southend tomorrow,' the redhead said.

Blitski gave her a disenchanted look and shrugged at me.

'Thanks for the offer. I'll try to make it.'

'Right. Bring Charlotte Corday with you if you like.'

He turned up at just four minutes before midnight that night, alone, even as I was sitting in the kitchen giving an account of the evening's events to Landau who, if he had approved of Blitski before, was now positively idolatrous.

'So the mob went for you, eh?' he said, grinning broadly. 'The bastards.'

Blitski sat in the wicker chair and said, 'Got any more of that wine?'

Landau shook his head. 'It's all down to cocoa tonight.'

'How's the nose?' I asked.

'Still growing.'

'You have to admit,' Landau said, making for the dresser, 'it was an easy target. No offence, of course,' and he rattled among the crockery in search of cups and saucers.

'I tell you what,' Blitski said. 'There must be some way two brilliant men like you and a genius like me can think of getting me out of going to Southend tomorrow and going through it all over again.'

I pretended to be shocked. 'Don't tell me you're ratting on the party.'

Landau spun round, a spoon of heaped cocoa in his left hand. 'You can't give up now. You've only just begun.' His face was furrowed with concern for the future of sedition. 'You wouldn't let one rotten potato end your career, would you?'

'Just watch me. I don't mind vegetarianism but this is going too far.'

This remark was far too obscure for Landau, who returned to his cocoa-brewing chores.

'The bus leaves at one,' Blitski said, 'and I'm going to be on it. And what's more, for the last time too.'

He took one of the three steaming cups from Landau and began sipping noisily.

'I suppose it was that redheaded chick who convinced you that you were a great public orator?'

Blitski flushed, so that for one incandescent moment his nose matched up with the rest of his face. Landau became curious.

'What's this about a redhead, Tom?'

'It's all right, relax. She's not your type. Is she, Blitski?'

'She's nobody's type,' he answered darkly. 'She doesn't go with men, she goes with theories. For the last two months she's been having an affair with Proudhon. Before that it was Jevons and before that Engels. God knows how many there were before me.'

Morosely he sipped his cocoa, feeling his nose from time to time to reassure himself that it was not still pouring blood. Suddenly he put down his cup and started laughing. His tiny body shook with the convulsions of some private joke, while we sat there staring blankly at him. Slowly he regained control of himself, rummaged in his trouser pockets and said, 'Well at least I got something out of it.'

He held aloft in his right hand a rather large King Edward potato, slightly misshapen and a little dusty but beyond all question a potato. Landau reached over and took it from him, turning it over in his hand, feeling its weight by lobbing it up in the air and letting it smack back into the palm of his hand.

Blitski watched him. 'I never knew a potato could be a deadly weapon.'

'Wait till you eat my mother's food,' Landau told him. 'Hey, that's it. Why don't we cook it?'

'Let him keep it. It's probably his first trophy.'

'I say eat it. Before he develops a big thing about it. What do you say, Blitski?'

'You're right. Only I have to leave in half an hour, so start cooking.'

Landau popped the potato into the oven and slammed the door shut.

'How about that? Revolutionary potato in its jacket. I bet you're the first martyr to eat the enemy's ammunition.'

But we never ate the potato after all. Perhaps symbolically it turned out to be rotten from skin to skin. So we returned it into Blitski's keeping when he straightened his tie and rose to go at ten minutes to one. Landau shook his hand rather too heartily and told him to come and see us again soon.

I walked Blitski to the street. In the courtyard he turned to me for a moment and said, ' Come on. You still haven't thought of a good excuse for ducking out of Southend to-morrow.'

'Tell them you've got concussion. You know, after-effects.'

'She'd never believe it.'

'But then it wasn't her who got it in the nose.'

'You're right. I don't know. *Epater le bourgeoise*, they tell you. So I do it and what happens? The *bourgeoise épaters* me.'

'Listen, why don't you find yourself a chick who loves you for yourself?'

'You must be joking. So long.'

When I came back to the kitchen Landau had his feet on the table, sipping his cocoa with a faraway look on his face. Without looking at me he said, 'He is a great man, Tom. A really great man.'

'I suppose in a way he is. A great booby.'

'He makes you want to go out and join in yourself.'

I looked at him in astonishment.

'Is that really what he makes you feel? You going to enlist?'

'Not exactly enlist. But it does make you want to start

doing something. Not speaking to the masses necessarily, but something. I mean, look how much he knows about things.'

'What things?'

'Oh, I don't know. Things. Writing. Books, that kind of stuff.'

'He doesn't know any more than I do.'

'Yes, but you're different. You . . . well, you don't do anything with it.'

'Well, just tell me what he does with it. He hasn't been to work for two years at least.'

Landau slapped the table. Then he stood up and stretched himself, still grinning. Who knows what fantastic portrait of himself he was now ogling in his mind's eye? Landau the Great Commoner? Landau the Sage? Or Landau at the Barricades? Landau the Messiah? It was hard to tell. As we trudged upstairs he said to me, 'I'm not sure about this yet, but I think I'm going to devote myself to something. You know, causes, big issues.'

'It doesn't happen like that. First you have to find the cause. Then, you join it when life seems impossible if you don't.'

'I can make my life impossible any time I want. Don't you worry about that part of it.'

We went into his bedroom. He looked at his bed as though for the first time, leapt on to it and stood upright. His head almost brushed the ceiling.

'Tom, I hereby announce that this is to certify that from now on I devote a certain amount of time every day to the problems of the world.'

'God help us all.'

'You're my witness. As true as I stand here, I promise.'

Then he jumped down and fished two bottles of beer out from under the bed. Within two days his vow was, of course, forgotten, but as it proved, two days was more than enough for him to land me in serious trouble.

5

SUNDAY was always a difficult time for Landau. His conception of the true professional was a man who worked twenty-four hours a day, seven days a week at his chosen art. The town corporation however, unmindful of his idealism, did not permit dancing on the pier on Sundays, and as I was required at the Arcadia seven nights a week, this meant that Landau was left to his own devices. Being an essentially restless creature, he soon found himself obliged to create artificial situations to fill in his time. Usually he would lie in bed till around noon, eat a belated breakfast with the worst grace he could muster, and then go off on a variety of mysterious jaunts which, to judge from his attitude on Mondays, never failed to misfire. Once he hired a car and drove himself along the south coast to catch a concert by a famous orchestra down at Portsmouth, but a spectacular misunderstanding with another driver just outside Worthing prevented him from ever reaching his destination. For a while this episode seemed to have discouraged him, but then came the soapbox interlude, which had evidently disturbed him more than I realised.

On the morning after Blitski's disastrous attempt to rouse the mass consciousness, I awoke to find a note pinned to the coverlet of my bed. For the first time that season Landau had elected to spend his day off in London. Clearly he was in the process of maturing one of his grandiose harebrained schemes, because the note ended with the ominous phrase printed in clumsy capitals, 'BIG PLANS'. I glanced at my watch. It said five minutes past ten. Whatever these plans were, they must be big ones indeed to tempt Landau out of bed this early. The tousled head on the pillow next to mine began to move slightly, and I wondered how, only seven hours before, I could possibly have considered a social call in the small hours from a cinema usherette to be the height of

eroticism. Her name was Annette, and already she had made
rash promises about getting me into matinées free of charge. I
tapped her on the ear with Landau's note.

'Landau's gone.'

She sat up slowly and blinked at me.

'Where?'

'London. Some scheme he's got going. He doesn't say
what.'

'He's too wild, that one. Always cooking up schemes,' and
her head flopped back on the pillow.

I pulled the covers back, swung my feet on to the floor
and worked my toes as I thought about Landau. His proclamation of the previous night came back to me. Perhaps he
had gone to London to open the new campaign of social
service? Impossible. The very idea was too uncharacteristic.
The most you could ever expect of him in that direction was
a three-month subscription to the *New Statesman*, certainly
nothing more. Then I remembered something that had happened a few days ago. We had been walking along the front
taking the early evening air before parting on the corner
of the main road to go to our respective bandstands.

A light breeze was blowing in from the sea, and although
we would never have admitted it, our egos were subtly gratified by the trippers looking round at us, their curiosity no
doubt stimulated by the awesome insignia of the black bow
ties and the silk lapels of our dress suits. We sauntered along
not saying much, stopping once at my request to watch some
boys playing beach cricket on a slender concrete strip under
the shadow of the West Pier, the other pier. But Landau,
whose sporting interests had never extended far beyond the
occasional desultory game of ping-pong, soon showed his
boredom, so we turned back towards the cheap end of town.
Soon we found ourselves approaching a small paved arena
down below us at sea level. A few people were whirling
round, their hired roller skates clicking sharply over the
grooves between the paving stones. Landau stopped abruptly,
gazing keenly at the innocent spectacle below. For a while
we leaned over the iron rail of the promenade, watching the
sport without speaking. It was pleasant to stand there taking
in the last impressions of the day before reverting to our

slightly absurd roles as Noveltones and Modernaires. The sea was oyster-grey tinctured with dots of reddening gold from the descending sun. The smell of the shingle drifted up, striking in me some poignant, elusive chord of childhood memory. The gulls wove lazy patterns above us, wisps of cloud moved imperceptibly towards the advancing dusk, the coloured lights on the far tip of Landau's pier blinked on, prematurely, their brightness reduced to pallor by the stubborn daylight . . .

'Now take this place, Tom.'

'Eh?'

'What happens to it? A few faces skate round from ten in the morning till ten at night or whenever it is they close. And then what? Nothing.'

'So?'

'So that means the Corporation is paying rates for a place that's unused for half the time. Twelve hours a day wasted.'

'It's not quite like that. I don't see how the Corporation can pay rates to itself.'

He brushed the point aside.

'Can't you see what I'm getting at? Midnight dancing. In the open air. You bung up a few Chinese lanterns, round the edges there, where the poles are, you put in a nice little quintet, me, you and a rhythm section, and you charge, what, say, half a crown a head. You could clean up.'

'First of all the Corporation wouldn't give you permission. Second, even if they did, they'd charge you money to hire the place and we haven't got any money. Third, you have to get a special licence for performing after midnight, and fourth, who in his right mind would chance the open air in a climate like this?'

'You're a defeatist.'

'I'm a realist.'

'It's down to the same thing. You won't even try.'

'No, but I'm not stopping you. I just don't want you to be too disappointed when you find out, that's all.'

'Well anyway,' he said, standing to his full height and yawning insolently at the sea, 'it was a nice idea.'

We walked on, but after about fifty yards he stopped again, peering intently at his own feet.

'I think you're wrong. I'm sure it's worth a try. What harm can it do to make a few inquiries?'

'None at all. But just don't start getting all brought down when you find out the way things are in this town.'

'But everything's dead here after eleven-thirty. They ought to welcome something like this. Good for the tourist trade.'

'Look, hasn't it occurred to you yet that the reason why everything goes dead here after eleven-thirty is because everyone prefers it that way, the Corporation, the residents, the watch committee, everyone?'

'That's because they've got no imagination. All they need is one little eye-opener. It wouldn't cost anything to ask.'

'Listen. It's five to eight. I'm going to be late for work.'

He walked off briskly in the direction of the pier, swinging his arms and whistling 'Intermission Riff' as he went, probably tabulating in his mind what two thousand half-crowns worked out at in pounds, shillings and pence. The way Landau did arithmetic there were sure to be some pence. He had never mentioned the subject since, but now, as I sat up in bed, it seemed likely that his sudden excursion to London might have something to do with his plans for enlivening the nightlife of Brighton.

I lunched with Annette in one of those small subterranean cafés on the front. The glare of the sun puckered our faces into sullen scowls. I was relieved when at ten minutes to two she went off to play her part in feeding to the locals the saga of Dorothy Lamour in 'Her Jungle Love' at a cinema which, for reasons best known to the management, called itself 'The Classic'. The rest of the afternoon went painfully slowly. I did a couple of crosswords, read a little, wrote out the melody lines of a few songs which looked promising for the aspiring improvisor, and then, at six, began to change for work as painstakingly as I could contrive. I made the shave last nearly twenty minutes, tied my bow tie several times until my arms ached and I had arranged the two ends in precise symmetry, polished my shoes, brushed my teeth, and then repaired my saxophone sling, which had snapped the previous night during 'El Cumbanchero'.

The Arcadia was quiet that night. Usually on Sundays people came in through sheer desperation, but this time they must have found somewhere else more stimulating to see out the week-end. By half past nine there were not more than fifty couples dancing, and when we went off for our second interval there was not even the usual polite patter of hand-claps. Crawford stood by the box-office, an anxious look on his face. But the ebb and flow of dance hall patronage is a nebulous thing. When we came back for the last session of the evening at ten-fifteen, the place had mysteriously filled up. The dancers, sagging slightly at the knees, had difficulty avoiding each other as they slid round, and the air, cool though musty only an hour before, was now oppressive with the smell of perspiration and cheap perfume. As I stepped on to the bandstand to pick up my instrument I noticed Crawford, beaming now, perhaps at the thought of the company's annual attendance bonus looming before him. He even nodded to us as we took over from the retiring rhumba band.

We churned through our programme, most of us by this time so familiar with the rigid order of tunes that we hardly bothered to glance at our music. I found myself clock-watching, eager for eleven o'clock and release. And then, at sixteen minutes to eleven, there was some kind of commotion at the main entrance. I knew it was sixteen minutes to eleven because we had just finished playing 'Lavender Blue' and were preparing to interpret the profundities of 'I Wish I Knew the Name of the Girl in my Dreams (So I could change her name to mine)'; several of the dancers turned to look at the party coming through the foyer into the hall. It comprised a noisy cluster of about a dozen people, and seemed to be heading straight for the bandstand. Then, as they came closer, I saw with horror that their leader was Landau, and that in his right hand he was carrying his clarinet case. The young men with him I did not know, although about one or two of them there seemed something vaguely reminiscent. The half-dozen girls who made up the deputation I had never seen before. The moment Landau greeted me I knew he had been drinking. His face was deeply flushed and his smile was flecked with all the signs of recklessness.

'Whatcha, Tom. Hi, Bertie. How about a little session, eh? Liven this hole up a bit.'

And before I could answer or Bertie step in his way Landau

63

had taken his place on the bandstand and begun to assemble his clarinet. Two of the men with him followed. One gently displaced our pianist simply by perching himself on the edge of the piano stool and then sliding along, while the other laughingly did the same to our drummer. Bertie began to protest, but even as the hysterical pleas began to pour from his trembling lips, Landau had shouted out to his allies in the rhythm section, 'After You've Gone', tapped his foot four times and was away on a noisy dixieland interpretation at least twice as fast as the regulation forty-eight bars to the minute which Happiness had laid down in its rules as being compulsory for quick-steps. The dancers looked confused for perhaps half a chorus and then, remembering their education at the hands of Hollywood, realised there was a given response to this kind of situation. They clustered round the bandstand and spurred us on by clapping their hands—naturally on the wrong beats. For two or three choruses I sat there paralysed, listening to Landau staggering drunkenly through the harmonies at a tempo so furious that already he must be regretting ever having started. But then it occured to me that the deed was done and that not all the decorousness in the world on my part could ever undo it. At the end of Landau's fourth chorus I began my own solo, blowing happily for several minutes. When I opened my eyes again and stopped playing, it was to see Bertie and Crawford in frantic conversation at the side of the bandstand. Through the shattering bombardment being put up by Landau's drummer friend, I caught incongruous fragments of what they were saying.

'. . . take over like this . . . open revolt.'

'. . . these bloody jazzers . . . more trouble than they're worth . . .'

'. . . never seen them before . . . just barged in here . . .'

'. . . just wait . . . stop soon . . .'

Crawford's jaundiced eye caught mine. I smiled happily at him. He seemed to go one shade paler and pointed me out to Bertie, who shook his head sadly. At eleven o'clock we played a distinctly jazz-tinged version of the National Anthem and trooped off. Landau and his friends congratulated each other and then joined the rest of their party, sitting at a table to our left, shouting noisily for more. Before I could slink off Bertie and Crawford had cornered me. They looked at each other, so bemused by the unconstitutional nature of the proceedings that they were unsure where to begin. It was Bertie who finally managed to construct something approaching a coherent sentence.

'What's happening? I mean what? What's it about? Who are you?'

'You realise,' Crawford said, 'that if the Union hears that musicians have been playing in here without payment there could be serious trouble?'

'Well, pay them,' I said brightly.

'You know we don't allow this sort of thing on our circuit,' Crawford added. 'Jazz ought to stay where it belongs, in the cellars . . .'

'Who belongs in a cellar, eh?'

It was Landau, still overjoyed with himself, who had come over to join in the debate.

'All freedom is born in cellars, but you won't keep it there for ever.'

'I know you,' Crawford said. 'You work down on the pier. Well, your employers may be interested to hear about your behaviour this evening.'

'Look, man, they loved it. Didn't you see their faces? Didn't you see the way they crowded round? They loved every minute of it. What are you so frightened about?'

'That's true enough,' I said.

'You keep out of this,' Crawford answered. 'You're in enough trouble already.'

'Why blame him?' asked Landau. 'He didn't do anything. If there's anyone to take the can back it's me, and as I don't work for you, why don't you drop dead?'

Crawford turned to him and said, with surprising dignity for a man of his calling, 'You're barred from here for the rest of the season. You so much as show your nose in here again and I'll send for the police . . . and that goes for your friend too,' he added, nodding at me. 'If you come in here again, he's fired instantly. Understand?'

I was astonished. The moment Landau had begun to play 'After You've Gone' I had assumed my own dismissal to be automatic. Landau, it seemed, had got away with it again.

'Come on, Tom. Let's get out of here and breathe some clean air,' and he headed back for his table, where the party was mustering itself for triumphant departure.

'Don't you forget,' Crawford called out to me, 'one more false step and you're out for good.'

But I walked on, already preoccupied by the fact that of Landau's party of eleven, there were six girls and only five boys. I stood chatting with the party for a few minutes, before leaving to return my instrument to a band-room hushed with awe at what had happened. As I cleaned my saxophone mouthpiece I realised that in a passive sort of way I might well have contributed to one of the legends of the profession. But then I reconsidered. After all, what had I done? Merely played a few choruses of 'After You've Gone', and not very well either. No, in a few weeks the whole business would be forgotten. I was too young in those days to allow for the embellishments of time and faulty memory. In ten years from now the musicians in that band-room with me would still on occasion discuss the events of this evening with joyous laughter, my own part in the farce having by then been inflated to the point where the whole thing was a plot on my part to undermine the policy of the company and strike a brave blow for jazz. The reputation I won in later years in the jazz clubs probably accounted for this, but that night, as I ran down the back stairs, my only intimation was that anyone who stuck around Landau for long enough stood a good chance of becoming a hero.

He and his friends were waiting for me in two cars parked in a side street at the back of the ballroom. I felt a slight pang of apprehension when I saw that Landau himself was sitting at the wheel of the first car, an old Buick with one of its headlamps missing.

'Jump in, Tom. This is Teddy and Des. That's Maureen, and the one with the legs is Paula. Eddie's in the corner there. Come on. I said we'd be there by eleven.'

I squeezed in next to him, and as he swerved through the streets of Hove tried to get some sense out of him.

'What was all that about? In there, tonight?'

'What was all what about? Just a little session. It livened the place up a bit, and you can't say it didn't need it.'

'Whoever heard of livening a dance hall up? You could have lost me my job.'

'Don't be mad. I only did it for you.'

'That was big of you, Landau.'

He sped on, one hand at the wheel, the other fumbling in his jacket pocket for a cigarette. He found one and asked me to light it for him.

'It was supposed to be a cure, that's all. Remember you said the Arcadia made you feel funny? Well, after tonight, I bet you it won't feel any different from all the other dumps. I bet we've cured you.'

'Maybe, but haven't you heard of burning the house down to roast the pig?'

His smile wavered for a moment. Then he half-turned to the others in the car, swerving wildly across the road in the process, and said, 'See? I told you he says the craziest things.'

'Actually I didn't get fired. But it was close.'

'Oh, come on. Is this all the gratitude I get? Here I am, sacrificing my one day off to rustle up a team to get you out of this mood, and all you can say is you nearly got fired. That's not the right attitude to go to a party.'

'Whose party?'

'What difference does it make whose party? It's a party. Some face with a big place near Lancing or somewhere. It's dead easy to find. You just go straight along the coast road.'

We got lost after that, and while Teddy and Paula got out to find somebody who knew the way I glanced at Landau. He was sitting there, gloved hands on the wheel, puffing contentedly at his cigarette. Every so often he flicked ash out of the open window with a nervous gesture.

'You know, when I read your note, I was sure it was something to do with that open-air dancing scene.'

'Open-air dancing? What scene?'

'You remember. The other night. You were talking about starting an open-air midnight dance club. On the front.'

He looked at me solicitously.

'That's ridiculous, Tom. How would I ever manage to do

that? It would be impossible to get permission, you ought to know that.'

'Yes, but . . .'

'This town really does unsettle you, I can see that now. Well, after tonight, you ought to be back to normal.'

He took a last drag of his cigarette and then flicked the butt out into the middle of the road. It rolled down the camber for a few inches, throwing off sparks as it went. Landau and I both watched it carefully until it had come to rest.

'How was I tonight, Tom? You reckon my playing's improving?'

'I don't know. I was so thunderstruck . . . actually you set the tempo too fast. We're not up to that kind of pace yet.'

'I know, I know.'

He was suddenly depressed, and I felt contrite.

'Still, perhaps that's a good idea. Only by trying can you ever learn how to do it, I suppose.'

'That's it. Only once you start, you have to keep on. You have to get yourself used to thinking at that speed, and how the hell do we do that?'

'You tell me.'

He stared out at the buff mansions of the broad street into which his careless navigation had landed us, anxious for one moment about his capabilities.

'You see, I play ridiculous, Tom. I haven't got any actual talent. I'm like a workman. I do what I can, and every note comes hard. I know that. I know I'll never play an original note. I suppose I'm a hack really.'

It was curious how Landau, an incorrigible dreamer regarding the world at large, could be capable of these bursts of sublime candour about himself. Although he busied himself with the pursuits of the moment, he was always fully aware of his limitations, and what was even rarer, took a genuine pleasure in the superior prowess of his friends.

'You're different, of course. I could hear that tonight. You really will be able to play. You're bound to get a lot better than you are now.'

I made the appropriate noises of modest denial, but was

68

naturally pleased. Not that his flattery took me in. I knew I was only a little less mediocre than he, and that it was the difference between us, slight as it might be, which had tempted him to overrate me as a musician. As we sat there in the car, discussing ourselves with comic earnestness while the strangers behind us listened carefully to the exchanges as though they were being allowed to eavesdrop on a Socratic dialogue, I realised that Landau, for all the tiresome persistence with which he rode his hobby-horses roughshod over the sensibilities of those around him, was fundamentally a person remarkably free of envy or malice.

'It was very good of you to go to all this trouble tonight.'

'What are you talking about? I had a ball.'

Teddy and Paula came back at that point, giggling, arm-in-arm, with the news that for the past three miles we had been travelling in diametrically the opposite direction to Lancing. Landau whooped with laughter, and then, with much grinding of brakes, reversed the car and set off down the right road. We arrived at the party soon after midnight. As we spilled out of the car I noticed something white protruding from Landau's jacket pocket. It was a copy of the *New Statesman*.

6

MY RECOLLECTIONS of the party are fragmentary. Never having been cursed with total recall I retain only a few dominant impressions of the event. The first was inevitably to do with Landau. I was both amused and impressed by his ability to go straight for his objective, regardless of all considerations of tact or courtesy. Within seconds of our arrival he had disappeared upstairs with Paula in search of an empty bedroom. I saw him falter only twice, first in the hall, where he was almost but not quite beguiled by the aromatic intimations of sausages chuckling on the kitchen stove, and again as he cruised past the lounge, whose doors were reverberating with the sounds of crude home-made music. But once he had negotiated the twin temptresses of food and jazz his steps were resolute. Like the true egocentric he always was, Landau went straight to the heart of the matter. It was understood that you went to parties to look for girls and then tempt them behind closed doors. He had come to this one supplied with his own girl, much as some of the more considerate guests had brought their own bottle, so that left only the closed doors. These he must have found within two or three minutes of entering the house. Somebody else gave me a lift home that night, and it was the following afternoon before I saw him again.

What surprised me much more than Landau's disappearance was my own realisation as I entered the crowded lounge that somehow in my few weeks at the coast I had drifted into the ranks of a loose-knit coterie which closed its ranks instinctively the moment it found itself in unfamiliar surroundings. Among the crowd laughing and dancing noisily I recognised several faces. Our drummer from the Arcadia was there. Apparently he had decided to overlook the ignominy of his disposal on the bandstand by one of Landau's imported virtuosi, and was thumping away at a side-drum, blissful in the knowledge that he had contrived for once to shake off the attentions of a relentless wife. Sitting alone in a corner by the bay window was one of Landau's ex-girlfriends whose name I never discovered. She smiled hopefully as I came in, but I shrugged my shoulders as if to say that for all I knew Landau was already dead and buried. There were also several of the Arcadia's regular clientèle, most of whom smiled or waved a greeting when they spotted me, and I noticed that Landau's London musician friends attached themselves to me in a vague kind of way most of the time.

The room's focal point was a large round walnut table, on which stood a kitchen bowl filled almost to the brim with what everyone kept referring to as the Punch. You dipped a huge enamel ladle into the mixture and tipped its contents into one of the chipped breakfast cups ranged round the table. Then you drained your cup and hoped for the worst. Compared to most of the revellers you could have called me abstemious, but the trauma of the recent invasion of the Arcadia was still with me, so I grabbed for the ladle. The punch tasted of highly potent and slightly rancid gin, and was probably responsible for most of the high spirits in the room.

I had just taken my first experimental sip when a bare feminine arm wound itself round my neck and a girl's voice, vaguely familiar, said, ' I knew you'd be here. It was ordained.'

I turned and found myself staring into the semi-glazed eyes of Vivienne the Occultiste. She seemed to be having slight difficulty maintaining her balance, and the arm round my neck to be serving a functional rather than a romantic purpose. Down the front of her white linen dress the punch had marked its progress in broad brown stains absorbed into the coarse weave of the material like ink on blotting paper. I must have looked startled at her sudden apparition, because she withdrew her arm and said in a slightly slurred voice, ' It's all right. You needn't look so panic-stricken. I don't fancy you, you know.'

' Thanks very much.'

' No, I'm not going in for callow youth this season. I like

the older men myself. But you must come outside with me for a minute.'

It was hard to tell whether she was serious, but after I had smiled uncertainly, she said, ' Well, you coming?'

' Where?'

' I told you. Outside. Somewhere where it's quiet. Come on. It won't take a minute. It's all right. The birds will still be here when you get back.'

She took my arm and led me from the lounge. My embarrassment was heightened by the fact that as we moved towards the door I recognised a friend of mine called Tommy Lawlor, leaning over the piano discussing something with the string bassist. Lawlor was a ship's musician on the New York run and was usually good for a few anecdotes about American musicians each time he came home. But Vivienne was quite determined that I should not escape. Brushing aside my request for a few moments' grace, she dragged me out of the lounge into an adjoining room in darkness, and silent except for heavy breathing at floor level, and pushed open some french windows leading into a small paved courtyard bright with moonlight. We sat down on a wooden bench and, with her arm still threaded through mine, she began to explain herself.

' You know I can tell the future, don't you?'

' I know you make a living saying you can.'

' No, but I really can. Oh, all that stuff on the pier is a load of lies, of course it is. But I do have the powers, even if I don't choose to use them professionally. It would be bad for business, you understand?'

' Not really.'

Loud guffaws of laughter came from the lounge. I was anxious to get back.

' Look, use your loaf. What's the good of telling a day-tripper from Bermondsey he's got six months to live? For seven-and-six a time you just tell them what they want to hear. There's a marriage in the family, a change of scene and all that. But apart from the pier, I have an entirely different field.'

' Oh really?'

She laughed with some bitterness. ' You sceptical bastard.

72

I suppose you're one of these rationalists.'

She was quite right. Not only was I one of these rationalists, but my fanatical disbelief in the occult amounted itself almost to a superstition. I found her claims preposterous and her attitude towards them rather obnoxious. Had she been a man I would either have insulted her or walked away, but because she was a girl, when she accused me of being a sceptic, all I said was, ' Who me?'

' Look, stop humouring me and listen for a minute. It might be very important for you.'

' Go on. I'm listening.'

' My grandfather turned up a couple of nights ago.'

I gathered this remark was supposed to prostrate me with awe.

' Don't you see? My grandfather. I saw him two nights ago.'

' I'm sure that's all very nice, but . . .'

' Oh, I forgot to tell you. My grandfather died of bronchitis in 1934.'

There was a loud crash from the lounge, the splintering of glass and more laughter. Vivienne had only been half-right about me. I was not only a rationalist but a moral coward too. My only thought was how to escape this half-mad, half-drunk charlatan.

' Now look,' she said, ' my grandfather can't afford to waste his time. He only comes to see me every once in a while. When there's some definite information, you understand?'

' Perfectly. Your grandfather's been dead twenty years and he gives you information.'

' Well, it's true.'

' How does he arrive? I mean, what form does he take?'

' A kind of messy white cloud. At the foot of my bed usually. Just when I'm dropping off to sleep. Of course with all that smoke I can't see his face.'

' In that case, how do you know it's him?' I said brightly.

' The voice, stupid, the voice. He came down two nights ago and you know what he told me? He said that the two musicians I met on the pier were coming into a lot of money.'

' What musicians?'

' I don't know. You and Landau I suppose. You're the only

two I've spoken to. He said there were definitely two of you and that before the summer was out you'd be coming into an unexpected source of money.'

' All sources of money are unexpected to a musician.'

' All right, so laugh if you want to. That's what he said.'

Rationalists are curious people. Had she told me something to do with my being handsome or sought after by women, or even to do with being a great saxophonist, I would have scoffed. I was well aware she was treating me like one of her day-trippers from Bermondsey. But somehow the mention of money put a subtly different complexion on the whole business. After all, she didn't have to tell me all this. She was charging nothing for the consultation, indeed I hadn't even wanted it. Why should she go out of her way to tell me a load of lies? Of course, it was all nonsense, but at least she was sincere.

' Did he give any details?'

She shook her head. ' He never stays long. So I don't know how you're coming into this loot. But I tell you this. He's never been wrong yet.'

I looked at her. She was staring gravely at the tub of geraniums just behind me. Then she sighed and looked up sharply at me.

' Go on. That's it. You can clear off now.'

' Thanks very much. But just one more question. Why bother to tell me all this?'

' It's nothing to do with me. I'm just the instrument. He just said, " Those boys are heading for money. Warn them now ". That's all.'

' Warn them? Why warn?'

' Look, I just deliver the messages. It's my responsibility to pass on the information. What it means is not my business. Mind you,' she said, changing the tone of her voice, ' when you do get the loot, you might feel you're entitled to slip me a few quid for being the one to let you know. But that's up to you.'

And without giving me another glance, she rose from the bench and stumbled through the half-open french windows. I remained on the bench for a while, and as I smoked a cigarette in the moonlight I wondered how Landau was getting on, and whether it was worth disturbing him to give him the glad tidings. I decided against it and made my way back into the lounge. There was no sign of Vivienne. The band was still playing, but some of the faces behind the instruments had changed. I filled a cup from the punch bowl and found myself a chair against the wall. For a while I watched the revels, but soon I got the impression that the males and females had paired themselves off with discouraging mathematical precision. I was wrong, however. A tall girl, her hair bleached almost white by the sun, came and sat on the chair next to me.

'I thought for a minute Vivienne had copped for you,' she said. Her voice was soft but coarse, with just a hint of a local burr.

'It was purely business,' I said.

'You don't want to have no business with that one.'

'Well, not business really. Just a story she wanted to tell me.'

'My name is Maxine. I know yours. Anyway, it's not important.'

We drained several cups of punch after that. It must have been her sex appeal that kept me sober. Some time later we followed Landau's excellent example and went to look for an empty bedroom. On the top floor of the house was a short, unlit corridor, with four doors leading off. We felt our way along the wall. She put her hand on a doorknob but I pulled her arm away.

'Not that one. There's a friend of mine in there.'

'How do you know?' In the darkness her voice was a whisper.

'You hear that humming noise? It's a vacuum cleaner. That means Tommy Lawlor's in there. He's a ship's musician, and he's so used to the sound of the engines that he has to have the noise with him before he feels comfortable.'

'You bloody musicians. You're all mad.'

'Not so mad that we can't occasionally find an empty bedroom.'

In the dark I had accidentally pushed open a door and been received only with silence.

It must have been about an hour later that we returned

to the lounge, by which time Maxine and I had given each other entirely bogus versions of our life stories and arrived at a state of temporary permanence with each other. In the lounge the crowd had thinned a little, but the music had become a little more serious. There was still no sign of Landau. Maxine performed the rite known as hanging about with considerable expertise. Everywhere I went she followed, implying a proprietary air without actually saying or doing anything. But I was more interested in the music. I began thinking again of the chaotic evening at the Arcadia and kicked myself for not having come to the party equipped to play. There seemed to be nothing else constructive left to do.

I listened for a while, measuring myself against the quartet blowing so strenuously, came to the modest conclusion that I could easily have held my own with them, and then quite suddenly became bored with everything about the room. I could not leave until Landau came back. I couldn't take part in the music making because my instrument was lying in the Arcadia band-room, and the thought of getting deliberately drunk did not appeal to me. Maxine came and sat by me for the tenth time that night and said,

' Fed up?'

' A bit. I wish I had my saxophone with me.'

' Bloody musicians. You're all the same.'

' No we're not. We're all different. For instance, I wouldn't have played the changes they just used in " Sweet Georgia Brown ".'

' Bloody mad, the lot of you. Want to go home?'

' Wouldn't mind.'

' All right. I'll see what can be done.'

She walked over to a knot of people at the far end of the room, conscious of the fact that I was enjoying her movements as she went. She talked earnestly for a few moments with someone whose face I couldn't see, a woman, tall and drooping slightly from the waist. The two of them seemed to come to some kind of agreement, and then the drooping one half-turned to give Maxine a set of car keys. I recognised her as the lone patron of the Arcadia bar, the one who sat smiling enigmatically all night, sipping gin till the last few dances, when she would always consent to be pushed around the floor by whoever it was she wanted to take her home. Now, in the half-light of the lounge, she looked more like a private investigator than ever. As Maxine took the car keys, the lone gin-sipper glanced at me, murmured something to Maxine and then they both laughed.

'My friend says we can use her car. She's got a lift. Come on.'

'Sorry. I don't drive.'

'Come on, useless. I do.'

'Maybe I ought to wait for Landau. We came together. Landau, he's a friend of mine.'

'Don't I know it. It took me days to find that out. Come on.'

We went out into the forecourt of the house and crossed over to a small red two-seater. There was a breeze blowing in from the sea which did its best to counter the effects of the punch. Maxine unlocked the car door. I jumped in beside her and we cruised out into the road. The moon was still high and the coast road deserted. For a while we drove leisurely along, and then something occurred to me.

'I didn't know you knew Landau.'

'Only in passing. I wanted to know if there was something wrong with you.'

'How do you mean?'

'Well, I'm not exactly a horror, am I? Am I?'

'Certainly not.'

'Well then. I come into the Arcadia every night giving you the office, and—nothing. You looked right through me.'

'So you're the one who was asking about me.'

'Why were you like that? You didn't waste much time tonight.'

'It's all very complicated. It's to do with my playing. I can't go into it now.'

She glanced at me and the car swerved across the road.

'Who'd have a musician?' she asked the night wind. 'You're all off your heads, the whole bunch of you.'

'Where do you stay, Maxine?'

'For the time being, anywhere you do.'

Before I could reply she laughed. 'You might as well take

advantage while you can. My friends say I'm fickle.'

'Well, I don't know. You can't just move in like that. We do have a landlady and she . . .'

'Mrs Stewart's an old friend of mine. She ought to be the amount of times I've ended up at number eighty-seven. Don't worry about her. She'll be glad to see me again. Any other objections?'

'None at all. Welcome home.'

For a while we cruised on in silence, the humming of the car only half-drowning the sound of the surf. Cloudmist began to obscure the sky, and under the indeterminate contours of the moon Maxine's face had a ghostly pallor which lent her features a grace they had not possessed at the house. I sat there idly balancing the arguments for and against falling in love. It would have been easy that night, in the car, and perhaps it was only Maxine's sudden desire to chat again which saved me from that particular indiscretion.

'Tell me what Vivienne wanted with you.'

'She a friend of yours then?'

'Not really. But she's been working the pier for three years now. We know each other, that's all.'

'She started telling me this wild story about . . .'

'See if I can guess. She told you her grandfather had come down to say that you were coming into some money, right?'

'How did you know?'

'You believe in all that junk?'

'Of course not. But I let her talk. She seemed to be happy just telling me about it. No harm done, I suppose.'

'Not till you actually come into the money.'

'What money? Don't tell me you believe it.'

'No. It's just that she shoots this line to all the men she can lay her hands on. Every summer the same routine.'

'But why?'

She stepped on the accelerator. The wind tousled her hair and mine.

'You're not very shrewd, are you?'

'No I'm not,' I said, 'I'm just a simple unspoiled boy.'

'Well, just imagine for a minute that what she told you tonight turns out to be true. What do you do when you get the money? I'll tell you what you do. You'd be so grateful that you'd go straight round and put her in it. Now wouldn't you? It's human nature.'

' I begin to see. Does it ever pay off for her?'

' Not very often. But it doesn't have to. Two or three strikes a year is enough. Last summer, for instance, she told the tale to some of the crowd that came down here for the races. One of them won three hundred quid the next day, so a hundred and fifty of it found its way into her pocket.'

' I see.'

Maxine moved into the house in John Street that night and stayed there, more or less, for the rest of the season, although it was not always me who was the attraction. When her friends said she was fickle, they were making the understatement of the year.

7

On the wet mornings, while Landau slept on alone in the empty ramshackle house in Kemptown, I pottered in the high-domed reading-room of the Public Library, composing ribald limericks and even on rare occasions scribbling a few pages of prose in a sixpenny notebook. Sometimes, when he requested it, I showed Landau the fruit of my labours. He would sit up in bed, eyes crusted with sleep and blinking sullenly against the intrusive noon light, scratch his head and look dubiously at my work. There was absolutely no point to these little literary charades. Landau had no critical faculty. Anything longer than ten lines always induced in him the same awestruck reaction and a smile of self-satisfaction as he drifted into his routine confessional about the slothfulness of his existence. He was toying with a theory that summer that marijuana was beginning to impair his memory, and would sup up great lungfuls of smoke with the air of an empirical scientist bent on martyrdom. I, who had never known him in the days of his innocence, was unable to argue the point, and he usually ended these orgies of mutual self-pity with a theatrical sigh and a remark to the effect that I was only able to consider the possibility of writing at all because I had the advantage of ' a good education ', by which I suppose he meant that I had contrived to avoid doing any work till I was twenty.

But these discussions were not entirely useless. The marijuana theory gave him a good excuse for what was really congenital forgetfulness, and the desultory readings exalted me to the status of author, if only with a readership of one. Landau's imagination must have been fired at least once by these sessions, because he returned for tea one afternoon flushed with the pride of a great achievement. Passing like a drifting ship through the narrow causeways linking the main streets of the town, he had been beguiled by the chaotic window display of a dusty junkshop masquerading as an antique parlour. It was quite untypical of him, but he had entered and been tempted to buy, and now he presented the spoils for my approval with the air of a man blessed by beginner's luck. He tipped up a large brown paper bag and dumped its contents on to the kitchen table, just as I had been tipping my own literary refuse on to his counterpane two or three mornings a week. I found myself staring at a heap of books, dusty and dog's-eared nineteenth century editions of the classics. I could tell from a glance at his face that Landau was convinced he had pulled off one of his authentic masterstrokes, and that his purchases were priceless.

' Look at that, Tom. *Paradise Lost* for eighteen pence. And *Selected Poems of Swinburne*, only ninepence. Can you imagine?'

Something occurred to him for the first time, and his brow furrowed in private concern.

' Who was Swinburne, Tom?'

' Like it says on the cover, he was a poet.'

' I can see that. But what was his scene?'

' I'm not sure. I think he died about forty, fifty years ago, and he wrote something once about the hounds of spring on winter's traces.'

' He did, did he?'

Landau tried to make something of that, and then forgot about Swinburne.

' What about this one, eh? Bacon's *Essays*. One shilling. And look here. Shelley, *Selected Poems*, for sixpence.'

He never got much further than the faded inscriptions on the flyleaves and perhaps a first stanza or two, but what little he did read he contrived somehow to remember, and he was for ever trotting out his quotations at the most incongruous moments. He kept the books with him for many years afterwards in his travels up and down Europe, talismans of a belated attempt at self-education. Ten years later they were still with him, on the marble shelves of his New York office, holding a place of honour between *A Pictorial History of Jazz* and the inevitable paperback edition of *The Doors of Perception*, every musician's apologia for contravening the narcotic laws.

These feeble literary stirrings had one other important effect on Landau. They undoubtedly prepared him for the turn of events at the end of June with the return of Blitski. Since the night of the scuffle on the promenade we had heard nothing of him, and had even begun not to talk about him. And then, one sunlit evening while Landau was conducting his daily researches into the art of tying a bow tie and I was polishing my brown shoes with the black shoe polish that my new station in life demanded, Blitski made his comeback. This time he was alone and carried none of the portable demagogue kit which had so astonished us earlier that summer. No collapsible soapbox, no subversive literature, no camp followers, no prepared speeches. His luggage this time consisted of a second-hand portable typewriter, the 1936 edition of *The Writer's and Artist's Year Book*, and specimen copies of thirty or forty periodicals. He had talked for years about ' crashing the market ', and it was now clear that he was about to make his bid at our expense.

Landau, still slightly tipsy on the wine of his first poetry readings, displayed a surprising charity towards him. The thought of numbering among his friends a political agitator had been stimulating enough. Now that the political agitator was to emerge from his cocoon of sedition to display the wings of authorship, Landau was really very flattered. For the next ten days he and I were obliged to throw ourselves into the campaign just as though the typewriter, the year book and the ambitions were communal property, which I suppose in a way they were. We came to a gentleman's agreement whereby we paid Blitski's rent until he sold something to somebody, on condition that while we were playing to the dancers, Blitski would remain indoors slaving away at the composition of masterpieces. I was interested in his methods, and when he expounded them to me they sounded reasonable enough. Leafing through the year book, he had realised that there were so many periodicals in print that it would be a virtual impossibility to write anything that somebody somewhere would not be interested in.

' I'm not aiming at any specific market, you understand. Doing that is the classic beginner's mistake. What I intend to do is to write the piece that happens to appeal to me at any given moment. Only when it is done will I look for the right magazine to send it to. With my range of interests it's certain that everything I write will find its own market.'

His first product was a short, and I think a humorous, essay entitled 'Satire and Metallurgy', which he posted off to a Canadian mining journal. He then embarked on a much longer, more ambitious piece called 'Symbolism and Nomenclature in the novels of Walter Scott', a work so abstruse that the editor of the *Scotsman* never even bothered to acknowledge its receipt. It was after this second failure that Landau's rights as patron began to obtrude. He demanded to see concrete proof of the campaign to crash the markets, at which Blitski, still supremely confident of his own powers, showed him the working notes for the Walter Scott epic. Landau began to settle down for a good read, but after only a few moments looked up at Blitski in bewilderment.

'Habakkuk Gilfillan, Saunders Mucklemackit, what's all this?'

'That's the symbolic nomenclature.'

'No it's not. It's just a string of mad names. What's it all supposed to mean? Tom, is this writing?'

'Ask him. He wrote it.'

'You expect to sell this crap? You actually think people are going to pay you money for it?'

'Walter Scott got money for it.'

'Never mind about Walter Scott. I'm not paying half his rent. Listen, why don't you write something people can understand, instead of all this pickle-bucket crap? You want to live on a soapbox the rest of your life?'

Blitski was cornered. Landau was indeed paying half his rent, and he desperately needed to buy more time in which to find the magic formula that transmutes manuscripts into publishers' cheques. He gave us his word that from now on he would concentrate on what he called trash for the masses. For a few days he seemed to be honouring the bargain, until we realised something I had sensed from the start, that gentlemen's agreements are only workable when dealing with gentlemen, and that assuming Blitski to be one was a grave tactical error. On the fifth night, Landau, returning home early from work on the trumped-up pretext of a sick stomach, spotted our protégé drinking noisily in a local cider bar. All Blitski's hurt insistence that he had been 'out collating local colour' was wasted on Landau, who didn't know what collating was but had a rough working idea of fraud. Blitski returned to London the next morning, bequeathing to us the selected periodicals, the first sentence of a short story intended for *Woman* which read 'Hermione undulated down the stairs, her hennaed hair floating down after her', a four-line ode to Engels, and a mysterious fragment of doggerel whose eventual purpose we never discovered, reading, 'The Medes and the Persians were busily casting aspersions'. But although Blitski never realised it, his short-lived literary pilgrimage proved to be one of the decisive acts of our summer.

One morning, just after his second departure, I was lying in bed, still half-asleep, when Landau poked his head round the door. Immediately my ego sagged. I was supposed to be the athletic one. You could tell from the way he ran for a bus that Landau had never been much of a sportsman, that he would be hopeless trying to anticipate the bounce of a ball on grass, that he would never kick any object with his left foot if his right were available, that he would never kick anything at all if he could possibly avoid it. And yet here he was, awake before me. It was a reversal of our roles and it interested me greatly.

He sat on the edge of his bed and sucked his tongue.

'Can't sleep.'

'Headache?'

'It's these teeth. I was born to suffer all my life with these teeth.'

His doleful expression and the intensity of his words were too much for me, and I burst into riotous laughter. Soon he joined in, rolling on to the floor, hand still clamped to his jaw. Then he suddenly grew serious again and said, 'If I had the whole lot out, what do you reckon would happen to my embouchure? I mean, I might never be able to play again. Hey, I've just thought of it. If you're a musician, your face is your fortune. Why don't you put that into one of your stories? Has there ever been a great saxophone player who had to swallow it because of his teeth?'

'Don't be so defeatist. One of my uncles had fifteen out

in one go, and he reckoned he went to heaven under the anaesthetic and came back to life again. He reckons that having your teeth out can be a great spiritual experience.'

' Oh, shut up. I'm in real pain.'

' It's all in the mind,' I told him, still laughing.

Landau punched the eiderdown in his frustration.

' Oh, no. Don't you start all that crap too. Not you. I had two hours of all that once from Eddie Perry when he got back from India. Three months of cocktail piano in a Delhi hotel and he thinks he knows the secret of life. You know what happened to him? He keeps telling us there's no such thing as pain, so Tommy Cooke hits him right up the arse with his trombone and tells him to think his way out of that one.'

I sat up and adjusted my pillows. ' Well go and see a dentist then. Or take something.'

He made no reply but lay across the foot of my bed on his stomach, staring down at the worn linoleum. A fine shaft of sunlight prodded the lobe of his left ear. A faintly maturing odour drifted up from his feet. From downstairs came vague scrapings and bumpings followed by fits of muffled swearing which meant the housework was being done. Traffic hummed beyond the open window and a dog barked in the back garden.

' Anything in the papers?'

Again Landau made no reply. He rolled over on to his back and surveyed the ceiling.

' What shall we do today Tom? Don't fancy the pier, it's getting me down, that room. Can't we do something different? You know what? Ever since Blitski went back I've had the feeling nobody knows we exist. I mean our work. What does it amount to? Your name in the trade papers in small print at the start of the season, and after that, nothing. Some of the boys on the pier have been doing that same job for ten years. Just think of that. Ten years on the pier.'

' At least they're working.'

' That's negative thinking. Remember what you said about negative thinking? You said it was for negative people. Well, are we negative people? I know I'm not.'

' What did you have in mind?'

'I don't know. There must be some way we can get known. In the profession, I mean. So that when somebody is looking for a musician, our names automatically come into their minds. You know how it is. Instead of them saying what have you done and who have you worked for, they just book you and no questions asked.'

'Who's They?'

'Come on, you know what I mean. And I think I know a way we could become real characters overnight.'

I looked at him with renewed interest. The toothache had been an excuse. It was not sore gums but a septic ego that was spoiling his sleep. He sat up, stared at the wall and smiled distantly, as he always did when observing the unfolding pageant of his own daydreams.

'Actually it was Blitski who gave me the idea. Now he came down here trying to write something for money, and you're always saying you can write just as good as him. Now, take a look at the trade papers. I was studying them after work last night, and have you ever seen such a big pile of crap in your whole life? Suppose you got something published, you'd be lifted out of the rut overnight.'

'What could I write about?'

'Anything, so long as it's not all that picklecrap stuff Blitski was on about. You could write about yourself. Or me, or the bands we're in, whatever you like, so long as it draws attention on to us.'

I was silent. Landau had inadvertently marched with hobnailed boots all over my literary soul. My writing was too sacred ever to be polluted by the taint of the dance band business. The things I was doing in the Public Library were pure and beautiful, and everything about the band business was impure and comically ugly. The trade press was produced by vandals for vandals, and the thought of their publishing anything of mine was enough to horrify me. At least, that is what I told myself. But I could hardly tell it to Landau, who believed in his innocence that good writing was good writing, no matter who published it.

'Let me explain,' I said, very patiently. 'The stuff you read in the trade papers isn't printed because it's well-written. It's printed because the people who write it are usually well-known musicians—I'm not talking about what are laughingly called the staff writers now. You've got the whole thing the wrong way round. You don't write something and then get well-known. You get well-known first and then you write something. If I sent them anything they'd glance at my name and then chuck it in the wastepaper basket.'

Landau sat up with an abrupt dramatic movement. He appraised me with eyes sparkling through the custard of sleep still stuck in their corners. Then he pronounced judgement.

'You are a genius. That was absolutely brilliant, what you just said. About having it the wrong way round.'

'I wouldn't go so far as all that,' I said modestly.

But for all his admiration for my lying sophistries, Landau continued to study the chances of a quick notoriety through the trade press. Usually his hare-brained schemes were forgotten from the moment you opposed them, but the thought of a literary assault on the music business appealed to him immensely, probably because it seemed like switching the point of attack, which is always appealing to an arm-chair tactician. The germ of the idea had been lodged in Landau's brain by Blitski's caperings and would not be displaced. That afternoon we went up to the pitch-and-putt course just outside the town, and every time I addressed my ball, Landau would gather his thoughts, making some exclamation about fame at precisely the moment I was about to make contact. The next day he ruined my tea by thrusting copies of the musical weeklies in front of me, and giving me a diverting review of their contents.

'There you are. Look at this whole page. Criticisms of records by people who've never seen the inside of a recording studio in their lives.'

Neither had we, but this did not seem the best moment to remind him of the fact.

'Now, what have we here? Pictures of birds trying to look sexy. And they don't even call them singers. Not even vocalists. You know how they describe them? Chirpettes. What kind of talk is that? Look at all this, who's appearing in which town, should Americans be allowed to play in England, it's not fit to wipe your arse on.'

And consumed by aesthetic disgust, he crumpled the offending sheet into a tight ball and lobbed it through the kitchen window. His aim was poor and the ball of paper bounced back and rolled under the table.

'You could do that kind of stuff on your head, you know that. You could write about standards of musical appreciation in our dance halls, how to educate the public to jazz, you know the kind of stuff. All right, so you haven't got a reputation. So write them a letter.'

The sound of the phrase communicated itself to Landau's mind. He always had to express his ideas out loud before appreciating the import of what he had said.

'Hey, that's it. A letter. They're bound to print it because it doesn't cost them anything, not like an actual piece, you told me that yourself. So, they print your letter, it starts a big row, and we're made.'

'Just tell me why you want to start a row. Why can't it be something peaceful, at least on the surface? You know, cold and distant.'

'No, what you need is the biggest argument you can think of. Libel someone, throw accusations around, something like that. It never fails.'

I thought about the idea for the rest of that day. Perhaps in his innocence Landau was right after all. He often had been in the past. But what did his plan for an insulting letter have to do with me? Does a man fall for Natasha Rostov just so that he can write about saxophones in trade weeklies? And what kind of recognition was Landau after? His trouble was not romanticism, but romanticism about the wrong things. His heart was in the right place but his eyes were slightly out of focus. He was keen enough about the music, but it was the mystique of the curious profession we had drifted into which really captivated him. Landau's sole desire was to become one of the demi-gods we now worshipped, and to play well happened to be only one of several ways of achieving this status. His attitude was tawdry, superficial, immoral and, I see now, utterly justified by the realities of the world we were living in. It was the trappings he was after, not the substance, his instinctive worldliness about such things telling him that there were many trappings and almost no substance at all. Usually this peculiar frenzied realism

88

of his was held in check by events, but at unpredictable moments it would burst through the very necessary veneer of humble decorum to transform him into a half-crazed propagator of his own lost cause.

One day that spring we had been crossing Coventry Street, involved in a violent argument about whether each key suggested its own colour. Landau was feeling unduly sore that day about the fact that the joys of the professional life seemed never to bring security with them, and I kept insisting that to expect both things, the joy and the security, was to misunderstand the nature of our position. I kept telling him that the music was supposed to be its own reward, but he would have none of it. He was convinced that life, at the same time it was a syncopated bacchanale, ought to be lucrative too. Jazz, he insisted, could be made as commercial a commodity as cheese or sex, so long as it was shrewdly presented. He foresaw musicians who were not only brilliant instrumentalists but captivating personalities, men whose magnetism did not stop abruptly the moment they laid down their instruments. Greatness according to Landau, true greatness, was indivisible. The great soloist should also be handsome, clever, compassionate and above all, colourful. What all this rigmarole had to do with colour associations in keys I have no idea, but most of the conversations involving Landau had a funny way of drifting far from the point.

At that moment two musicians tumbled up the steps of the subway. Each carried an instrument case and each sang as he went. It was not ordinary singing, but the strictly functional kind based on a harmonic sequence, the kind that young jazz musicians often preoccupy themselves with in public places. They wore dark suits and sunglasses. Black silk gloves flopped over their wrists. They swept past us like conquerors, purposeful, self-important, intent on an object significant because unknown. In a few moments they had merged into the crowds of shoppers swirling about us. But in their wake they left the dust of their own pursuit, and it choked Landau insufferably. He stood dazzled on the pavement, the light of dawning hero-worship in his eyes, while my own mind, the usual rag-bag of literary allusions, immediately conjured up Toad and the yellow motor car. Landau peered down the street for one last glimpse of the heroes from the promised land, turned to me and said, ' Now they were the boys. The real boys.'

We walked on towards St James's Park. Landau was silent, a smile of beatitude flickering softly about his features. I think it was the black silk gloves that really did it. They seemed to stand in Landau's mind for an impregnable professionalism on the part of their owners, for a sophistication that could only be won after a thousand and one nights in the constant twilight of palais de danse, that sophistication which Landau yearned for so fervently. As my mind rummaged again among its literary references it came up this time with Sherlock Holmes. Landau had taken those gloves just as Holmes took Mortimer's walking stick in *The Hound of the Baskervilles*, deducing from them everything about their owners. By the time we reached the neatly barbered lawns of the park, he had formed a picture of our two strange musicians, right down to their musical styles, their sexual ethics, their bank balances and the places they lived in. The picture enchanted him, and he tried for a while in stumbling phrases to describe it to me, without much success.

Probably the two musicians were no better established or more highly talented than either Landau or myself, but we caught them at a moment when their earnest pursuit of somebody or something perhaps no more exotic than a bus might easily be mistaken by an impressionable rival for poise and maturity. It was precisely this kind of professional acceptance that Landau longed for, and it had nothing to do with playing well or making money. Had the dream been frankly mercenary I might have been more sympathetic, but his hero-worship of players outside our tiny circle always maddened me. If he was so eager to admire other musicians, why couldn't he admire me instead of being patronising about what he called our mutual faults?

The next morning, while Landau slept, I retired to the reading-room, took up my usual seat by the Natural History shelves, and began composing a letter to one of the most prominent of the musical weeklies. For an experienced, if unpublished writer like me, a few hundred words would be child's play. I, who had actually read *War and Peace*, was about to condescend to my illiterate fellow-tradesmen. The satire wove sinuously into my first sentence as though it were creating itself. Even as it took form on the paper, the cadence of my closing line presented itself. I would sign off with, 'The musician of integrity is the one who eats'. The fact that I was not sure what I meant was by the way. I returned to thoughts of my opening paragraph. The second sentence was less impressive, the third downright mediocre. The fourth refused to come at all. I sat there staring at the rich cinnamon binding of *The Voyage of the Beagle*, wondering why it was that the things I was always saying refused to become things I could write down. It took me four days to write five hundred words, and when I showed the final polished version to Landau he never even bothered to read it. In his life four days meant half a dozen newly discovered unholy grails, and at first he could not even remember what the letter was supposed to be for.

'You took your time about it, I'll say that.'

He crumpled the sheets of copper-plate handwriting into his band jacket and promised faithfully not to forget to post them on his way to the pier that night. As he walked out of the room I had sudden misgivings. There was still time to call him back, still time to stop the machinery we were about to set in motion. Would it be so prudent after all to send the letter? I had only to tell him further revisions were needed, and he would hand it back to me without a thought. Probably he would never mention the matter again. But I was inhibited by the thought that perhaps after all the letter really was a literary masterpiece. You could never tell. Then again, there was always Landau's execrable memory. Perhaps despite his assurances to the contrary, he would forget to post it. I sometimes wonder what would have happened that summer if he had.

8

It was said of him by his friends that Blitski's tongue rendered Marconi's life work redundant. If ever you trusted him with a confidence you soon found consolation, not only in his sympathy and understanding, but in the concerted sympathy and understanding of everyone in his vast social orbit. Once, in an unguarded moment, I had happened to confide in him my acute anxiety about the reaction of my lip muscles to long bouts of saxophone playing. Months later, at a Saturday night engagement he had wangled for me for the annual celebrations of some obscure sect of Utopian Socialists, I had hardly assembled my instruments before I realised that he had peppered the audience with an assortment of week-end osteopaths and what he called secular faith-healers, all equipped with purely theoretical panaceas for my troubles. I was as polite as the occasion demanded, but I remember being very irritated later that evening by the patronising way the dancers belittled my playing and then made generous allowances for me because of my unfortunate affliction.

I had come to realise over the years that these vicarious revelations of Blitski's seemed to be governed by a vague mathematical law, which said that the more precious the confessional, the wider its dissemination. To do him justice, there was no malice or mischief-making in all this. It was simply that once his frustrated creative impulses began gilding the lily of plain fact, he was too pent up with excitement not to convey his visions to those whose companionship he valued. In fact, this liberality with the privacy of others was the only manifestation I could ever detect of his living by the stern socialistic theories he propagated.

The longer he cut himself off from our hospitality the more succulent its delights must have tasted to him, and after three weeks away from us he must somehow have magnified our modest little ménage into a sumptuous pleasure-house open to all. At least, I can think of no other explanation for the rising tide of callers who deposited themselves on our doorstep hopefully waving the credentials of a vague association with him. During late June and early July we must have turned away from our doors half the unemployed renegade utopians in London. Some staggered under knapsacks, others only under the burden of their own fierce incorruptibility. A few wore beards, one or two were bald. There was one fat man I remember whose walk up the modest incline to the house had so distressed him that he hardly had the breath left to tell me, as he stood there with one sandalled foot in the door, of his belief in stringent dietary laws as the only salvation from the political and economic confusions of capitalism. Not all our visitors were young, and very few justified themselves by being beautiful. There were at least three girls whose plain features and grave demeanours magically rendered them skinny rather than slender. But all of them had that same indefinable yet unmistakable air about them of people eager to demonstrate their contempt for the principle of private property by invading somebody else's.

Probably the six bottles of *Nuits St Georges* had sprouted into six crates inside the vineyards of Blitski's well-meaning head. The beds on the floor must have ripened into elegant boudoirs, and the bread-and-jam at five o'clock into a soup-kitchen for gourmets. But whatever the legends Blitski managed to weave out of his brief experiences at the house, hardly a day went by without either Landau or myself backing away and slamming the front door with indecent haste. I thought it very unfair of Landau to blame me for all this.

'After all,' he said, 'he's your friend, not mine. It's your responsibility to tell him.'

'Tell him what?'

'To stop sending all his pals down here. What does he think we're running, a youth hostel?'

'Personally, I think it's best to leave well alone. If we don't say anything about it, the whole thing will die down. I think we're over the worst already. Anyway, you must remember that he probably thinks this is what you want.'

'What I want? How do you mean?'

'Well, the first thing you have to keep in mind is that Blitski is one of those people who thinks in terms of types rather than individuals. He could see you liked him, and he probably thought it was because of his politics, his idealism, or whatever you want to call it. So that now he can't be with us, he keeps trying to fill the gap with substitutes.'

'But none of this lot is anything like him.'

'Oh, we know that. The question is, does Blitski know it? You know what? I think Blitski regards you as promising revolutionary material.'

Landau beamed. 'You reckon so?'

'And if you are, that means you're entitled to keep open house for all the comrades he can find.'

'I'm not that promising. They can all go and get stuffed, the whole lot of them.'

'Agreed. And we haven't been caught yet. All we have to do is keep on shutting the door first and ask questions afterwards. So long as we do that, we're safe.'

'All the same, if we should get lumbered, remember what I said. He's your friend, not mine, so they can kip in your room.'

A week or two ago this kind of veiled threat would have had no effect on me. But the truth of it was that since Maxine had moved in, I had become rather sensitive about the place I lived in. It is not poverty which makes people ashamed of their homes, but sex. I had tried for the first time that summer to make my room less like a pigsty and more like a place where human beings might feel inclined to co-habit two or three times a week. The day after the party I had stacked my books in two neat piles under the window, had repaired the dressing-table mirror by stuffing back numbers of the trade papers behind the frame, I now washed my dirty underwear in the bathroom down the passage instead of in the sink in my own room, and I had taken to making the bed every other day instead of twice a week now that Maxine seemed likely to be sharing it with me. And then, after all these stringent reforms, Maxine had insisted on camping in the box-room on the top floor.

'I always use that room when I stay here, and anyway, it's a good thing for a girl to have a bit of independence.'

I went through the motions of protesting, but I was secretly relieved she would not be under my feet all day. This was how I arrived at the ultimate lunacy of making my bed more frequently from the day I began using it less often.

I had no idea what Maxine did with her time and did not feel inclined to ask. She worked the afternoon shift at the restaurant a few doors down from the Arcadia, but there were occasions, once or twice a week, when she never came home at all. On the other hand, I told myself, when she did come home there must presumably have been another base of operations from which she was absent. She still frequented the Arcadia at night, and was a little put out by the fact that although she had somehow contrived to get me on to the free list for lunches at the restaurant where she worked, I had not even attempted to do the same for her at the Arcadia box-office. So far as I was concerned, this was not a bad arrangement, as it gave her that very useful thing, a focus for her sense of grievance whenever she felt the need to complain about my treatment of her. Blitski's callers she found neither interesting nor irritating, but merely the kind of crazy manifestation to be expected in any situation involving the mad musicians she had decided Landau and me must be.

One afternoon I came back dispirited from one of Bertie Fields' very rare and utterly pointless rehearsals to find her perched on the kitchen table painting her toenails.

'What's happened to the restaurant? I looked in for a bite of lunch about half past one, but I couldn't see you, so I ducked out.'

'That's a choice greeting if you like. He hasn't seen me for two days and all he can talk about is food. Typical.'

'If I haven't seen you, whose fault is that? You disappeared without a word on Monday night and . . .'

'Stop snooping.'

'Was I snooping?'

She performed the last flourish on her toenails, slid off the table and undulated like Blitski's spectral Hermione towards the door, trying to make her exit as dramatic as possible.

'There's a man in your room.'

'That must be a situation you're more used to than me.'

She pouted. 'That was a cowardly thing to say.'

'I know. I only said it because it's true.'

'All right. Now I'm going to make you feel really lousy. I bought you a shirt. It's on your bed.'

'You shouldn't go spending your money on me like that. What size collar?'

'Seventeen. Go on. He's waiting.'

I became anxious as I saw she was serious about the visitor.

'There's not really anybody up there, is there?'

'I just told you. He's been waiting about half an hour.'

'You're joking.'

'Am I? You just go and look.'

'Maxine, you rotten cow. You know how hard Landau and me have been beating off the callers. Why couldn't you tell him I'd left and you didn't know where I was?'

'Because if I'd said that, you'd probably be having a go at me right now for being rude to your friends.'

I should have known it was impossible to argue with her.

'Let me guess,' I said wretchedly. 'Knapsack, beard, no socks, undernourished.'

'Wrong, wrong, wrong, and wrong,' she said truculently. 'As a matter of fact, this one's not bad looking. That's one of the reasons I let him in. Course, I haven't decided if he's my type yet, but he had a collar and tie, dark grey suit, clean fingernails, polished shoes, sharp haircut.'

'Christ,' I said. 'It sounds like Gregory Peck. You're sure there's not some mistake?'

'Course there's no mistake. He particularly asked for you. I'm going to have a bath.'

She slammed the kitchen door behind her, nursing some mysterious hurt of her own. I listened to her clattering up the back stairs, drag her heels along the upstairs passage and shut her bedroom door. By now I knew who my visitor must be. I buttered myself a slice of bread, gulped down a mouthful of milk from the bottle on the table and went upstairs. On the first floor landing I peeped through the grimy lace curtains. Their dust made me sneeze. The Ford Anglia parked in the road confirmed my theory. When he heard my foot-steps coming up the stairs Victor must have jumped up from my bed. By the time I opened the door he was half-way across the room to greet me. His gaunt features realigned themselves into a broad smile.

'Victor. I was just thinking about you. What brings you down here, as if I didn't know?'

He laughed and took off his thick tortoise-shell spectacles, which he began polishing with the edge of my towel dangling from the rail under the sink.

'Actually the crisis is over. But the strain was too much. I felt I needed a little rest.'

His long, lean body, thrust slightly forward at the left shoulder, described a gesture half-shrug, half-shiver. I opened a couple of bottles of beer, handed him one and sat on the edge of my bed, chewing the last of my bread and butter. He stood leaning against the open window tapping his finger-nails on the beer bottle.

'Who was it this time?'

'This secretary, at head office, see. I knew I shouldn't go near that place. Every time I put my nose inside the door it ends up with trouble. After about a week she started talking about leaving her old man for me, so I thought I might as well disappear for a while.'

'Very sensible. Where's your bags?'

'Oh, I won't be staying. I have to be in town tomorrow morning to get the invoices in and make the weekly report. Actually, I'm here on a whim. I was working the South London area this morning and I was driving over to Streat-ham with some samples. I don't know. The sun was beating down, I thought what the hell. So I kept on driving till I got here.'

He took a long swig from the bottle and wiped his mouth on the towel. Then he looked at me and added, 'I can come back tomorrow afternoon though. If it's all right with you and Landau.'

'Certainly. Welcome to the club.'

He seemed immensely relieved by my invitation. His mood instantly soared. In one moment he had dumped his samples, torn up his invoices, shed several years and reinstated himself in the ranks of the adolescents. He grinned the special grin which melted frustrated secretaries by the dozen and asked, ' Who's that blonde? The one who showed me up?'

' Her name's Maxine and I get the feeling she's going to show us all up before long. Officially she's kind of half-staying with me at the moment.'

' I take your hint.'

' There's no need. She's got a mind of her own, if you can call it a mind. If she thinks you're more interesting than I am, just watch out, that's all.'

He drained his bottle and placed it carefully on the windowsill.

' How's it all going down here? The music, I mean?'

' All right I suppose.'

He looked disappointed. ' I thought this was the big time, this was it. You know, a professional musician at last and all that. You ought to be on top of the world. I came down here expecting you . . .'

' Easy on. You sound like Landau. He's the one you want to see if you're looking for the big time. He's been walking about like Duke Ellington ever since he got here.'

' And you?'

' Well, it turns out to be just a job, really. Only instead of packing your instrument up after the National Anthem, you leave it in the band-room and come back again the next night.'

But Victor, with his incurable romanticism, was determined to be starry-eyed about my rise in status.

' Never mind. At least you've proved you can hold down a full-time job.'

' Hold it down? There's nobody else who wants to pick it up, that's all. I'll tell you something that'll surprise you, Victor. The standard here is lower than those Saturday night municipal dances. How about that?'

' I don't believe it.'

' Do you know, the first night I got here, we play " Woodchopper's Ball ". And it turns out I'm the only one in the whole band who can play a blues in D♭. I was shattered.'

That shut him up for the moment, and I immediately felt sorry for having deflated him. Poor Victor, who needed somebody else's triumph so desperately to keep himself going. He worked as a traveller for the paper handkerchief department of a large cosmetics combine, and although he detested the world of commerce more even than Blitski, having been victimised by it at first-hand, he was sadly lacking in that fine contempt for convention which gave Blitski the moral strength to queue up at the National Assistance Board in unpressed clothes. By environment and heredity Victor should have been the prototype of the man who waits forty years to get his gold watch from the chairman of the board. And no doubt he would have been had it not been for the accident of his temperament and the exposure during his teens to the pernicious influence of myself. From the day he staggered from my front room, drunk with the brandy of Muggsy Spanier and his Ragtimers, he had become a convert to the curious belief that only jazz musicians live beautiful and worthwhile lives. The music must have given him a dazzling glimpse of another, highly-coloured world, and he believed for ever after that to play an instrument for a living was very nearly an ascent to godhead. At seventeen he had gone to the length of buying a second-hand clarinet, on which after two weeks of my coaching he was able to play the first six bars of 'Whispering'. But unlike the rest of us, he had no talent for sponging on his parents, and so, with sad reluctance, he sold the clarinet, took a job as an insurance clerk, graduated through the cavernous shipping offices of Leadenhall Street to the cosmetics business and confined his musical ambitions to overseeing the welfare of myself, and later Landau.

But even though the salesman's life disgusted him, he devoted much of his unquestioned intelligence to aping its methods to beat the System. Realising after a few months that statistics are the mathematics of falsehood, he had invented a method of making his invoices look twice as conscientious as they should have done. After a short time with the paper handkerchiefs he had managed to build up a network of chemist's shops whose buyers were females under the age of forty. By flashing his smile at them at fairly regular intervals, and something more impressive when the occasion called for it, he had persuaded them to agree to the practice of buying three months' supply at once, and then splitting the orders into fortnightly doses, each of which would represent the diligence of a personal visit on his report sheet. It was a simple scheme brilliantly executed, and it gave him that freedom three days out of five which his spirit craved. Life had withheld permission for him to be a jazz musician. Very well, he would at least have the pleasure of not being anything else. The Victor Split-Order system gave him a chance to cultivate what he regarded as his real talents, which were being courtly to an endless succession of young girls who didn't deserve it, doing the round of the local dance halls, and wandering across the plains of the London parks with people like Landau and me who had nothing better to do.

Landau liked him for obvious reasons. Anybody who could join the enemy and then cheat them every Friday was a man after Landau's own generous heart. Moreover, anyone who knew an author as well as Victor knew F. Scott Fitzgerald must be a benign influence, picturesque to have around. In Victor's London bedroom Fitzgerald was a constant but ever-absent guest. 'Scott' was introduced freely into the conversation, as though he were an acquaintance not seen for some time but likely to walk through the door at any time. At first it was all an affectation, but in time affectations, as Scott himself once observed, become instinctual. As the years drifted away, Victor digested the entire litany, beginning with *Gatsby,* a book he always read with the background of Chicago jazz ringing in his ears, through the other novels, into the short stories, the letters, the fragments, the aphorisms, Schulberg and the biographers, and then back to *Gatsby* again and so on. Whenever he discussed Fitzgerald with me in Landau's presence, the greatest romantic of them all would sit at our feet with that wide, delighted grin on his face, while Victor and I tried as best we could not to play to the gallery. After one of these impromptu lectures, Landau resolved to do some homework, and turned up a few days later with the first purchased book of his adult life, a second-hand edition of Edward Fitzgerald's translation of *Omar Khayyam.* Its pages understandably baffled him. He spent hours searching for what he had heard Victor call the retribution that follows frivolous amorality, and managed to come up with nothing more apposite than ' a jug of wine, a loaf of bread and thou '. He complained bitterly about this to me.

' You build me up for a big immoral thing and what do I find? A load of crap about bread.'

I explained he had got hold of the wrong Fitzgerald, and his reaction was typical. So overwhelmed was he by the subtlety of a world in which there could exist not one but two writers called Fitzgerald that he immediately began a one-man cult on behalf of his own candidate. He quoted its couplets in every dance hall we worked in, brought his obsession down to the coast with him and even staggered half-drunk into a bakery one midnight demanding to be presented to the thou who was supposed to go with the bread. The bakers got rid of him eventually by stuffing a doughnut in his hand, leading him back into the street and pointing him in the general direction of the sea. When I told Victor of Landau's mistake concerning the two Fitzgeralds, instead of laughing, he reacted with all the bitterness of a man who feels he has been cheated by contacts with literature.

He counted himself the victim of an intellectual fraud, even though he admitted the fault was his own. In late adolescence he had suddenly fallen upon the set of presentation Dickens his father had bought from the *Daily Herald* during the pre-war circulation wars, and then moved on to the great Edwardians under the mistaken impression that life, or at least literature, had changed very little since. He had read Shaw and Wells and been completely overwhelmed, and almost without realising it, adopted their platforms with blind faith. It apparently never occurred to him that the first of the wars to end war, the one that had sent his own father home with half a lung, might have rendered obsolete much of what he took to be inviolable truth. He grasped at Fabian socialism with trembling fingers, only to find on the day he entered the insurance office, that life was not quite like that.

And so he became a curious anachronism, bemoaning the death of a past he had never known, being nostalgic, and this time with no affectation, for days that had vanished before any of us were born. He read and re-read the early

Wells comedies, and cursed him roundly for having elected to become a teacher instead of a creator of endless strings of Pollys and Hoopdrivers. He tried Lawrence and found morbidity. He tried Proust and found only verbosity. He tried Henry James and found nothing at all. There was no longer anyone he could trust to carry him across the borders of full consciousness into the world of substantial moonshine. Often he used to ask me, with little hope in his voice, ' Read anything good lately?' meaning had I read anything similar to *Tono-Bungay* or *Clayhanger*. I would offer a few names, which he would copy down into his diary, but whether he ever bothered to read any of my nominations I never knew. Certainly he never mentioned any of them to me again.

He stayed in my room for about an hour that afternoon waiting for Landau to put in an appearance, but at six o'clock he heaved himself off the bed and said he must be going. We were to expect him the following evening, but the next morning he sent a wire saying that business had detained him. He told me later that somebody at head office had questioned his report sheet, and that he had only managed to stave off dismissal by giving the company a line for their new advertising campaign. They gave him a £20 bonus for his contribution to the paper handkerchief crusade, and about two years later, long after there was any necessity for him to be conscientious, hoardings all over England showed a négligéed girl on the brink of a sneeze reaching for a paper handkerchief and saying, ' Ah, tissue!'

9

AT THE back of the house in Kemptown was a large, sprawling garden matted with the flora of long neglect. It began fairly respectably with two long, narrow flowerbeds, declined into a scarred and bumpy lawn, and then ran quickly to seed in a riot of weeds, rotting timbers and a cracked enamel bath filled with household refuse, old shoes and bundles of mildewed newspapers incongruously tied with neat pink tape. At the far end, backing on to a disused sports ground and protected from it by a crumbling brick wall, was a halfwrecked summerhouse. In the small clearing between the wall and the summerhouse door bonfires had evidently once been lit to dispose of the accumulated rubbish, and the grass by now was charred beyond redemption. Here on the bald turf, we would sit around on dry afternoons, discussing ourselves and each other with cautious candour, aware always of the disturbing presence of the nearby sea. The smell of brine was in the air, and when the wind was up you could just discern the rumour of the shingle being sucked back with the retreating breakers.

From where we sat the house, exhausted by contact with too many indifferent tenants, took on a surprising air of quaintness. Because it straddled the hill, the base of its kitchen windows was on a level with the lawn, giving the structure the whimsical air of a man whose trousers are falling down. Perhaps that was why we all felt such an affinity with the place. It seemed to be as hopelessly bewildered by the slow tide of events as we were. A spectacular success of any kind within its walls would have been unthinkable, and even Landau agreed with me that there were better places to practise the arcane arts of seduction.

One afternoon, a few days after the party, Victor and I were sitting on two old arm-chairs propped against the wall. The arm-chairs had been Landau's outraged response to what he called the poverty-struck look of the faded deckchairs huddled inside the summerhouse. He never told us where he acquired them, or for how much, but simply arrived with them in a small van one afternoon. Probably he had picked them up in the junkshop which kept dumping the poetry books on him, and perhaps also this was why whenever he made some attempt to read the battered, dusty volumes he would always settle himself down in one of his arm-chairs. For Victor, however, they were rapidly becoming the hot seat for his conscience. It was now his fifth day away from the paper handkerchiefs, and already his mind was beginning to drift back to the insubstantial world of samples and invoices. As usual I tried to lure him back.

'There's no point in leaving yet. You've only just got here. Besides, who buys paper handkerchiefs in June?'

'That's just where you're wrong. You know, when they put me on tissues, they gave me this Snot Ordnance map to work from. It shows you the incidence of hay fever all over the country. According to the map, there are more sneezes per nose of population in this country in June than at any other time. Instead of sitting around here listening to your troubles, I ought to be out on the road knocking up big fat commission fees.'

I abandoned Landau's arm-chair and flopped out on the grass, contemplating without much enthusiasm the prospect of spending several weeks down here with neither Victor nor Blitski to divert me. Of course there was always Landau. Landau was a fine fellow, but there were times when he was inclined to live solely for himself instead of solely for me, and so far he had shown little talent or inclination for the subtle pleasures of mutual introspection.

'I tell you what to do. Why don't you get a doctor's certificate and send it up to your office?'

I sat up and watched his face hopefully.

'No good. I've used that one up already this year. In March, with that bird on the tandem. Remember? Anyway, they're not fools, you know. They'd take one look at the Brighton postmark and suss the whole scene in five minutes.'

'No, no. Landau's got this doctor straightened in London. He can fix it so that the certificate comes from London without you having to go near the place. That should be good for at least another week.'

' It's no use. Look at me. Healthy as an ox. How can I tell them I'm not well enough to sell packets of paper?'

' Well, quote their own research at them. Tell them you've got hay fever. Show them on their map.'

' Thanks all the same, but I think I'll have to get back.'

He smiled uneasily, as he always did when he felt the ethics of my world, with their tumbledown routines and apparent disregard of any kind of discipline, impinging on his own family tradition of strict devotion to the most trivial commercial obligations. It was not the paper tissues he was scurrying back to, but the ordered world of working hours comfortingly defined. Evidently in his infancy, someone had instilled in him the curious delusion that selling an object for more than you paid for it was more respectable and necessary than blowing a few choruses of the blues. He started to tap the sides of his arm-chair with the palms of his hands and asked me one of those nervous rhetorical questions which were a signal that he wanted badly to change the subject.

' You're staying on till the end of the season then?'

' Don't know. You've heard the band. People are always telling you in this business to get experience, but that kind I can do without. I reckon six months with that team at the Arcadia could put me back a year at the very least. Probably more.'

All this was highly disturbing to Victor, who worried about the welfare of his friends almost as much as he did about his own. His idea of Utopia was a place where everybody he liked had a pensionable job or an independent income. The news that I had finally stumbled into a regular job had really delighted him, not only because I was the last surviving bearer of his ambition to cheat the system and live a romantic life, but because now he could stop worrying, at least for a while, about where my next month's rent was coming from. I knew that this was precisely the thought going through his mind now, and the one he was trying to express without offending me when he said, ' But you have to start somewhere. And at least the money's regular. What else could you get in town in the middle of the summer?'

'Nothing, I suppose. But then I'm used to that.'

This time he had no counter. We had performed our usual trick of reducing all existence to a mockery. He sat slumped in the arm-chair sadly contemplating the awful gulf between life as it was turning out and life as we had once fondly imagined it.

'When do you go back then?'

I asked the question less out of curiosity than from a desire to take his mind off the daunting problem of my future.

'Not sure. After lunch, tomorrow, maybe. I'm not sure.'

'All right. I tell you what. We'll have lunch together, tomorrow . . .'

The hysterical screech of Landau's clarinet suddenly cut through the somnolence of the afternoon. He was evidently still in pursuit of those 420 hours. Victor laughed.

'I'll say this for Landau. He's a trier.'

I took this as a reproach to me, especially as I knew that I too should have been practising instead of wasting the days away sitting around like this. I sprang to my own defence.

'He hasn't got any method. He just blows. Anything that comes into his head. I don't see how that can be much good to him in the long run.'

'Come on. Practice is practice. You're always saying that. Any playing must be better than none at all.'

'I don't know about that any more. Take this job at the Arcadia. I see now that there is such a thing as playing that spoils your playing. Now just you listen to that for a minute and tell me what possible good it can do Landau.'

We paused to concentrate on Landau's attempts to achieve the last soaring flourishes of Artie Shaw's 'Concerto for Clarinet'. Time and again he went for his top C and time and again the note degenerated into a squeak. After a dozen attempts Landau went back to his doodling.

'You see? He tries to run before he can walk. It's like picking the tiles for the roof before the foundations have been laid.'

'Well at least he's working harder at it than you are.'

'Listen. I was saying. About tomorrow. Why don't we have some lunch together and then I can come and see you off.'

' Great.'

We both felt better after that, having pushed back the tide of dreary events by twenty-four hours. The conversation lapsed. Landau continued to impose his invisible presence with his drunken arpeggios. The late afternoon sun slipped behind a great leaden bank of cloud and the wind's shadow swooped across the lawn towards us. The two tall elms behind us shivered in the sudden gust of wind. In a few moments the whole character of the afternoon had changed for the worse. The light began to fade and the sea seemed to take up a lament for our predicament. Our surroundings no longer looked idyllic. And still there came the persistent resonance of Landau's minor chords. Victor chuckled again.

' He doesn't give up easily.'

' Landau is a very fortunate man. He doesn't have quite enough talent to realise he hasn't got any talent. Only two kinds of musicians manage to keep on practising, the very good ones and the very bad ones. He's one of the very bad ones.'

' What about you?'

' I, as usual, am stuck right in the middle. I do still practise, you know. I haven't given up altogether. But I must admit it's getting harder all the time to see the point. It's this job down here that's been the real eye-opener. I mean, what's the point of working so hard at it when all they ask you to play is rubbish?'

' Oh come on. You knew all that before you started. You used to say all that to me before, word for word.'

' I don't think I knew anything before I came here. I knew theoretically, but you always assume your own case is going to be different. Then you actually get involved, you actually do it, and then . . .'

I could see my attitude was distressing him almost as much as his own truancy. I kept forgetting that I was his last chance of some kind of spectacular success, some picturesque escape from the commercial treadmill he brooded about so deeply and yet could not muster the strength to defy. For me to confess disillusionment now would be the final acknowledgement that the world of paper tissues was right, and he and I and Blitski and Landau hopelessly, disastrously wrong. I was still considering how I might be able to contradict myself and revive his waning spirits when my thoughts were interrupted again by Landau. His clarinet reeled all over the keyboard, spluttered and then was silent, leaving a gaping hole in the range of our sense-impressions. Now that the noise had stopped we seemed more conscious of it than when he had actually been playing. Victor looked up at me.

'He must have heard us talking about him.'

A moment later Landau came striding out of the back door across the lawn, waving something in his right hand. He looked exultant, always an ominous sign for those of his friends who preferred the comparative safety of the status quo. He came crashing through the undergrowth like a hungry tiger and stood over us, feet astride, that distant grin lighting his face.

'That's not real practising,' I said. 'Running up and down the E minor arpeggio like that. More like self-indulgence.'

He made no attempt to argue but simply stood there grinning down at me. I know from his expression that one of those events must have happened to convince him that he was at last performing the indeterminate act he was always referring to these days as taking life by the throat. I think he came across the phrase in some Victorian novel I gave him to read, and he had never forgotten it. He sat down on the grass and flushed with pure pleasure.

'Tom.'

He was bursting with eagerness.

'What's the matter?'

'Tom, they printed it.'

I noticed for the first time that the object he had been waving and which now protruded from his hip pocket was a copy of the weekly trade paper.

'You serious?'

'They printed it. Word for word. I told you.'

'Show me. I don't believe it.'

Victor smiled inquiringly. 'What's all this? You never told me you were writing something for publication.'

'He wrote a letter to the paper,' Landau explained.

'Just for a joke,' I added hastily. For some reason I felt

wretched and ashamed in front of Victor. After all my talk about writing, a mere letter in a trade paper . . .

'As a matter of fact, I only wrote it in the first place because I didn't think anyone would take it seriously.'

'They took it seriously all right,' Landau said. 'Seriously enough to print every word.'

He smoothed out the paper on the grass. Look at it. The "Week's Star Letter".'

We gathered round. There it was, about twenty lines of print. I felt horribly exposed. The phrases seemed to be graced by none of the congenial wit I could have sworn they possessed when I wrote them down. Print had rendered them impersonal and strangely arrogant. Mildly facetious phrases had somehow bloomed into monstrous libels. In fact the letter now expressed nothing I had intended. I suddenly realised, squatting there staring at my creation, that for the desired effect to be made, I should have enclosed with the letter a photograph of my genial grin and a potted autobiography.

'I don't know about this sort of thing. Is it important?'

Landau looked at Victor. 'Important enough.' Then he returned his gloating eyes to the paper. It seemed more his triumph than mine. But then, he was not answerable for my libels.

'I like that bit about the bow-tied popinjays,' Victor said, 'but how is the management down here going to react to it?'

'That,' I said gloomily, 'is a very interesting question. I think the problem of whether or not I decide to see the season out is going to turn out to be purely academic.'

Landau looked puzzled. 'What does that mean?'

'It means I'm sure to be fired.'

'Good. Let them fire you. It's the best thing that could happen. Then we can go to the Union and kick up a right stink. How about all that publicity? We'll be made.'

'If it was publicity you wanted, I could have stuck a meat-hook in your neck and we'd all be famous overnight. I never thought of it before, but this letter is going to type me as a troublemaker, not the right type they want in our ballrooms. Do you realise what I've done? I've gone and blackballed myself out of a profession I've only just got into.'

'I'll tell you what you've done,' Landau said. 'You've spat in the face of the system, and it was about time somebody did. They'll probably write folk blues about you one day. You know, like that cat John Henry, who defied the railways. You've defied the system. You'll be like him.'

'Thanks very much. But what do I do in the meantime?'

'Oh, stop worrying. I don't care if we do get the sack.'

'We? What's it got to do with you? It was only your idea. It's my name at the bottom. You're in the clear, as usual.'

'What are you talking about, Tom?' and he thrust the paper in front of me. The letter was signed by both of us.

'You didn't think I was going to miss out on this, did you? Anyway, it was my idea, like you said, so I figured I was entitled to half the glory. Right or wrong?'

'Oh, absolutely right.'

'So you see, we're in this together.'

I turned to Victor. 'I told you if you hung around here long enough, something was bound to happen.'

Landau looked up sharply from the paper. 'Why, is he thinking of going home?'

Victor smiled his uneasy smile again. 'Can't take too many liberties, you know. Not like you lot. Still, perhaps just one more day . . .'

'One more day is about all it will take.' Landau grinned happily. He actually seemed to be looking forward to the prospect of losing the job he had fought so hard to acquire only a few weeks before. As it happened, it took even less than a day for the repercussions to begin. Within hours of publication, my letter had become the most infamous document in the profession, a kind of syncopated Zinoviev Letter. Musicians' Union officials phoned three times before we left for work that evening, only to be rebuffed by Landau, who in a peculiar accent supposed to convey aristocratic hauteur, insisted they contact his solicitors, Messrs Roebuck, Cohen and Abercrombie. When I asked him how he managed to think up such an absurd name, he said it was because Messrs Roebuck, Cohen and Abercrombie were absurd solicitors, who had eased his father out of many awkward corners with regard to the purchase on credit of large stocks of cotton trousers.

When we left the house to go to work that evening, we found ourselves trampling local reporters underfoot in our attempts to reach the end of the courtyard. Landau, drawing on his copious stocks of Hollywood folk-lore, brushed them aside with the authentic head-down posture, saying, as he pushed me into the street, 'We have no statement to make at this time.'

We ran down the hill laughing.

When I arrived at the Arcadia there was a note from Crawford awaiting me at the back door. I opened it.

The musician Gray is to report to the manager's office as soon as he enters the premises.

I folded the note and tucked it in my jacket pocket. If Crawford wanted to see me as badly as all that, let him come and find me. Clearly I was doomed this time, but there was no point in making Crawford's job any easier for him. The Arcadia was almost empty that night, although I noticed the dark lady sitting at her usual table sipping gin in enigmatic solitude as always. When I passed her on the way to the bandstand I caught a whiff of her perfume.

There was no question that the atmosphere in the orchestra was subtly different. The other musicians avoided my gaze and said not a word to me between numbers, but kept smirking to themselves, like model schoolboys who know that somebody else has been caught breaking the rules. Bertie himself was white-faced, and tried not to look me in the eye. We had been puffing away for about half an hour when Crawford came marching across the almost deserted floor. He was wearing his double-breasted yachting blazer, the one with silver buttons and the Royal Artillery badge on the outbreast pocket. A purple handkerchief, a cream shirt, green tie and brown suede shoes, completed the ensemble of the man described a few weeks earlier in the local press as 'dapper'. He arrived at the bandstand and stood directly in front of me, hands on hips.

'You. I thought I told you to report to my office?'

I immediately laid my saxophone on the floor, stepped off the bandstand and began walking across the ballroom floor. Crawford came after me and pulled my arm.

'Where do you think you're going?'

I knocked his hand away. 'Before we go any further, are you going to give me the sack? Because if you are, I might as well have the satisfaction of punching you one. If, on the other hand, you show willing to forget the whole business, I'll behave accordingly.'

Crawford backed off two paces. I followed him. He backed away two more paces. I followed him again. The word quadrille seeped into my mind.

'Do you come here often?' I said.

This time Crawford stood his ground. 'I specially asked you to come to my office. In my note. You did get my note?'

'I got your note. But that isn't what it said. It said that as soon as you came into the building, I was to go to your office. There it is, read it for yourself. That's exactly what it says. You know your trouble, Crawford? You're illiterate. You ought to have a great future in this business.' He clutched his note without bothering to look at it. He was utterly baffled, as well he might be. There was nothing in the Happiness Guide for Ballroom Managers about dealing with inte'lectual arrogance. There was also the awkward fact that I was three inches taller than he was, much younger and much fitter. He decided to try the man-to-man approach.

'Now look here. Just tell me something. Are all you jazz musicians mad? Don't you want to earn a living?'

'Mind your own business, Crawford.'

'Why in heaven's name did you go and write a letter like that? Just going around causing trouble for everybody. You must have known it would leave me no choice. I've got to fire you.'

'Oh, so it is the sack after all?'

'Now don't go doing anything you might regret.'

He backed away another two paces. 'A letter is one thing. Trespassing and grievous bodily harm are another.'

'No they're not, they're two other things. I told you Crawford, you're illiterate.'

By now the few customers had gathered round waiting hopefully for the first blow to be struck. I noticed that the dark lady remained at her table, watching the argument with bored amusement.

'I wrote that letter, Crawford, because I was sure you couldn't read. I still don't think you can read. You must have got someone to read it to you. Who's the one who read it to you, Crawford? He's the one I really ought to punch.'

By now he had realised he was dealing with a hooligan, and so naturally became one himself.

'If you're not out of this building in two minutes, instruments and all, I'll call the police.'

A knot of ballroom louts on the balcony jeered and blew a few raspberries.

Each time Crawford spoke they threw pennies into the ring.

'If you will permit me to retrieve my instrument . . .' and I walked back to the bandstand to pick up my saxophone. The eyes of the other musicians remained averted, except for Bertie's, which looked at me in sorrowful reproach. I told him I was sorry and that it was nothing personal. Then I began dismantling my instrument, methodically, painstakingly, as slowly as possible.

'Ninety seconds,' Crawford chanted. Another shower of raspberries and small change. I packed the instrument in its case and clicked the locks shut. Then I turned to my ex-fellow-workers.

'I just want to tell you what an honour it has been for you to have me here. I shall always . . .'

'One minute.'

I shook Bertie's limp and sweating hand with as much solemnity as I could muster and made my way through the knot of spectators towards the front door. Crawford could not resist one last threat.

'You'll be hearing from me.'

It is not often in life that enemies set up an authentic Groucho Marx exchange, and I could not ignore this one.

'Do that,' I said. 'Even if it's only a postcard.' As I skipped down the front steps of the building the last thing I heard was Crawford shouting 'Thirty seconds' and the sound of money splashing on to the floor. It was still light in the streets. The esplanade was garish with the corporation coloured lights competing with the last parting wisps of a ruddy sunset, and most of the holidaymakers were still *en route* to their evening's destination. The night, as the lyrics to one of Landau's favourite songs went, was young. The obvious place for me to make for was the pier, if only to compare notes with my fellow-author. I walked slowly, celebrating a tremendous sense of release which might have been more exhilarating had it not been for the weight of my instrument case. I deposited it with the turnstile attendant, wondering whether Landau too had met with defeat. But down at the end of the pier everything seemed to be running smoothly enough. A fair-sized crowd was shuffling round to the sound of Landau's clarinet solo in 'Diane', his bandleader was waving his arms at the musicians and smiling glassily at the couples floating past the bandstand. The painted sailors on the walls still smiled imbecilically at the girls in summer dresses, and the ship's mast still pointed up at the now darkling sky.

Nothing seemed to have changed since that first tea-dance when I had come looking for Landau. But when he caught my eye Landau winked, and as soon as his solo was over, he grinned and ran his forefinger across his throat to indicate his fate. I made the same sign back and his grin broadened. I waited till the interval to compare notes with him, but when the dancing stopped, instead of coming over to me, he immediately ducked into the men's lavatory, where I found him trying to climb over the back wall to escape the recriminations of two girls who each claimed proprietary rights over him. It was not till later that he told me that he had fared better than I, two weeks' notice instead of instant dismissal, and the faint hope that exemplary behaviour during those two weeks might earn him a reprieve.

10

I RETURNED to the ranks of the unemployed with a confidence
born of long practice. In fact there was almost no adjustment
to be made. Instead of going to the Arcadia to play, I went to
the pier to listen and watch. There was something inexpress-
ibly relaxing about the music wafting out to sea, melting away
in the murmur of the tides. For one thing it was a most
convenient way of dispersing the wrong notes and the sour
harmonies. It was during this period that I discovered that
even the worst music sounds better in the dark. You could
squat on the wooden floor with your back resting against
the wall of the bandstand, quietly sipping beer, watching the
moon rise, and nobody would know you were there. Except
Landau, who kept a keen proprietary eye on everything that
went on down there. At first he disapproved strongly, insisting
that what I was doing was like an out-of-work actor hanging
around the dressing-rooms.

' There's no dignity in it, Tom.'

What he meant was that he was worried about my trying
to steal his job, but after a few nights it must have dawned
on him that I had no such intentions, and he even began
to welcome my visits, especially if the nightly intake of girls
happened to be hunting in pairs.

Most of my days were spent with Victor, who was by now
beginning to reveal himself as the dedicated wage-slave he
really was. His current bout of illicit freedom had now lasted
eleven days, and I knew from experience that his limit was
never more than fourteen. On his twelfth day away from
the paper tissues there was a sudden decline in his morale, and
I sensed that the non-existent call to non-existent duties was
beginning to ring in his ears. That afternoon he groaned when
I suggested a visit to the county ground at Hove, so I went
alone, leaving him and Landau arguing wildly about the
advantages of taking a married woman as mistress. Victor

proved to be right about the cricket, and by four o'clock I found myself walking back up the hill towards the house. I arrived there to find us all plunged into fresh crisis.

As I trudged home, struggling against the drifting tide of trippers, I spotted a splash of bright colour standing out against the greys and dark blues of the tea-time crowds. It was Landau's turquoise beach shirt, and as I drew closer, I could see that he was standing, seemingly without purpose, side-on to the stream of humanity about him, hands thrust deep into the pockets of his canvas trousers. So engrossed was he in his own studies that I came to within a few feet of him without his noticing me. I was surprised to see that he was contemplating the glum stare of the dead whiting on the marble slab of the fishmonger's. He was utterly absorbed in his own thoughts, and when I slapped him on the back he started as though roused from a deep sleep.

'Does that remind you of anybody?' he asked, nodding at the fish.

'Practically everybody. Come on. You've been reading the poets again.'

'No, I mean anyone in particular.'

'Well let's see,' and I edged closer to the bulging eyes.

'My mother,' said Landau. 'It's uncanny. That fish looks exactly like my mother. I don't like it, Tom. Let's get out of here.'

We walked on up the hill, golden in a burst of late afternoon sunshine. Landau consumed the ground with quick nervous strides, as though it were vital to put as much distance as possible between himself and that fish. Soon we began to leave the town behind. Terraced shops gave way to expansive crescents of buff-coloured mansions. The crowds dropped away, and as we drifted on into the suburbs, Landau's tempo gradually slowed down. He scuffled along, staring at his own feet, shaking his head as he went. Once or twice he smiled gently to himself. I knew he was conducting one of those long wrangling debates between the various psyches inside his head, and waited patiently for my cue. At last it came. Unable to contain himself any longer, he muttered, 'I wonder what she'd say if she knew?'

'Who?'

'My mother. That she looks like a dead fish.'

'You can trust me with the secret, you know that.'

'What secret?'

'You know. Not to tell her. That she looks like a whiting.'

'What are you talking about, Tom. I said she looked like a fish.'

He gave me an anxious glance, as though he was seriously concerned for my sanity.

'I tell you I don't like it. First the fish, now you talking rubbish. Everything's getting out of hand.'

'Come on. Let's go back and get something to eat.'

But the thought of food was repugnant to him, and it was not until, by a supreme intellectual effort, he had resolved his problem about the fish, that he would agree to go home for tea. After we had covered perhaps a mile he stopped abruptly, smiled into the distance, and blurted out in his absurd melodramatic way, 'Of course. Reincarnation. That stuff Blitski was on about the other day. You remember?'

'I remember.'

'My old lady's going to come back as a fish.'

Having established his theme, he now began to improvise, and it occurred to me that he did it much better than he usually did with a clarinet in his hands.

'No, wait a minute,' he cried, 'hold on. This is even wilder. The fish has come back as my mother. Of course, that's the scene. Come on,' and without bothering to look at me he swung round and turned for home. His spirits had vaulted with amazing speed. He could cast off the gloom of metaphysical speculation quicker than any man I knew, and yet his self-examinations were always perfectly sincere. Now that he had ironed out the creases in his universe, his face was wrinkled in a mischievous smile, and by the time we tumbled noisily down the back stairs into the kitchen, he was his old self again. He sat himself at the table, tapping his fork in a beguine rhythm, humming to himself while I foraged in the pantry.

'When they begin the beguine,' he sang, and then broke off. The fork froze in mid-beat.

'What a tune, eh? Who wrote it?'

'Cole Porter,' I shouted.

'What a man.'

He resumed his recital. Then he stopped again to reconsider his position.

'No,' he hissed with great vehemence, and threw his fork on to the table. It struck the butter dish and pinged out a concert F.

'You know what? I've just twigged it. A beguine rhythm is a crutch for a crippled melody.'

I poured the tea while Landau buttered the toast. The back doorbell rang.

'I'll go,' I offered. Landau grunted and threw five lumps of sugar into his teacup.

I opened the kitchen door and there were Victor and Maxine standing on the steps looking vaguely embarrassed with each other. Maxine had been sunbathing. Her face glistened under suntan lotion and her body smelt of the beach. Victor leaned against the wall wearing his droopy unbuttoned look. His tie sagged down his chest and he was smoking feverishly. He seemed suicidal to me. Maxine swung forward into the room.

'You'd better talk to this one,' she said, tossing her head in Victor's direction. 'I don't know what he's got himself into, but he's well choked about something.'

She brushed past me. Her mules clacked down the kitchen steps. Victor made no move.

'You coming in?'

He pushed himself off the wall and ground his cigarette savagely under his heel. He was acting his part as hard as he knew how. I waited for him to come in, closed the door after him and resumed my seat at the table. Maxine was already eating and drinking.

'I found him walking up and down West Street like some old brass,' and she draped herself across the arm of the sofa, munching toast as she went. Victor stood with his back to us, staring out through the kitchen window, saying nothing and contriving to convey a mood of deep self-pity without showing his face. Landau doggedly worked his way through a mound of toast, sublimely unaware that it might just be within the bounds of possibility that everybody was not quite as absorbed as he in the lesser joys of life. After his third cup and his sixth slice, it occurred to him that perhaps Victor was not after all quite at his best.

'What's up with you then?'

Victor spun round and slumped deep in the cushions of the sofa.

'Disaster. Complete, absolute disaster.'

Landau beamed. 'It's about time something happened in this crumby hole. What kind of disaster?'

'I lost my job, that's all.'

Landau's face registered disappointment, mild but unmistakable.

'In that case, welcome to the club,' and he buried his face in his teacup. He supped the dregs and then looked up benignly at Victor.

'So you lost your job, eh? Well, well, fancy that.'

'It's not the same thing as for your crowd, you know. Before I get something else, I have to have a reference, and this time I won't be able to get one. For me this is real trouble.'

'Listen, Victor, that's nothing. Wait till you hear what happened to me today. This afternoon I made a fantastic discovery. Did you know my mother was a fish? How about that? My own mother a rotten, stinking dead fish. Of course it explains a lot I never dug before, but it's disturbing, don't you think?' Victor looked at me in mute appeal.

'It's true,' I told him. 'I saw the actual fish myself.'

'Anyway,' Landau said, 'it's all for the best. Now you don't have to rush back to town. And another thing, it's a good excuse for a celebration.'

Victor waved his arms in rejection of Landau and said to me, 'What's wrong with him? Doesn't he understand plain English?'

'He understands it, but he doesn't think much of it.'

Victor went and stood over Landau and shouted at him, 'I lost my job. Today. I was fired. Thrown out. You understand? I lost my job.'

'Hey, baby, that's great, take another chorus,' Landau muttered, and started to cut a large sultana cake into thick slices. Victor stared at him for a moment and then shrugged his shoulders.

'He really is impossible,' he said and sat on the sofa.

'Look,' Landau replied, 'when a man, a grown man in the best of health and sexually normal, loses a job flogging paper snotrags, isn't he entitled to celebrate? Isn't he?'

Victor tried to smile and failed.

'I just want to know one thing,' I said. 'How do you get the sack sixty miles away from the office?'

Landau looked up from the teapot. Maxine licked the butter off her fingers, swung both legs across the arm of the sofa and peered at Victor. For a moment there was a hush in the room. Although getting the sack interested none of us, the technicalities of how you got it fascinated us to the point of morbidity. Victor sighed deeply, as though he had already explained twenty times before, and recited the details of his tragedy.

'I went up to the Regent for the tea-dance. I didn't fancy going to the cricket with him, so I went to the tea-dance. It was your idea, Landau, remember? You said it was the sexiest dance hall on the south coast.'

'And so it is,' replied Landau sagely. 'Especially when I'm inside it.'

Maxine sniggered.

'Well, I go up to this girl in the fox-trot medley, and who's she dancing with but Willie Marshall.'

'Do I know him?' Landau cut himself another wedge of fruit cake.

'Willie Marshall. He's my managing director. He takes one look at me and he says " I'll see you at head office Monday morning. Do try to be there, because it will be your last visit ", and then he walked off the floor and that was that.'

'What about the bird? What was she like?'

This was too grave an affront for Victor to bear. For a moment even his deep respect for Landau's exalted status as a real live jazz musician crumbled.

'How do I know what she was like? You think I was worried about birds at a time like that? I walked straight out of the place and I came back here.'

'A mistake,' Landau said, still oblivious of Victor's exasperation. 'A serious mistake. That makes one less possible chick on your list. I'm surprised at you. You should never have done that.'

Maxine slid on to the cushions at Victor's side.

'I tell you Willie Marshall's trouble. He's frustrated.'

'Everybody's frustrated,' Landau said. 'I keep telling you there isn't enough to go round. That's exactly why he shouldn't have walked off the floor like he did.'

'No, but this one is really frustrated,' Maxine insisted. 'You just haven't got any idea, you especially. You can't imagine what a poor fish he is.'

'Hey, did I tell you my mother's a fish?' Landau beamed happily as he leaned back, balancing his chair on its two hind legs. 'That's really far out, eh? My mother's a fish.'

'A whiting,' I added.

Landau glared at me and rode forward on his chair. Its two front legs thumped on to the carpet.

'Look, don't you start all that whiting crap again. It was a fish.'

'That's right, a whiting.'

'Listen, it's my mother and I say she's a fish.'

'What is all this?'

Maxine seemed bewildered by the turn the conversation was taking. So were we all. One of Landau's more endearing qualities was his gift for cancelling out the normal rules of communication. Day after day throughout that summer we had been chasing his false hares, snapping at his red herrings, following his mad syllogisms until by now we were all reduced to a dreamlike acquiescence. The conversations we lived by from hour to hour possessed only their own highly subjective logic, and at moments of crisis it became increasingly difficult to wrench our thought patterns back on to the conventional tramlines of sanity. We were no longer capable of the simplest deductions, and now, instead of grasping the import of what Maxine had said, we drifted into a constrained silence, not realising for the moment that the pivotal event of the season had just occurred. Outside in the back garden a stray dog bayed at a passing aeroplane. The kitchen clock wheezed its way round its own tired face. Landau munched ruminatively on the fruit cake. It was Victor who finally brought us back to hard facts. He had been watching our little pantomime with pale concentration, and now he stood up to confront Maxine.

'Just a minute. I was talking about my boss, William R. Marshall. The man . . .'

'Ooh. He never told me he had a middle name. Deceptive old sod.'

'I mean Willie Marshall, the man I work for. The one who gave me the push this afternoon.'

'So what? You might say I work for him too. As a matter of fact, I bet I know him a bloody sight better than you do. He comes down to see me at least once every month. Sometimes he stays the whole week-end. I can usually count on a tenner from him.'

Victor stood there struggling to reconcile a vision of an old roué forking out ten pounds to sleep with Maxine, with his own image of a stiff-collared dictator who drove his minions relentlessly up and down the country helping the great British public to trap its own streptococci. We were all young enough in those days to believe implicitly in the watertight compartments of our own private experience. Overlappings astounded and delighted us, but we never counted on them.

'Listen, Maxine.' Victor's voice was a soft croak. 'What's he look like, this friend of yours?'

'Well, he's got a pot belly for a start. As a matter of fact he's got a pot chest.'

Landau laughed. Cake crumbs flew out of his mouth like lava from the lip of a volcano.

'Let's see. Very white stomach, and lots of it. Oh, yes, a brown birthmark near his crutch.'

'What about his face?'

'I knew a girl once,' Landau interrupted, 'who had this birthmark right . . .'

'Let her talk,' Victor said. 'Go on.'

'Well, I don't know really. Sort of blotchy face, with those funny little purple veins round his bugle.'

'About five feet eight?'

'About that.'

'And that's just his nose,' Landau said. Victor brushed him aside.

'What else?'

'Thinning hair . . .'

'What's his voice like?'

'Oh, he's a bit of a loudmouth all right. I'm always having to tell him to cool it. He'll get me slung out one of these days, ranting away.'

Victor crashed back on the sofa.

'Jesus Christ! Marshall of all people.'

'See?' Landau said. 'I knew there was nothing to start sweating about. All these people, all these little dictators, you just have to find their ackle's heel, that's all. They put the finger on you. You put the finger back on them. That's how the world goes round these days.'

'Well, it's interesting, I'll say that,' and Victor grinned for the first time that afternoon. 'But I can't see where it helps me.'

'Look, don't be so soft,' Landau said, forgetting even about food in the urgency of the moment. 'He puts pressure on you. Maxine puts pressure on him. Result, retreat of both parties. It couldn't be simpler.'

But the thought of slovenly, easy-going Maxine putting pressure on the formidable William Marshall was too much for Victor.

'That stuff's all right in the pictures. This is real life.'

'Ah yes. Life is a dream. When we sleep we are awake, and when awake we sleep.'

'What are you talking about, Landau? That's a lot of crap.'

'It's Montaigne,' Landau replied, 'but you're right about it being a lot of crap.'

'Whatever you say, Willie Marshall caught me red-handed and that's all there is to it.'

'Nobody who's been making it with Maxine is in any position to catch anybody red-handed,' Landau insisted. 'Except possibly himself.'

'He's right, darling. If I tell old Willie to cool it, he cools it, double quick, I can tell you. I'm the last one in the world he can afford to cross.'

'But how do you put it to him? What do you say?'

'Easy. "Willie," I say, "how would you like me to cut you off without a penny, sexually speaking. And let your old lady see a few hotel bills? Well, Willie," I say, "just you forget you ever saw Victor down here and nobody is going to get hurt." And if he's got any sense, which he has, I'll say that for him, he'll reply, "Victor who?" and that will be the end of that, and you can go on flogging your merchandise for ever if you want to. See?'

'But that's blackmail.' Victor sounded horrified.

'Well, if you're going to get all moral about it, forget the whole thing and let's get on with our tea,' and Landau returned his attentions to the cake.

'But what do I do? Where do I come into all this?' Victor still couldn't grasp the situation.

'You?' Maxine stared at him. 'You don't do anything. It's me he's been making it with, not you. He's exposed his flank, you might say.'

Landau said, 'So you've been unfaithful, eh?'

He daubed quince jam on another slice of fruit cake.

'Mmm,' he said, munching thoughtfully. Cake crumbs flew out of his mouth, speckling the tablecloth. 'Can't deny it, you know. You've been unfaithful.'

'Just as well,' I reminded him.

'As a matter of fact,' Maxine retorted, 'he's not at all bad for a man his age. In bed, I mean.'

'Where else?' Landau asked.

'Oh, shut up Landau,' she said, surprisingly stung by his accusations of faithlessness. 'Listen to me, Victor. Just stop worrying. Act like it never happened. It's all arranged. Just leave everything to me.'

Landau beamed benevolently round at us all. 'Little Miss Fixit. What a set-up this is turning out to be, eh?'

'What surprises me,' Victor said, still baffled, 'why I was so shocked to see him at the Regent, is that he should be down here in the middle of the week. I don't remember him ever being anywhere in the middle of the week except head office. He's the original nine-to-five man.'

'You're right there, darling. He comes down to see me the last Friday in every month, goes back last train Sunday night. Never misses. But I think he's combining business with pleasure this time. There's some deal on.'

Victor looked up sharply. 'Oh? How do you know?'

'I heard him chatting on the phone last night. His team's trying to take over some other team just outside Brighton.'

The last chunk of Landau's jam-daubed fruit cake dropped from his hand and plopped on to the carpet. I remember noticing on the day we left the house at the end of the season, that the stain was still there. The smile on his face disappeared, to be replaced by a kind of predatory snarl.

'What place are they taking over?' His voice was quiet, strained, wholly uncharacteristic. 'What place?'

Maxine remained unimpressed by his melodramatics. 'How should I know?'

Landau turned to Victor. 'What place, Victor? What place is your lot trying to take over?'

'I don't know. It must be Filox. They're the only ones in that line of business down this way. They've got a big place somewhere near Worthing. Littlehampton, something like that. They're in hand lotions, detergents, that kind of stuff. It must be them.'

Landau was satisfied at last. The crisis was over. He sat back in his chair, balancing it on its hind legs again.

'Well, chaps. That's it. That counts game. We've made it.'

'Made what?' I asked, not daring to say what I was thinking.

'Whatever we feel like making,' Landau shouted. 'Take-overs. They're kid stuff. I've heard my old man talking about it. He seems to understand it, so it has to be kid stuff with his brain. Listen, you buy the shares before the bid goes in, then you sell them after the bid. Everything's worth three times as much by then, and us, we'll we worth ten times as much. Isn't that right Victor?'

'In theory, yes. But you've forgotten one thing.'

'What's that?'

'Capital.'

'Hey, Tom. Tell him about my old man. Listen, Victor, my old man's so well stacked, he's got money he hasn't even spent yet. Don't you worry about capital.'

Victor now made a general appeal to the rest of us, no doubt feeling that the discussion was drifting far away from his immediate problems. 'It's all happening too fast for me. Half an hour ago I had the sack. Now you're telling me I'm about to own a piece of the firm. It's not possible.'

'Nothing is impossible. Read the newspapers. The Duke of Wellington said that, and the Duke was no schmock. Impossible? On the contrary, it's certain. Absolutely, utterly certain. Maxine, who else knows about all this?'

'Nobody I shouldn't think. He's very secretive about his work. If he knew I heard him on the phone he'd go off his head. I made out I hadn't heard a thing, but you know how it is. He asks me to leave the room while he makes a phone call, so naturally I listen outside the door.'

'Maxine, you have done sterling work. On behalf of the skint members of this community, I salute you. I assure you that in our hour of triumph we will not forget that it was you who was earwigging when Marshall made his phone call. We will pay our tribute. In other words, we are going to put you in it.'

He broke off and picked his fruit cake up from the foot of his chair. Dusting it carefully with that distant smile on his face which meant supreme self-satisfaction, he popped the morsel into his mouth with a decisive gesture and licked the tips of his fingers. As he munched he beamed at Maxine.

'Isn't she the greatest thing?'

Something else occurred to him and he laughed.

'Listen, Maxine, since you're fixing things for everybody, you couldn't put in a word for my old lady while you're about it? Right now she's lying dead on the slab in the fish shop downstairs,' and he laughed so wildly that his chair overbalanced and sent him sprawling into the dresser. The Reluctant Shepherd rattled violently on its perch and almost fell off. Landau lay on his back, exulting in the waves of mad laughter enveloping him.

Maxine looked profoundly shocked.

'How can he be like that, with his old lady lying dead downstairs?' she asked, with real scientific interest. But Landau's laugh was always too infectious for his friends ever to resist it, and our tea-party subsided into hysteria.

PART TWO

The Speculators

11

LANDAU lay on his back shielding his eyes from the sun. I sat cross-legged next to him fiddling with the pebbles. We were on Landau's secluded patch, sheltered from the masses by a cluster of beached fishing boats and a stone breakwater. Our distance from the popular beaches muted the sounds of the morning and bestowed upon us a curious unreal sense of isolation which perfectly matched our mood. The shrieks of distant bathers floated across the foreshore and diminished to a tinkle before they reached us. A few children squatted on podgy haunches and improvised in the warm shallow pools left by the receding tide at the wall of the breakwater. The sound of the surf itself seemed subdued in deference to our thoughts. Once an aeroplane swooped low over the pier and tempted Landau to raise his head for a moment. Small grains of grey sand fell from the tuft of hair over his right ear, and a rivulet of perspiration coursed in fits and starts down his right side as he changed the angle of his body. We were abroad in a muted world, and the spectacular fortunes Landau had experienced the previous night had left us both lightheaded. He rolled on to his side and caught my eye. I knew from the way he was smiling fondly at the pebbles that he was savouring the enormity of his indiscretions.

'How about that Van Rhodes, eh? Calling me a bolshie. I wouldn't have minded if he'd said commie or red. But a bolshie. He's so square, that Rhodes, it makes you sick.'

He started to chuckle. 'You know something, Tom? He'll never be anybody, that Rhodes. I can see his whole life stretching out before him, right now as I sit here. Twenty years' hard labour on the pier and then a semi-detached in Peckham or some carsy like that. And you know the biggest drag of all? That people like him get into show business. You know what he's really suited for? Coalheaving.'

'Well, you can't blame him for that. If he can get away with it . . .'

'No, no, listen, Tom. We are musicians, professional entertainers. We are the people the masses adore. How can anyone in his right mind adore a creep like Rhodes?'

'Who adores you then?'

'Look, stop bringing personalities into it. We are supposed to be larger than life. That's what they're paying us for. Take the average man. He goes to work, he comes home, he goes to bed, year in, year out. Where's the jolliality in that? There isn't any, and that's where we come in. We are the ones who have to give the glamour to them. We've got to act colourful, Tom, we have to make the big gesture, live it up big. We are the entertainers of this world, and we mustn't forget it's a responsibility, something that people like Rhodes don't even understand. If I told him all this, he wouldn't know what I was talking about. I said to him last night, you can get boys who knuckle under any time. How many times can you find somebody like me to take your wages and spit in your face at the same time. You ought to think yourself lucky you found me, I said.'

'What did he say to that?'

'He said to get out.'

He stared out to sea and thought about his responsibilities.

'No,' he said. 'The way I see it we have to be larger than life.'

It struck me then that it was certainly true that Landau was larger than life, much larger, but whether he was fitting the theory to suit his temperament or consciously trying to make himself conspicuous I never discovered. I thought about it for a moment before getting back to practicalities.

'Are you going to work out your fortnight's notice?'

He stared thoughtfully at his toes, working them among the pebbles.

'I think I might. No point in turning down two weeks' money. Milk the squares for what you can get, that's what I say.'

'It's not what you said when you told me it was a good thing they sacked me on the spot.'

But he ignored this cowardly remark and plunged on with his own plans.

'Listen, Tom, you could easily stay on here till I'm finished.'

'I wouldn't mind the rest, as a matter of fact.'

'It's a funny thing,' he said, 'when I first landed the job down here, I had the whole thing worked out. I was going to save enough loot to see me right through the winter without having to steam into the old lady. Do you know what? I wasn't even going to try to look for work till two weeks before the pier closed. So what happens? It's the end of June and we're both out. That's what I mean about this business. You can never tell.'

I said nothing, but recalled the triumphant afternoon that spring when I met him after his successful audition for Rhodes. At that time neither of us had managed to rise higher than the semi-professional week-end bands who play at weddings and municipal dances. And then, out of the blue, Landau had broken into the enchanted circle of professionalism. Even egocentric Landau had sensed that the grand gesture was required, and he made it by taking me to tea at the Regent Palace Hotel, where he scandalised even the pillars of the jewsoisie with the violence of his gesticulations as he conducted the symphony of his own triumphant progress. He had come away from that monumental audition with an aura about him of the professional musician. It positively shone across the room, and in case anyone doubted his status there was the signed contract in his pocket to prove it. In his right hand he clutched a sheaf of orchestral parts which, he had decided, unless he practised them diligently, might give him trouble, and he insisted on going over them with me, note by note, ignoring the clatter of teacups around us, pointing out the complexities facing him with masochistic delight. He was too absorbed in the upsurge of drama in his own life to notice the lack of it in mine, and when I timidly inquired whether there were any other vacancies, he gave me an odd look and replied, 'I was the last one to get in, Tom. There was just the one place going, and that was it.'

His elevation to a higher rung in the professional ladder had a surprising effect on him that afternoon. Instead of playing the great virtuoso as I had anticipated, he insisted on being abject, the apprentice with the lily of aesthetic endeavour clutched in his tiny fist. He kept telling me that I was the better musician, that it was only a matter of time before something turned up for me, that my future was assured, that if a punk like him could get on, then it was all a foregone conclusion for me. In the meantime he was going away to work for twenty consecutive weeks and I was not. On the way to the hotel he had darted into a newsagent's and bought a diary at reduced spring prices. Now he sat forward, resting the diary on our tea-tray, filling in the bottom of each Saturday page with the amount of money he expected to save. Against the space for 28th September, he drew a thick line and ringed round the sum of £90. Then he began to divide the total by thirty shillings, the amount we usually earned for Saturday night casual labour. He looked up at me with a puzzled frown as he said, ' According to my calculations, one-pound-ten into ninety goes eight. That can't be right, surely?'

' It goes sixty,' I said.

' Sixty, eh?'

His eyes gleamed at the thought of the riches to come.

' That means I can hold out for thirty weeks in the winter and live on the money for two gigs a week without actually getting any work at all. Then, next summer, if I want to, back to Van Rhodes. Tom, I'm set up. I can afford to be independent now.'

The amazing thing was that he really believed all this nonsense, never having realised that he was one of those men who would always contrive to spend roughly five per cent more than they earned and then collect the balance from the family. But the delight he obviously derived from filling in the diary was so pure that I had not the heart to disillusion him. Soon he drifted into the realms of the metaphysical. He thumbed through the virgin pages of the diary and looked at me.

' Just think of all the events preparing themselves to go down in these pages, all the people who will be packing suitcases and buying tickets, applying for holidays right this minute, and who will go down here.'

He was then silent, having stunned himself for the moment

with thoughts of the future rapidly converging on the pages of his diary. I knew it was one of the great days of his life.

And yet, if the afternoon of the audition was a landmark for him, it was one for me too, although not of the same kind. It took the shock of his coming departure into the ranks of a real orchestra to bring home to me the extent to which I leaned on him, for professional advancement as well as for a stimulating social life. Without Landau to talk his way into and out of a thousand ridiculous situations, how would I ever manage to earn any money? He had been accurate enough when he told me I was the better musician, but he might have added that an embarrassment in the face of money would do more damage to my career than any of the technical solecisms he committed every time he picked up an instrument. I think he must have had a vague feeling that day that he was about to desert me, and it was this twinge of conscience which must have prompted his remark from the carriage window the day he left for the coast. ' Don't worry. I'll put you in it.'

And now it was the end of June and we were both back where we started. Indeed, in one way you could say we were worse off than ever before. Landau's diary, with its rash entries of money he was destined never to earn, was there to mock him. And worst of all, worse by far than no start at all, was our disastrous beginning. Probably we had black-balled ourselves for life. Landau lobbed a large pebble into the ragged fringes of the surf.

' Who'd have thought it, eh, that we'd be sitting here like this, out of it all?' he remarked.

We both started laughing, rolling about on the stones, hysterical and in a way deliriously happy, because although we were in financial difficulties once more, we had at least escaped the treadmill for a while without having to make a decision for ourselves. Rhodes and Crawford had obligingly made our decisions for us, and who could reproach two musicians who had tried their best and still been dismissed? We knew there would be no casual work in London for at least two months, but we would be able to spend all the time we wanted pottering about in his front room trying to com-

133

pose original songs or evolving new musical combinations, hunting girls in the milk bar on the corner of Landau's road, transcribing famous solos from borrowed recordings. I would return, at least for a few weeks, to the spartan practice routine I had invented for myself, and there would be better players to study and worse ones to deride. And above everything we would do, hovering like a pink cloud, was the promise that one day there would come that phone call, the one which would transform us magically from geese into swans, double our ability, quadruple our prestige and give us security doing what we wanted to do, although what those things were neither of us was very clear about. After all, it was not such a bad prospect.

'It is better to travel hopefully than to arrive,' I said.

'That is pure crap,' Landau replied. 'Philosophy is strictly for when the money is coming in. When you're out of work, forget it.'

'That is not the true Platonic attitude.'

'I don't agree with anything Platonic.'

I must have dozed off after that. When I awoke the sun had escaped from the banks of steely clouds cloaking it all day. The sea mirrored the bright glare. Landau was still sitting up, hugging his knees, frowning into the summer light.

'I've just thought of something,' I said. 'You realise that we've ruined the rest of the summer for Blitski and Victor? We were their bolthole for the rest of the season.'

'What?'

He was craning to the left, observing the jiggling thighs of two girls in bathing costumes hopping gingerly over the pebbles. Their style reminded me of the anguished tread of the exhibition dancers we sometimes played for. I joined him in his study of pure form until the girls climbed over the breakwater and disappeared from our view.

'What I mean is, when we're gone from here, there'll be nowhere for Blitski and Victor to run to.'

Landau dragged his mind back. 'The blonde one was best. The waist was a shade too thick, but she wasn't bad really. Let Blitski and Victor find their own scene,' he said irritably. 'We've got enough to worry about looking after ourselves.'

'Tell me honestly, do you think we'll ever live this down? Maybe no bandleader will ever employ us again. We're branded.'

'Don't be mad. Granted that at this minute we look like a couple of commies. Granted that all bandleaders are fascist dogs. But you can stop worrying. For a start, give it a few weeks and nobody will remember a thing about all this. And second, if there is anybody left who does remember, they're sure to think we're such characters that they won't be able to resist finding out what we're really like. Listen, if I was a bandleader and I was looking for musicians, I'd be fascinated to find out what you and me carried on like. As a matter of fact I'm glad you brought this up. If nothing much happens in the next fortnight, I think you ought to write another letter. You know, a kind of follow-up to keep the pot boiling.'

I sat up and stared at him.

'Landau, you're out of your mind. Another letter? That really would put . . .'

'Oh, that reminds me. There was a letter for you this morning. You went out so sharpish you beat the postman.'

He reached for his trousers and pulled from the hip pocket a crumpled buff envelope with a London postmark. While Landau lit a cigarette I turned the envelope over in my hands, looking for clues.

'It's typewritten,' I said. 'Who do we know besides Blitski who would send me a typewritten letter?'

'I got a great idea, Tom. Why don't you open it and find out?'

I tore open the envelope. Landau puffed at his cigarette, propping himself up on his elbows and squinting through the smoke out to sea with a bored air. 'What's it say?'

'It's from the paper. The one that printed the letter.'

Landau looked round sharply, his interest kindled. 'Go on then. What's in it?' He craned over my shoulder to get a better look. I pushed him off and read the contents aloud.

'Dear Mr Gray,
        In view of repercussions following our publication of your letter, it may be as well for us to discuss possible

135

future developments. I am free most afternoons at this office, and would appreciate it if you phoned on the morning of your visit,

Yours faithfully,
Ray Knowles, Editor.'

Landau grunted. I could see he was disappointed. The letter's contents were far too mundane for him.

'The least he could have done was bung you a fiver. You filled up one of his lousy columns didn't you? And why didn't I get a letter as well? He put both our names at the bottom, didn't he?'

'What do you suppose he means by possible future developments?'

'Oh, that's just routine editor's crap,' Landau said with the air of a man who has been in Fleet Street all his life. 'What he probably means is that if he gets sued for libel, you'll have to pay.'

'And you. Remember, he put both our names at the bottom.'

'Oh, it's all a load of nothing.'

He flopped back on the pebbles, utterly disenchanted with the morning, the sea, the letter, his own company, every circumstance of his existence.

'A right crumby paper that must be,' he said, 'letting you choose your own time for an appointment.'

'What if we do have to pay? We haven't got a light.'

'So we go bankrupt. Undischarged bankrupts at twenty-one.'

He brightened up at the thought.

'Hey, that's quite something. It took my old man till he was nearly thirty.'

'What disadvantage is it to be an undischarged bankrupt? There must be one.'

'Well, you can't have a bank account for a start. That's why my old lady signs all the cheques at home.'

'But we haven't got bank accounts anyway.'

'Oh, don't drive me mad. Anyway, it might not be about that at all. Maybe he's going to offer us a job.'

'Us?'

'Sure. Remember he printed both our names at the bottom.'

'So you think I ought to go and see him.'

'Of course go and see him. How can you resist a challenge like that? There is a tide in the affairs of men. Sometimes I just don't understand you.'

'Always I don't understand you. I might be walking straight into a hot case of libel.'

'Look, I just explained. You're in the clear. The great advantage of being boracic is that nobody can take anything from you. You're laughing, don't you see?'

'All right, Landau. Be it on your head.'

'Oh, come on. None of that Roman crap. You got a letter. A man asks to see you. So you go and see him. No big deals.'

Landau swiftly recovered something of his previous good humour.

'Actually, when you think about it, it's fate. This letter, I mean. I've been wondering what to do about the old man, so now we can both go up to town together. While you're getting sued for libel, I'll be putting the bite on the old man. With any luck we should break even.'

'How much you reckon your old man for?'

'Oh, I don't know. I suppose a few grand. Nothing too strong.'

A gang of children rushed across us, hooting and kicking up sand as they went. Landau started to curse them, but they were across the breakwater and out of sight before he could rouse himself.

'Little bastards,' he grunted, and spat grains of sand from his mouth. I was still staring at him in horror.

'Did you say a few grand?'

'I was thinking in terms of three thousand. A nice round sum, don't you think? The old man's definitely getting a bit senile these days, so we don't want to go and get him all confused with pounds, shillings and pence, now do we? So I reckon if I just ask for a nice plain sum, something he can understand, he's going to feel much better about it. What's wrong with you?'

'Nothing. I just didn't have any idea there was that kind

137

of money involved. To be honest, I didn't think your old man had that kind of money to lend.'

' Listen, Tom, there's no point in messing about with this Filox scene, specially as we're both out of work. It's the chance of a lifetime. Who knows, perhaps we'll never get another one like it for years. So we have to steam in big while we can.'

' I know. Only I was thinking more in terms of . . . oh, I don't know, a few hundred, something like that.'

He snorted in disgust. ' A few hundred? Where do you think that's going to get us? Split that four ways and there's just about enough for ice-cream cornets all round. No, if this is going to be a killing, that's what it's got to be, a real killing.'

' It'll probably kill your old man for a start.'

' Funny you should say that, because that's exactly what his defence is every time I try to put the bite on him. He actually starts pretending he's going to die.'

' How do you cope with that?'

' Play him at his own bent game and pretend I don't care if he does die. I can tell you now exactly what will happen, move by move. Everything will be cool, see, till I mention the money. Then he'll keel over and put his hand inside his shirt or something like that, and my old lady will start screaming and run for the pillbox. But don't you take any notice. It's all a great big moody to keep my fingers out of the till. I know how to deal with . . .'

The old-fashioned filial piety must have been showing in my face.

' Look, don't get this wrong. I like the old guy as much as the next man. I mean, if he really flaked out, that would be different. But this is all an act. Mind you, I can understand why he does it. He's like everyone else. He wants to keep his loot and he'll stop at nothing. I want to get hold of some of it so I stop at nothing too. Don't worry about it for one minute. It's all right. Nobody's going to die.'

' Even so, I'm glad I won't be there to see it.'

' What are you talking about now? Of course you'll be there to see it. I need you there. You're my diversion to draw off the main attack.'

' I just don't understand any of this.'

'Well, you see, it's all down to human nature. Even my mother will have to cool it a bit with a stranger in the room. If there's just the three of us there, she'll have hysterics, crying, throwing pots and pans, the full production. Now, if you're about, it's bound to embarrass her just that little bit and keep the conversation on the ground. I mean, she'll still behave like a mad pig, but at least she'll see she has to control it a bit. And every bit helps, you see?'

'I can never figure it out,' I said thoughtfully. 'Either you or me is a half-wit. Sometimes I think it's you and sometimes I think it's me.'

Landau was highly flattered. 'You mean I'm kind of a special case? Like Shelley?' he inquired eagerly. 'A test case, or something like that?'

'I reckon you're a special case because you're out of your mind, and I'm a special case for telling you.'

But this was much too devious for Landau, who beamed with pleasure at the empty beach, revelling in his new status. We sat there watching the lips of the rollers, flecked with foam, curling up on to the wet shingle, gurgling at the wall of the breakwater, hissing under the loose pebbles, whose creamed surfaces gave me a sudden mental picture of Landau's mother frothing at the mouth with thrift. The gulls wheeled in. One of them gathered about him the cloak of his wings and settled on the wooden rib of the breakwater. Landau lit another cigarette.

'No use hanging around. Let's go up to town this week. You go and see this editor of yours in the afternoon, and then in the evening, we both confront my old man. How does that sound?'

'I suppose it'll do.'

'Agreed then. This week it is.'

He sat there smoking for a while, taking in exaggerated deep lungfuls of sea air between drags of his cigarette. Landau always believed in the outdoor life, so long as it was not too arduous. I kept thinking about his poor unwitting father who, had he only realised it, was booked one evening this week for the greatest performance of his career. Landau took a last draw on his cigarette, jabbed the butt into the pebbles, and with much grunting and groaning, stood up, stretching himself luxuriantly in the warmth of the afternoon. Then he hitched up his swimming trunks, ran across the loose stones into the water and dived in head first. He disappeared under billows crystalline in the bright glare of the sunlight. After a few moments he came spluttering to the surface, wiped his eyes with his knuckles and trod water with his back to the horizon, surveying the town behind us.

'It's shifting, Tom. The whole town is shifting. It must be that heat haze thing Blitski was telling us about. It's a good omen,' and he plunged back under the surface. I agreed about the omen, but not quite in the way he meant. I found myself frightened to move from my spot on the pebbles, in case even that slight movement should disturb the precarious equilibrium of our situation and cause the whole town to cave in on top of me. Suddenly the joke was no longer a joke. Landau reappeared and shouted, ' I'm coming on, eh, Tom? How about the way I slipped in that bit of poetry before, about the tide in the affairs of men, eh?'

He wiped his face on the back of his arm and said, ' Shelley, actually.' Then he turned and began swimming out to sea.

Three thousand pounds. Trust Landau to get everything out of proportion. I sighed and followed him into the water.

12

WHEN HE cared to live in it, Landau's London home was a semi-detached redbrick house backing on to the River Lea, identical in the cowardice of its conception and the ugliness of its design to tens of thousands of distended dolls' houses all over England. It was a house built by dullards for dullards, and his parents thought it exquisitely beautiful. Upstairs Landau enjoyed what seemed to me the sybarite luxury of his own room, but whenever I came visiting he commandeered the lounge, because here, by the french windows backing on to the garden, stood the grand piano, a lord of creation so cluttered with the petty spoils of domestic routine, the lace doilies, the wedding groups in gilt frames, the empty silver salvers, the ashtrays and the vases, that it always put me in mind of a rhinoceros with a cluster of small birds on its back. It had been purchased second-hand from a distant cousin during Landau's childhood, in one of those spasms of parental ambition when for a few short months visions of floral tributes and the concert halls of Europe had clouded the family judgement. Now it was used only for our intermittent bursts of songwriting.

We were safe in the lounge, and suffered interruptions by Landau's mother only for tea and honey cake, wheeled in on a trolley shining like a gilded chariot. Landau always used to say he was surprised she had never had knives fitted to the wheels. He had long since learned that every act of apparent charity in the house masked a sinister ulterior motive, and knew that the tea and cake was only his mother's pretext for badgering us about our prospects and wheedling out of us how much we were making in this mysterious profession of ours. Although I discovered years later that I was quite mistaken, I was convinced at the time that Landau's mother considered me a malign influence on her son, who, but for me, might have been treading the paths of righteousness instead of arming himself for the battle of life with nothing more substantial in the way of deadly weapons than a clarinet and a saxophone. There was about her nagging an undoubted air of heroism born of a sorrow at her husband's lack of animation. Somebody had to defend her son's interests, and if the old man persisted in reading the *Draper's Record* in the kitchen all day, then it was up to her, and whatever else she might have been, Mrs Landau was not the kind of woman to flinch from her responsibilities.

Landau's father was a passive, paunchy little man who only once in all the time I knew him was ever goaded into any kind of emotional outburst, and characteristically the passion which transported him on that unique occasion was impotent rage. One evening Landau and I were conducting a daring experiment to discover the possibilities of two clarinets improvising together without accompaniment. After about fifteen minutes Mr Landau, whose only previous connections with art had been selling cheap drill trousers to the residents of a North London suburb, crashed into the room at a speed and with a flushed urgency of which I had never dreamed him capable, and started to scream. He never actually said anything. It was more like a musical effect, a high-pitched wail underlining the weakness of our clarinet tones. Misunderstanding the situation, as usual, I assumed he was trying to join in, and shouted some words of encouragement. However, after a few bars the prominence of the veins on his forehead told me I was wrong and that he was trying to deliver some kind of adverse criticism. While these thoughts were going through my mind he stopped screaming, glared wildly round the room, as if the familiar furnishings and ornamentation might reassure him as to his own sanity, and then left as abruptly as he had arrived, leaving the residue of his rage echoing round the room, now dramatically still and peaceful.

Landau waited a few moments and then, with sad deliberation placed his clarinet on top of the piano among the pots and coverlets. Then he perched himself on the stool and stared gravely down at the dragons of the fitted carpet. Shuffling his feet, he said with comic bitterness, 'Look at the critic. Canvas trousers he knows about. Cheap underwear he's a connoisseur of. Music? He's a bloody ox.'

By now I was laughing in delight, but Landau seemed genuinely horrified at this gross breach of aesthetic decorum by a member of his family.

' I'm ashamed,' he said. ' You'll have to forgive them. They just don't know any better.'

But apart from this one isolated incident, it was Landau's mother who really dictated the course of events in the household. As time was to prove, even she was no match for Landau when he really hit his stride, but everyone else who lived with her quickly learned to acknowledge her authority. Her most deadly domestic weapon was a shattering self-confidence born of complete freedom from any kind of sensitivity. I remember her as an insistent woman with a strident voice forever asking people questions she never gave anyone time to answer, and whose inspiration was an insatiable appetite for the economic facts of other people's lives. Money as a topic of polite conversation held no horrors for her, and on each of my visits I was rigorously interrogated about my income and asked how I could possibly exist on so miserable a pittance. I believe she had in her own mind a kind of platonic ideal of a reasonable income, and towards those like myself, obliged by circumstances to struggle along on perhaps a tenth of this purely arbitrary sum, she adopted an attitude which was an irritating blend of contempt and solicitude. She would wheel in her tea-trolley with the dignity of a pallbearer and, while dispensing her charity, would cunningly wheedle out of me the monthly treasurer's report.

' You mustn't mind her,' Landau would say, after she had retired in perfect order. ' She can't help what she does.'

It was his desperate attempt to bridge the vast gulf between his own ideas of social decorum and the realities of his mother's relentless assault on the sensibilities of all his friends.

' You see, she has to know what you earn for her own peace of mind. I mean, if she didn't know what your bank balance was, how could she possibly sum you up as a person?'

And indeed there did seem to be some unspecified property

qualification required before you won her full acceptance. When in the previous summer her motherly love had driven Landau to the refuge of two rooms over an Indian restaurant in Gerrard Street, one of the greatest pleasures of his new life had been to invite her to tea, so that for once it was her sensibilities that were being outraged. He exulted in the squabbling rats behind the skirting, the oppressive aura of yesterday's curry wrapping the house like a shroud, the tap protruding nakedly from the kitchen wall, the peeling paint, the grease-clotted gas-ring on which he prepared his daily fry-up of egg and sausage, the anonymous brassières and girdles abandoned in the passage.

For him the episode was at once a gay bohemian gesture and a merciful release from his mother's unremitting hygiene. He stayed there for nearly three months before surrendering to Mrs Landau's tearful pleas to erase the stain on the family honour. He always insisted afterwards that the Gerrard Street holiday had been a turning point.

'Tom,' he once confided, 'those three months were the formative years of my life.'

Perhaps he was thinking of the time when the girl with the biggest breasts in show business had stayed with him there for three days. He had to throw her out eventually because she had no conversation.

Landau's return home was his mother's unconditional surrender. He won every concession he asked for, and soon the house on the river became a glorified rehearsal room through which trooped the bedraggled legions of his lost ambitions to become a bandleader in his own right. For a while his mother was glad to accept any conditions so long as he was living under her roof once more, but the extent of her patience shrank as the size of his bands steadily increased. Uncertain pleasure modulated into panic. One evening, when Landau brought home a fifteen-piece band complete with two girl singers and a bandboy, she made her last stand and threw everybody into the street. Landau's parting shot that night, delivered from the safety of the road leading down to the local bus terminus, was to call her a stinking bourgeoise, and from that night on he never lived at home again for more than a few days at a time.

But the stinking bourgeoise was not downhearted. Although she sensed that she had lost her darling boychild for ever, there was still one dream left untarnished by events. Oh, of course, it was sad that she should lay her head on her pillow each night wondering where her little boy was and what he was doing, but all might not be lost. It was this last all-pervading dream which put us on to the Victoria train one afternoon soon after our talk on the beach, the one dream which might make Landau's preposterous plan workable. All her life Mrs Landau had prayed that one day her problem son would ' have a business '. She was not an unreasonable woman once her conditions were acceded to, and never cared what business, so long as there was ready money coming in, so long as her son might always have a pound or two in his pocket and be able to cheat a little on his income-tax returns. The two obsessions of her class, medicine and accountancy, she had reluctantly discounted many years before. The mere thought of Landau with a scalpel in his hand or somebody else's money at his disposal was so horrific that even Mrs Landau, doting parent that she was, knew they were out of the question. And so the matter of Landau's future finally resolved itself in her mind into having a business.

The music profession she loathed with all the loathing of a woman with a guilty conscience, because she knew very well that but for her own insistence on piano lessons in Landau's childhood, he would never have thought of a career in music at all. She had had sweet visions of a velveteen cherub playing the ' Indian Love Lyrics ' to the Ladies' Guild of the local synagogue. Instead there was this demented saxophone player who, she suspected, and perhaps rightly, would murder them all in their beds if he thought the act would help his embouchure. And now, after all these turbulent years, her fondest dream in life was about to be realised, although she didn't know it yet. For her darling boy was going into business after all. Landau sat in a first-class carriage of the *Brighton Belle,* tapping thoughtfully with his fingers on a third-class ticket. His feet were propped up on the opposite seat, and he was gazing out at the Sussex countryside.

'Tom, I'm going to please her at last. Think what that means. I'm actually going to do what she wants. What *she* wants, Tom. You know, it makes me feel sort of . . .'

'Warm inside?'

'That's it. Makes me feel warm inside.'

He swung his feet off the seat. They clumped on to the carriage floor, raising a barely discernible cloud of polite, first-class dust.

'You know, I've realised something in the last few days thinking about all this. We don't think enough of our parents. I mean, if it wasn't for them fancying each other, where would we be? Nowhere, that's where we would be. Nowheresville, boy. We wouldn't even be alive. And yet what do we do? We go along and take them for granted and we think they've got no feelings at all, just because they haven't got much for us. All my life she's been saying get a business, get a business and she was right. How about that? My mother, my nosy, loudmouthed mother was actually right about something. It's a very funny world.'

Our train lurched to a halt outside some railway sidings. Across the track some ancient engine belched out maps of South America in drifting steam. For a moment the sky outside our carriage window was clouded by rags of smoke. We jolted forward again and the blue returned. Landau said, 'I'm about to make her a very happy woman.'

When we arrived at the house by the river, the unwitting beneficiary of our visit bellowed out a greeting which echoed out across the mud flats of the Lea. The lounge was the same old mausoleum of pink mirrors and cream leather furniture, apparently disused since that last disastrous experiment with the clarinets in the previous winter. After a moment the star of that memorable night came in. With a tired sigh Mr Landau settled himself in one arm-chair while his wife occupied the other. They looked like some ghastly caricature of a king and queen spending a quiet night at home on the second-best thrones. Landau and I took the sofa opposite. I perched uneasily on the edge of my cushion, ready for a quick getaway, focusing my attention grimly on the winking street lamps away on the far side of the river, out beyond the twitching gauze curtains of the french windows. Landau leaned back luxuriantly on his half of the sofa, apparently perfectly at ease. For the purposes of our business he adopted his most patronising air, the one he usually reserved for objectionable relatives and the stray girls he wished to impress with his worldly wisdom.

'Now Mum and Dad, I want you to listen carefully to what I've got to say. And when I say carefully, I do mean carefully.'

He paused for a moment, trying to remember the lines he had been silently rehearsing all the way up in the train. His parents looked at him not knowing quite what to expect.

'I've decided to take the advice you gave me a long time ago. To cut a long story short, I'm going into business.'

The effect of this mild remark was electric. Mrs Landau immediately clasped her hands together high in the air, half in applause, half in supplication to the Lord God of Hosts whose patronage the family enjoyed through its five guinea annual subscription to the local synagogue. They never actually attended except once a year on the Day of Atonement, but still managed to draw an invaluable supply of moral superiority from their subscription. So far as religion was concerned, the Landaus were absentee landlords. But at this moment of Landau's declaration his mother was so delirious with joy that she would willingly have attended the synagogue every day for a year had rabbinical law permitted it.

'Morris, you heard him?'

Morris had heard him all right. He was all too well acquainted with the utter hopelessness of his son's cause, and knew also by a kind of obscure family chemistry that this startling development could only cost him great anguish and possibly a considerable sum of money into the bargain. He licked his lips and asked, 'What kind of business, son? Something reliable?'

Landau grimaced in exasperation.

'No, something unreliable. Of course it's reliable. If it wasn't, why would I be going into it. Look, Dad, I've waited a long time to make this move, you know that. Would I make it without weighing up the chances carefully first?'

The answer to this question was obviously 'Yes', but Mr Landau was too exhausted and disenchanted a father to say so. Instead his wife leapt from her chair and took her stand by his side.

'My son, he's so clever, bless him,' she yelped. 'It's the right thing to do. You'll never regret it. Look at your father.'

We all looked at his father, who was beginning to appear very sick at heart, trying helplessly to make some kind of sense out of this awful contradiction of the known facts of his world. There must be something wrong somewhere. His son, his mad son, going into business? Perhaps it was one of those hallucinations that Dr Burman had warned him to expect? The business wasn't invented that his youngest son could go into. Perhaps on the moon, possibly on Mars, but not down here, not his last-born, not . . .

'Your father, he started a business, and look where we got to. Our own house, a car, a daily help three times a week and three lovely sons.'

It was a curious inventory, delivered in such a way as to make it sound as though the three lovely sons had been bought out of the profits. The recital continued.

'Lennie, I tell you you'll live to bless the day you decided to listen to your mother.'

'I got no choice, Mum. You're talking so loud.'

Mrs Landau brushed his objections aside and sprang forward to crush him in a tearful embrace. Landau, usually not in the least particular whose arms enfolded him, recoiled smartly, pushed her away and began striding about the room, making himself a moving target. He winked at me, lit a cigarette and began to recite the main body of his speech.

'Now you understand of course, that when a man goes into business he needs capital. You'll appreciate that, Dad, being a bit of a businessman yourself.'

'There's your life policy,' his mother said. 'Morris, how much is his life policy?'

'There's a few hundred quid there, anyway, boy. Take it. It's yours.'

'A few hundred quid? A few hundred lousy quid. Look, I'm not talking about petty cash. I mean real money. You have to think big these days if you're going to amount to anything. Times have changed quite a bit since you started out, Dad. Look, who's the one the bank manager respects the most? The one with the biggest overdraft. Right? You told me that yourself, remember?'

But Mr Landau preferred not to remember, and sensing the way things were going, gazed round at his wife like a trapped animal.

'Now, it's all quite simple,' Landau went on. 'All I'm asking for is three thousand quid.'

At this I looked up and regarded Landau's father with great interest. Sure enough, just as his son had predicted, on came the big scene. The old man released a compromise between a rattle and a gurgle, slid gently out of his chair, rolled on to the carpet, where he spluttered feebly, twitched a little and then lay still, his eyes closed, his chest heaving strenuously. Landau's words in the train came back with a rush . . . 'It's amazing. Every time you mention money to him, he has one of his turns. He doesn't need a doctor. What he really wants is a good accountant.'

But at this moment of crisis, Mrs Landau subscribed to different theories. At her husband's collapse she ran shrieking from the room, returning a few moments later with a cut-glass decanter brimming with brandy and a small bottle of pink pills. As she forced the liquid between her husband's lips she screamed reproaches at the two of us.

'You'll kill him before you've done. I always said you'd kill him. You know what his heart's like. I tell you, you've killed him this time.'

She was glaring at us all this time, so that the brandy intended for the corpse's lips slopped over his face and down his shirtfront. His eyelids fluttered and he struggled to sit up.

'Bertha, what are you doing with that brandy? He's trying to scare me to death and you're trying to drown me.'

He snatched the bottle of pills, deftly unscrewed the cap and threw two of the little pink pellets down his throat. Then he picked himself up, brushed aside his wife's helping hand and sat himself down in his chair once more, bracing himself for the next assault.

'I don't understand you, Dad. I try to talk sensibly for a minute and you start getting all melodramatic. No wonder nothing ever gets done in this place. All I want to do is start a little business of my own, and to start it I need three grand, that's all. And what's more, you can have the lot back in three months.'

Then he glanced quizzically at me and said, 'Two?'

I shrugged.

'There you are. You get it back in two months. Now I can't say any fairer than that, can I? I tell you what. I'll go even further. You can have interest on the top. It'll be more of a temporary loan really. The money's as good as in the bank.'

Mrs Landau, finally satisfied that the widow's weeds were not yet upon her, now clicked into gear. Not for nothing was it said that only she had made Mr Landau the uncrowned cotton trouser king of Turnpike Lane. Her business acumen, as she liked to call it, now brushed away the tears of joy and grief alike that she had already shed in the course of this brief but bumpy interview.

'What's it for? What's the business? Is it ready money? Where's the shop? Leasehold or Freehold? Retail or Wholesale? Any living accommodation? How much staff? Perishable stock? What's the . . .'

'Look, if you're going to start getting hysterical again, we're not going to get anywhere. Now listen. There's no shop. There's no stock. There's no ready money. Plenty of profit but no ready money. As a matter of fact it isn't really a business at all. It's more of a . . . well, a kind of investment club with the profits absolutely guaranteed, wouldn't you say, Tom?'

'Never mind what he says,' Mrs Landau snarled. 'What are you buying and selling?'

'I told you. I'm not buying or selling anything. It's the chance of a lifetime, and if I don't move soon it'll be too late. Will you do it or won't you? Let me have the money for two months and all this music stuff is finished for good. I give you my word on that. It won't be necessary any more. You stake me just this once and I'll be set for life.'

His father, still breathing heavily from his exertions on the carpet, said 'What's all this " stake me " talk?', turned to his wife in real bewilderment and asked, 'What's happened to him? He sounds like a cowboy.'

'Now you listen to me, son,' Mrs Landau said. 'Your father had to slave for years to make three thousand pounds. It's a lot of money, an awful lot of money. You don't even know what three thousand pounds means. You can't walk in here and expect him to hand it over just like that, just for the asking. We have to know more about it.'

But by now another idea had permeated Mr Landau's brain.

'Listen boy, what you up to anyway? It's not another one of your bloody bands, is it? If that's what it's for you can go and beg for it. I wouldn't give you three thousand pence for one of your bloody rotten bands.'

His voice rose to a croaking crescendo. Landau snapped his fingers in tempo on the offbeat, looked admiringly at his father and said, 'Yeah, Dad, take another chorus.'

'If you think I'm going to put money into one of those bloody bands of yours, you've made a big mistake. I'm not putting any of my money into your bloody bands.'

He broke off, frustrated by his own inability to express his contempt, looked at me and said cryptically, 'Him too.'

'Now look,' Landau said with a well-rehearsed air of finality. 'Let's get this straight once and for all. You're not putting money into anything. You're just letting me have a loan. And for not longer than two months. And for this you make a big scene. You make me feel ashamed before my own friends in my own home. For the last ten years all I've ever had from you two is get a business. You never once stopped. When I bought my first clarinet—out of my own earnings, I might add—it was get a business. When I gave you my first money towards the housekeeping, it was still get a business. When I got a regular job, six nights a week, mind you, in one of the biggest entertainment centres in the country, still it was the same old cry, get a business. All right, so I decide to get a business, and what happens? You try to welsh on the deal.'

'What deal?' asked his father. 'I haven't made any deal.'

But it was the last feeble shot in the family locker, and it bounced off Landau's impenetrable hide like a peanut. We left the house that night with a cheque for £2,750, Mrs

Landau's famed business acumen having insisted on an immediate twelve and a half repayment on the capital borrowed. Landau literally danced down the tree-lined road pointing back to the city. Automatically I made for the bus terminus, but he grabbed my arm and sang out, 'What are you thinking of? Buses? Come on. We're rolling in it.' Soon he had hailed a taxi, where, once inside, he sprawled all over the seats and sang all the way back to Victoria Station.

For some reason the train had a sobering effect on him. As we sped through the dark towards the sea, his gaiety dissolved and he began to gather his scattered thoughts. In the carriage gloom I watched him staring out of the window at the anonymous roofscape of the suburbs. He pulled the cheque from his inbreast pocket and studied it.

'What a responsibility this is,' and he flapped the cheque across his face, as if to catch a reassuring whiff of the riches it represented.

'I tell you one thing I discovered in there tonight. Money brings with it certain responsibilities. I mean, who knows how many pairs of cotton pants this represents?'

'We must pay him back, you know.'

'It's not up to us, Tom. If the deal comes off, of course he can have it all back, plus interest. But if we lose out, we won't have anything left to pay him back with. In a way, we're speculating with his money for him.'

'So what does he get out of it?'

'I told you. There's the interest. Here, what's three per cent per annum on £2,750 for three months?'

'I worked it out in the cab. Thirteen pounds, fifteen shillings.'

'And how many pairs of cotton pants does *that* represent, eh?'

With this truculent remark, Landau appeared to have cleared his conscience once and for all. From this moment on, I never once saw him showing the slightest concern for his father's rights, either as parent or moneylender. The train ground to a halt on the southern fringes of the river. Peering out of the window I became acutely aware that this journey had been a ridiculous vanity. I had a wild premonition that our train would never arrive at Brighton or anywhere else. There was no boarding house in Kemptown, no Mr Landau in his pink lounge swallowing pink pills, no cheque, no Filox Investments, no nothing.

Falling away behind my window to the left was a cavernous chapel lit with the lamps of doom. Their dull beams accentuated the dark rather than dispersed it. Next came a breaker's yard, scattered with the debris of boats abandoned among orange boxes, scrap iron and moulting mattresses. The crust of suburban roofs was broken here and there by the piercing line of a chapel spire or swollen by the round of a vague cupola, the faded gesture of some nameless Edwardian architect. And across the whole darkling vista lay a pall of soot and grime and shifting river mist which somehow softened the jagged contours of the landscape into a subtle water-colour, towering yet elusive, solid and three-dimensional and yet a shifting rumour fading away behind the carriage windows. The train jolted forward a few yards and almost flung Landau into my lap. He grunted and settled back in his seat. The racketing of the train wheels died away again, and the small noises of the night drifted into the carriage. A chorus of boys' voices, their stridency diffused through the distance, echoed across the dark. Then the train stumbled forward again and the voices were washed away in the ponderous syncopation of the wheels, rolling on out of the suburbs. Already our plans had gone further ahead than had seemed possible. Let the whole thing stop now, before we were hit by a terrible disaster. So long as Landau and I sat in this carriage nothing could go wrong. We would drift along in suspended animation, he and I and the cheque. Brighton might be a million miles away . . .

Suddenly the carriage lights flickered on, died, flickered again, almost died again, and finally asserted themselves. All at once the gloomy symbolic view from my window was wiped out by my own reflection, comically serious under the crumpled blue beret. Landau sat there blinking against the raw light. Facing me on the wall behind his head was a reproduction of the foreshore at Porthcawl so vacuous that even Landau's face seemed a more rewarding work of art by comparison. I had been to Porthcawl once, for one night, with a band. It had been bitterly cold and the rain had slanted down the whole time we were there. In the reproduction over Landau's head, honey-coloured sunlight bathed the rocks and gulls wheeled in over the friendly surf. The painting was about as real as our prospects. I started to ask Landau what he thought about railway art, but his eyes were closed. Soon he was snoring heavily. I pulled down the window-blinds and closed my eyes. The rhythm of the train wheels kept shifting from three-four to four-four, three-four to four-four, three-four to four-four . . .

I awoke as the train cruised into Brighton station. Landau was still asleep and snorted resentfully when I shook him. I noticed that the first thing he did on gathering his scrambled wits was to feel for the cheque. It was still lying there in his lap. He grunted with satisfaction and muttered something about taking life by the throat.

Before we went to bed that night we had one more conference in Landau's bedroom. Or rather we sat there and stared dumbly at the cheque. Just before he turned in Landau, who had placed our entire financial assets with loving care under his grease-stained pillow, thought of something. He sat up, dragged out the cheque yet again and scrutinised it minutely. Then apparently satisfied, he returned it to its place under the pillow and sank down in the bedclothes. The last thing I heard him say before I went back to my room was, 'A wonder he didn't put the wrong date on it. Just like him to do something like that. If he tries to stop payment, I'll disown him.'

I had just slid into my own bed, wondering how long it would be before my sorely troubled mind would allow me to escape into sleep, when Landau's head appeared round the door.

'If you want something on account, you know you only have to ask.'

'Sure. Let's sleep on it.'

He nodded. The head disappeared again and my door clicked shut. I switched off the bedlamp and tried to recapitulate the evening's events, but it was too much for me. All I knew was that Mrs Landau's advice had been heeded at last. Her son was going into business. With three partners. That night a great wind swept in from the sea, swaggering through the dusty streets, rattling the window-panes of the sleeping town. I heard the church clock chime three before I fell asleep.

13

THE PIRATICAL escapade of the cheque brought with it a curious aftermath. Whatever success Landau had scored, he had been obliged to score it off his own family, and the knowledge troubled him. Dearly desiring to stand on his own feet, he had for some time been fighting a self-conscious battle to disengage himself from what Blitski had taught him to think of as the dear octopus, and it irritated him to know that in a moment of financial crisis he had had to come back, cap in hand, to those whose standards he found so odious. His mother's insistence on choosing his boarding house for him that summer had been the last straw in a veritable thatched roof of petty indignity, and after it Landau ruthlessly cut himself off as completely as he could. So convinced was he that salvation lay in making himself as nearly an orphan as possible, that the idea soon became an obsession. He felt that in going home for money he had in some obscure way ratted on his dearest principles, and that therefore the price would have to be paid. Within twenty-four hours he was proved right.

On the afternoon after our trip to London there was a melodramatic shift in the weather. I remember that when Landau and I started walking the sun had dried out the evidence of the previous night's storm. The paving stones were hot under the thin soles of our sandals, so that every few hundred yards we were obliged to sit on corporation benches to rest our feet. There is no doubt that on that first afternoon as practising capitalists we were both heavily intoxicated, not so much by the possession of the money as by the thought of the wild act of commercial brigandage the money would make possible. As we threaded our casual route through the crowds, I sensed that at last we really were different from everyone else. Now we were speculators. We were men of affairs and could afford to take leisurely strolls like this one. The fact that we were no longer leading the professional life seemed to matter very little. Each time the pangs of conscience assailed us for forsaking our beloved muse, the thought of that cheque, now snuggling cosily among the reeds and mouthpieces of Landau's saxophone case, restored my poise. No longer obliged to practise our instruments, we could afford for a while to become theoreticians, to think about making jazz purely in the abstract.

By the time our walk was in its third stage we were already involved in a confused and rather pretentious argument about the importance in music of relaxation. Landau, intrigued as always by the mechanics of his own body, was convinced that the soloist who relaxed himself physically was at once an improved soloist, whereas I was equally certain that mental self-confidence while improvising could have the most surprising power to relax tense muscles. In our preoccupation with this vital dispute, we wandered further afield than usual and soon found ourselves strolling along a part of the promenade overhanging an unfamiliar stretch of beach. We must have passed the West Pier without even noticing its existence, and soon the buildings across the road had modulated into the expansive tans and greys of Hove. By this time Landau had finally arrived at his King Charles' Head, the question of whether or not he possessed a chin. He knew that an embouchure to a saxophonist was as important as hands to a pianist and was trying to excuse the undoubted lack of resonance in his own playing by suggesting that the unusual structure of his jaw and chin was to blame.

'Look,' he said, stopping in mid-stride, 'you tell me whether my embouchure is tight enough.'

'How the hell do I do that?'

'I'll open my mouth and you put your finger inside. Just like it was a mouthpiece. Go on. It won't hurt.'

I looked around. People were swirling past us apparently just as intent on their own affairs as we were on ours. Landau was my best friend. We were apprentice members of a unique brotherhood. I poked my finger in his mouth. 'Go on,' I said. 'Blow.'

Landau blew. A fine spray of spittle burst from the corners of his mouth.

Keeping my index finger on his lower lip I stepped back to examine the ring of muscles forming the vital embouchure.

'It looks fine to me.'

He pushed my finger away and wiped his mouth. 'Never mind what it looks like. How does it feel?'

'I don't know. I'm not a mouthpiece. But I shouldn't worry if I were you. I'm convinced your chin is adequate.'

But this afternoon, plagued by his self-betrayal of the night before, Landau was bent on martyrdom. He walked in silence for a while, every so often shoving his own finger in his mouth and blowing hard. Finally he abandoned the experiment and tried to recapture the high spirits in which we had set out. For a while he talked about the beauty of the cheque, but it was no use. The shadow of his own faithlessness had fallen between him and the bright sun, and nothing I could do or say made him feel any better. At last we drifted to an indecisive halt and debated whether or not to turn back. Landau was insistent on retreat, and I very soon understood why. I also began to understand other things, including his readiness to jump into the deep waters of high finance on so flimsy a pretext as ours. We stood there arguing for several minutes, I urging him along the coast road, Landau standing there on the tessellated pavement stubbornly refusing to take another step forward. And then the incident occurred which he must have been dreading all summer. A young man in a beach party under the stone breakwater recognised him and called his name.

As we descended the bleached wooden steps leading down to Landau's friends, a change came over him which I can only describe as remarkable. All his characteristic insouciance melted away, to be replaced by a kind of distracted sulk which wiped the hint of that perpetual grin from his face. The new mood was quite different from the comical despair of the embouchure incident. Over his face there now spread an absent frown, as though he were the slow-witted butt of the company we now joined. I wondered at first whether he had merely miscalculated the extent of our isolation down there on the coast. Ever since I had arrived I had sensed that Landau was living and thinking as though the fifty-eight minutes by train which separated us from all the old cycles of hope and disappointment, ambition and frustration, confidence and defeatism, comprised an unbridgeable chasm which rendered him immune from all the old influences. He had reacted to the town rather as I had to the Arcadia, looking for magic in the most commonplace faces, believing that the enchanted inhabitants of this new world accepted him on the terms of his imagination rather than his achievements. Perhaps the fact that he had been recognised by the old world was upsetting him now. He spoke only in monosyllables, kept staring out at the skyline and refused to sit on the chromatic array of beach towels spread out before us, doggedly ignoring all the conversational skittles his friends set up for him. But it was only when the girl spoke to him that I realised the full extent of his demoralisation. I had noticed her the moment we started walking down the wooden steps, and by the time we reached the party had reluctantly concluded that the closer you got to her, the less did she resemble the dream-figment which the inner eye of my imagination, strongly indoctrinated by celluloid childhood affairs with Hedy Lamarr and Paulette Goddard, had always demanded. Whether she might be Landau's type I had not the remotest idea. At this advanced stage of our association I had admitted to myself, not without a certain envy, that for Landau there were no types, only women, and that therefore a far wider field of philandering was open to him than it was to me. But there was no denying that the girl sitting before us in the sky-blue swimsuit with mules to match looked a highly stimulating proposition. She was squatting in a way which would make it impossible for Landau to conduct his customary anatomical survey, but at a guess I would have said she was well enough proportioned to meet even his stern demands. After the introductions, made by a sallow young man who turned out to be Landau's second cousin, the girl asked what kind of music we liked playing. I looked to Landau, but he appeared to be intrigued by the contours of a small fishing boat out on the horizon. So I replied, 'We play the kind of music you would probably hate. We play jazz.'

'Oh? I'm not so sure about that. Why would I hate it?'

She had that sing-song intonation which made me want to grab a sheet of manuscript paper and notate it. And Landau, keeping his eyes resolutely on the horizon, said, 'Because you're stupid, like most people when it comes to the arts.'

And that was his sole contribution to the small-talk. The girl's logical processes were obscure. Having been insulted by one stranger, she now did what she could to insult the other and when I told her that musicians in our field rarely earned much money, she replied, 'Yes, I thought you looked a bit poverty-stricken when I saw you walking along.' I barely resisted the temptation to introduce the theme of the cheque.

The sallow second cousin hastily changed the subject, but Landau still refused to take any further part in the uncomfortable little drama we had stumbled into. An inquiry about the welfare of his family drew only a slight shrug of the shoulders, and attempts to get him to talk about his work met with no response at all. I, on the other hand, was beginning to enjoy myself. Usually it was Landau who carried the ball, but now, because of this untypical fit of sulks, I was able to behave very airily towards people whose opinions of us did not interest me and whose code of etiquette I sensed might be even more imbecilic than our own. When we first joined the beach party I had been confused about its frame of reference. Who were these people? What was their connection with Landau, and why had their very presence disconcerted him so badly? And then, in the very first stages I sniffed the dust of a familiar battle. These people seemed to assume a superiority over us simply because they were richer than we were, and were groping for some way to assert that superiority in conversational terms. From the moment I realised this, the situation presented no difficulties. I sat there in the sunlight boxing a few desultory rounds in the class war, highly relieved now that I had not after all fallen in love with the girl in the blue swimsuit. I had learned from the experiences of Blitski that when fighting the class war it is always better to be emotionally withdrawn from the enemy, and when she interrupted me on a point of ethics, I told her as much. I was beginning to feel confident that my virtuoso display of bad manners would amuse Landau and stir him into action, but I was wrong. For him it was a tortuous fifteen minutes, and when at the end of it he pleaded more pressing engagements he told the lie with real desperation. As I rose from the crumpled rainbow of towels and dusted myself down, I could see he was counting every second of the time till we would be out of sight and earshot of the beach party, which, apart from his cousin, had included a few old school friends. After we had made our escape, he walked along in silence for a long time, hands thrust deep into his trouser pockets, eyes staring at the ground. Neither of us broke the silence till we came in sight of a cider house in one of our favourite side streets.

'Fancy a drink?'

He asked the question with the air of a man who has already seen a dozen reasonable suggestions spurned, and is trying to humour an unreasonable world. I nodded and we went inside. The bar was refreshingly cool and shaded after the fierce glare of the beach encounter. I sat at a corner table while Landau went to the bar. I watched him leaning on one elbow staring into space till the barmaid came across. Soon he came back carrying two pint glasses of cider. He took a great gulp from one of the glasses before he sat down. Then he lit a cigarette, exhaled with relief and stretched his legs to their full extent. He studied the tips of his toes through the open ends of his sandals and started trying to explain himself.

'You see, Tom . . .'

He broke off and swilled the cider round his glass. He was beginning to act a part now, and that meant the worst of his mood was already past.

'You mean those people?' I prompted.

'You see, what do that lot know about music? Did you see the jewellery my cousin was wearing?'

He began to pat the table in time to the recital of the catalogue.

'Identification disc, ring, wrist watch, necklace, charm bracelet. I ask you, what kind of a person is that, who wears an identification disc down here? A boy who's actually worried about getting lost on Brighton beach. Just like a dog.'

'Why do you go so strange when you meet a team like that?' I asked. Perhaps I knew the answer better than he did, but it was quiet in the bar, and it might be pleasant to spin out the conversation for a while. For a few minutes he waffled on about art and capitalism in the best Blitski manner, but I could see he had no intention yet of providing the real answer to my question. Like the true artist he was, Landau would only deliver the real confessional when he reached the climax of his act. I knew that any encounter we might have with the jewsoisie always underlined the inadequacy of our own predicament. Our fame, if ever we won it, would be restricted to our own little world, and our earnings, if ever we managed to get any, would always sound like petty cash to people like those in the beach party. To the accountants and dentists and dress manufacturers who had grown up with us, we would always seem like naïve vagabonds who remained blind to the one truth that really mattered, which was that the more money you acquired, the better it was for your soul. As Blitski put it in one of his rare anti-clerical diatribes, easier for the camel to get through the eye of a needle than for the poor man to get his name inscribed on the synagogue wall. The graffiti of pietism, Blitski called it. Whatever he meant by that, it was certainly true that the beach party people believed that when it came to a choice between sensibilities and hard cash, the sensibilities could always be crushed. Money, and money alone was what really mattered. Court it, covet it, marry it. Music? What was music? Only a diversion that everyone understood instinctively, without the drudgery of learning about it.

'And that's what makes me ashamed,' Landau said, head bowed under the incongruous twilight of the cider bar. 'The fact that, knowing all their ideas are so bent, I still get brought down when I meet them.'

There was very little I could say to comfort him. I knew as well as he did that our ivory tower was unbreachable only so long as we never ventured outside it. Every time we exposed our flanks and measured ourselves against the

162

society we despised, we felt beaten and ludicrous. On the face of it Landau's defences should have been more effective than mine. Having been raised among the philistines he should have been less impressed by its list of battle honours. In fact he was far worse than me. He had two older brothers, one an actuary, the other a wholesale grocer, and he made a point never to say anything to them which was not an exasperated insult at their maddening alliance of money and denseness. Landau knew he could become one of the beach party simply by selling his instruments and going back to the house by the river, whereas I had always been sunk in a comparative poverty so natural to me that I had not for years realised it was poverty at all.

' Listen, Landau, I can't follow you. Are you brought down because you hate them, or because you envy them?'

' What do you mean, envy them? You know me better than that.'

' Well, there's one thing you've overlooked. If you're a jazz musician, you're déclassé.'

' What's that?'

' It means classless. If you're going to play the saxophone for a living, play jazz that is, you don't have any class any more.'

' So?'

' So, that means that the rules of no particular class apply to you any more. Don't you see? You're free of all that crap.'

' I'm sorry. I don't understand what it's got to do with those people we met.'

' All right. Put it another way. You're depressed because you feel some kind of failure when you see your friends living it up. But what you're forgetting is that you can't expect to do well in that particular race because you're not even entered for it. See?'

With this I had given him his prompt for the climactic line, and out it came with comical predictability, except that it wasn't quite the line I had anticipated.

' That's just it. I *am* entered in the race. So are you. So is everybody. The only difference between us and them is that we're riding a different kind of horse.'

163

I took a few moments to digest this surprising remark and then said, ' You realise that this puts a different complexion on everything?'

' Why?'

' Well, it seems that you actually expect to make money out of being a jazz musician.'

' Don't you?'

' No, not real money. Come on, Landau. You know as well as I do there's no real money there. I thought you just loved playing.'

' I do. Playing's my life, you know that. But it ought to be possible to beat that crowd at their own game without descending to their level.'

' And what level is that?'

' You know. Thinking about money the whole time.'

' If you're so against thinking about money the whole time, just tell me what we're doing throwing three grand into the Stock Exchange.'

' Ah, that's different.'

' Tell me why.'

' Because we're doing things the jazz way. Look, in everything we do there's the jazz way and the square way. What we're doing with Filox is making loot the jazz way.'

' You mean without working for it.'

' No, no. We live strictly as jazz musicians and what happens? Filox falls right in our laps. We just had to take the chance, to show them.'

' Show them what?'

' That saxophone players can be shrewd.'

It was one of the most revealing conversations I ever had with Landau, and goes a long way towards explaining how he arrived, not so many years later, at the spectacular compromise, not between art and commerce, but between what he conceived as art and commerce.

' You know what, Landau? I don't know what you're talking about.'

He looked at me and we started laughing. We sat in that bar for a long time, sipping cider in gradually diminishing draughts—for neither of us were real drinkers—allowing the cool air and the mock Tudor beams to perform their therapy

164

on our battered egos. It took Landau a hundred and ten minutes and three pints of cider to recover his aplomb. When we emerged into the street at last, he was singing one of his pet chord sequences, slapping his hand against his thigh to hold the tempo. He never stopped singing all the way home, even though long before we climbed the thronged hill to the station, great isolated spots of rain began to spatter the dusty pavements. Landau was like that. He could shrug off a major defeat within hours. He reacted more violently than I, but his powers of recuperation were proportionately swifter. With me the experience on the beach might fester for weeks.

There was, of course, a postscript, although whether it was accidental or contrived I never discovered. In the small hours of the following morning Landau came strutting into my bedroom obviously fresh from some great triumph.

'Guess where I've been.'

'Give up. Where?'

'As a matter of fact I've been out speculating with our capital.'

I dropped the paperback edition of *How to Make Money Work For You* I had been studying and sat up in alarm.

'Landau, what have you gone and done?'

'It's all right. No need for alarm. I got in a poker game.'

'Landau, you got no right . . .'

'Stop panicking. I told you it was all right.'

'I refuse to believe you till you give me all the details.'

Of all the men I have ever met, there is no question that Landau was the least qualified to play the devious game of bluff and counterbluff demanded by good poker. His features were an infallible guide to his emotions, and even five minutes' acquaintance with him would be enough for a shrewd gambler to distinguish the nervous grin of a full house from the mad elation of a running flush.

'Go on. What happened?'

'Well, guess who I met in the Metropole Bar? Those relatives of mine. You remember, that creepy cousin and his crowd. They had this poker scene going, see, and they talked me into joining them.'

'Landau,' I shouted, 'for chrissake, what happened?'

Instead of answering he performed the gesture he must have been rehearsing all the way up the hill. He pulled out his comb, dragging out with it crumpled sheafs of banknotes which fluttered to the floor around his feet.

'How much?'

'Two hundred and fifty, sixty, I'm not sure. I haven't counted it yet. Anyway, it brings up the investment fund to a round three thousand. How about that?'

'You might have lost,' I said, staring fascinated at the money on the carpet.

'Don't be silly, Tom. How? I was playing with credit. If it had gone the other way, I would have knocked them,' and he stooped to gather in his winnings!

I think I can guess now what happened to Landau that night. For just one moment in his life, he became an invincible poker player by grace of the hatred which froze his features. I see now that all he needed to do to conceal the truculence of an unbeatable hand was to look his hated friends in the eye. His face must instantly have turned to stone and the enemy been hopelessly confounded. In later years Landau built up the fiction in his own mind that he had won by using marked cards, but that couldn't have been true. Landau never had that much sense.

14

It was a night too hot for sleep. The town clocks had just struck two, and I was sitting on the edge of the children's bathing pool dangling my bare feet in the water when along the deserted promenade Landau came marching. I picked up the distant tap of his footsteps long before he came into view, his tall drooping body silhouetted firmly against the saffron glow of a full moon. His bow tie was gone and his shirt unbuttoned halfway down his chest. So intent was he on his own business that he strode past without noticing me. When I called his name he spun round like a man who has been shot in the back.

'Tom!'

He exclaimed my name as though surprised to discover that anybody but himself had the initiative to be out so late. Despite the hour and the deserted seafront he had been stepping purposefully along like a man late for a luncheon appointment. He was in no physical condition to run, but the anxious rapidity of his patent leather shoes on the warm stone of the promenade had implied a great throng of milling pedestrians impeding his progress. He slumped on to the wooden bench behind me, so I gathered my shoes and socks and joined him.

'Whooo.'

The air burst out of his lungs as though long imprisoned.

'What's all the panic, Landau?'

'Do I seem panicked?'

'Don't you know?'

He shrugged his shoulders in a vague gesture of self-disgust and said, 'Of course I know. What am I bothering to pretend for? It's that nurse. Remember the one I told you about? I just wanted to put as much space between her and me as possible, that's all.'

'Just a minute. I thought you said she was a great

167

woman. Yesterday morning, wasn't it?'

'That was yesterday morning. This is today, tonight. It's all finished, and I might tell you it's a relief to get away from her.'

He waved his arms against the sky in disgust, not at himself this time, but towards his once beloved nurse.

'Do you know what that cow went and did?'

'What?'

'She gave me a false name. Remember I told you her name was Laura? Well, it isn't. Go on, guess her real name. I defy you.'

'How do I know? You said it was Laura.'

'Well, the bitch was lying. It's Flora.'

He took a deep breath and simulated a shudder of repugnance. 'Flora, what kind of a name is that, Tom?'

'I don't see what difference it makes. I mean, she's the same person you've been pulling for the last two weeks, isn't she?'

'How can she be the same person if her name's different? Just answer me that.'

'No, but her face hasn't changed, has it? Or her figure? How can it change anything?'

'I'll tell you how it changes everything. For a start, every time I want to speak to her I have to say Flora instead of Laura. Second, if a chick can lie about her name, she can lie about anything.'

'What is this, sociology or something? We all know about chicks lying.'

'No, it's terrible, it's all wrong. Look, why do you think there's a song called " Laura " but no song called " Flora "? Imagine calling out to the rhythm section, " Flora in C ". No, Tom, it's all ridiculous. I'm definitely not having any more of that.'

He leaned back, resting his hands on the nape of his neck against the ribs of the bench, gazing up at the cloudscapes drifting across above us.

'What are you doing here anyway?'

'Just cooling off. Been trying conclusions with one of the waitresses from the Arcadia.'

'Any good?'

'Waste of time. She said I was self-centred.'

'They're all bloody mad,' Landau said darkly and took another deep breath.

He stared at the clouds and then smiled.

'Great night, eh?'

'Mmm.'

'Look at that sky. Vast.'

He grinned more broadly at the thought of the sky being bigger than he was. Soon the noise of our laughter sent ripples of sound out across the still waters of the empty pool.

'There's all this,' Landau said, flinging his arm generously towards the rippling path of golden light stretching across the sea to the horizon, 'and I'm worried about a nurse. I must be mad.'

He seemed quite overcome by the magnificence of our location. The whole town was our backdrop and the brightness of the moon our lighting effect. He suddenly pushed himself up from the bench, threw off his shoes and socks, and started to trudge across the shallow waters of the pool.

'It was funny the way it came out.'

'What was?'

'About her name. How I caught her out. It was pretty smart when you come to think of it.'

He was down at the far end of the pool now, and began shouting to make himself heard.

'She was wearing this brooch, see, with F.W. on it, so I asked her if she'd nicked it from somewhere. Just kidding about, see, so she starts crying and then she says that F stands for Flora. So you know what I said? I said, " Good-bye Flora ".'

He had waded back to my end of the pool by now, and clambered out laughing at the thought of his brilliant parting shot. His bare feet slapped on the pink stone tiles and he settled back on the bench again, wiping his toes with his handkerchief. His face was grave in concentration, and graced by the moonlight playing on his right profile. As he worked his way along the toes of his left foot he said, 'How about that, eh, Tom? " Good-bye Flora ".'

His mood changed abruptly again and he started to laugh

uproariously, and I joined in. We wiped our eyes as the clocks struck the half-hour, and then sat back in silence for a while sharing my last cigarette.

'Shall we cut out?'

I nodded. Landau bent down and began working his socks on. As he tied his shoelaces he sang to himself, 'Goodbye Flora' and chuckled as he came to the end of the chorus. He was relaxed now and made no attempt to walk at the pace he had been using when I spotted him. We ambled back, speculating on what might be concealed behind the curtains of the few lighted windows we passed, and deciding with some reluctance that the mysteries were hollow ones. When we arrived at the house we went into Landau's room. He opened the bottom drawer of his wardrobe, produced two bottles of lager and deftly opened them with a gadget on the end of his penknife. Then he threw himself full-length, face upwards on his bed and began to swill the cool liquor around his mouth. I perched myself on the end of the bed and sipped my beer.

'Listen Tom. I've been thinking about this business. We can't waste much more time, you know. We've got to work out the next move.'

'I know. As a matter of fact I've been doing a bit of research myself,' and I pulled from my jacket pocket a paperback edition of *Tono-Bungay*.

Landau sat up and reached for it. He skimmed suspiciously through the pages. 'What's it about?'

'Well, there's this old guy who puts coloured water in bottles and sells it as a health tonic.'

'Does this Filox team make health tonic?'

'No, I don't think they do. But the principle's the same.'

'How do you mean?'

'Well, when this old guy makes his fortune he starts buying and selling shares, floating companies, the whole scene, including takeovers.'

'That's good. That's very good. Where's that bit? What page?'

'Well, actually, it's not much help. I thought it might be, but when it comes to the actual details it's a bit vague. You know. It just says that they buy this company and sell that one, but it never explains what they actually, physically do when they play the market.'

Landau lobbed the book back at me and sank back on his pillows. 'It's like sex passages,' he said.

'What is?'

'What you were just talking about. Just like sex books. You wade through a whole load of crap to find out what sex kick the hero is on, and when you get there it's all left to your imagination. That's no good to people like me, Tom. We haven't got any imagination. That's why we read books, to enjoy someone else's.'

'I suppose we could get hold of one of those manuals. You know, a *Simple Guide to the City*.'

Landau's frustration stung him into violence.

'Guide to the fucking city? What do you think this is, a sightseeing tour? What we need is technical knowhow.'

'All right. You tell me where we get that.'

'Well,' he mused, 'we've got to do something. And quick,' and he began by draining his bottle.

'Don't look at me. I told you when this whole thing started that I don't know anything about all this.'

'That's not the right attitude. You'll have to learn. Do you remember what you once told me, that time we got slung out of the counterpoint classes? You said that education was knowing how to learn. So learn about the market. After all, you're in business for yourself now, you know.'

'Yes, but what exactly do we do?'

'How do I know? You're the educated one. You tell me. Look, you can't tell me there aren't ways of finding out. It's not as if this business is illegal or secret or anything like that.'

'Why don't you ask your old man?'

'Him? He can go and get stuffed. No, we're going to do this all on our own, just the four of us. And I'm not putting my old man in it. We go to him, and in five minutes the old lady's on the scene, and once that happens, forget it. Look, it's ridiculous. There's thousands waiting to be picked up, and here we are not knowing how. It's like them ads you see in the personal columns of the papers. Hey, that's not a bad idea. "Wanted, experienced business adviser to show four skint members how to pick up loot"!'

171

Landau collapsed in hysterical laughter again. I walked over to the open window and stood there staring at the sea now silver in the moonlight. I was angry at Landau's persistent hysteria but half-inclined to join in. After a few moments he managed to control himself. He sat up and made a visible effort to be serious once more.

'This whole situation is mad, Tom.'

He spoke now in that brusque voice he reserved for serious occasions, as though he had only to adjust his intonation for all the problems of the world to fall neatly into place. For no particular reason his sudden change of manner had a profound effect on me. Months and years later I was to recall, several times, that it was in this moment, for the first time since Filox Investments had entered our lives by its circuitous, libidinous route, that I felt excited at the prospect of becoming involved in an adventure with Landau at the helm, drunken perhaps, and half out of his head, but still, at the helm. Out beyond my left shoulder the moon glinted on the sea and the backwash of the breakers reduced itself to a sibilant murmur. Landau drummed with his fingernails on his empty beer bottle and swept me away on the coat-tails of his mad scheme for the first time. He dropped the bottle on the bed, clapped his hands like a chairman calling the meeting to order and began to get down to hard facts.

'Now. The first thing is to find out who to get in touch with.'

I was too exhilarated by my change of feelings to be serious for the moment.

'No. The first thing is to find out how to find out who to get in touch with.'

'Oh, come on, for chrissake. Be serious for one moment. I'll find out who to contact. I'll get some good advice from someone we can really rely on. The only really important thing is the outlay, and we've already raised that. Thanks to my old man.'

'The one who can go and get stuffed?'

'Right. And don't you worry about him changing his mind. If he starts trouble I'll make his life an even bigger misery than it was before.'

'All right. So we get the capital and make our contact. What then?'

'It's coming, Tom. It's coming.' He stood up and began pacing about the room, no doubt imitating the choreography of some half-remembered Spencer Tracy film seen in childhood whose impression had never quite faded.

'We've got the money. Right? So we go and open a bank account. That's the first thing. We can't go looking for brokers with a sackload of money on our backs. A fine thing if all we get out of this deal is a hernia. So, that's settled then. We open a bank account.'

'What about references?'

Looking deeply pained, Landau stopped in mid-stride.

'References? What are you talking about? With a cheque for three grand in the drawer, we need references? Any bank in the country would welcome us with open arms.'

'All right. So we open a bank account. What then?'

'Then we go and see the bank manager and we ask him about brokers and buying on margin and all that crap.'

'One thing we must make sure of is that there aren't any leaks.'

'What do you mean, Tom? The entire Stock Exchange is based on leaks. What do you think this is we're involved in now?'

It was one of his typically disconcerting remarks. While the rest of us inched cautiously round the perimeter of pure reason, he would occasionally perform one of those wild but masterly diagonal slashes of intuition which cut straight to the truth none of us could see. I said nothing, in case my remarks might disturb the train of his thought, which really was beginning now to sound practical. But he appeared to have shot his bolt, and none of his pacing, his play-acting, his reasoning out loud to himself, his accusatory finger pointing at me demanding a useful suggestion, none of this moved us beyond the decision to throw ourselves on the mercies of an understanding bank manager. For the next hour we ran through the list of our acquaintances who might know something about the machinery of buying shares, without success. I was rendered useless because of my class background, Landau by his wholesale renunciation of his. Finally we came round to bandleaders we knew, well-appointed girl-friends, people in and out of the music business, but none seemed likely to be of any help to us. And then Landau, who had stretched himself full-length on the floor to aid his concentration, slowly raised himself to a sitting position, grinned slyly and exclaimed, ' Of course. Why didn't I think of it before? Why don't we ask Bella Herbert?'

' Why not?' I said, grinning back.

It was symbolic of Bella Herbert's peculiar prestige among us that, without the slightest evidence to support us, we should have regarded her as the answer to our problem. We had known her for about a month before this sudden divination of Landau's about her talent as a tycoon, and the only data we had collected on her was sexual rather than commercial. Landau, who knew her best, probably understood her least, but in the course of a brief but frantic idyll, he had conceived an immense regard for her abilities, real or imagined. It was his old propensity for hero-worship coming out again. Landau was always impressed by the good taste of any woman who happened to fancy him, although it was an approval which instantly subsided the moment he ceased to fancy them. Bella had apparently been something of an exception, whose aura lingered on long after her body had lost its attraction for him. Landau was just twenty-one that summer, and I think she must have been his first older woman. As she was therefore a prototype in his life, he rapidly endowed her with all the mystical qualities which prototypes always have. When he first met her he could talk of nothing else, and struggled desperately to convey something of her appeal in and out of bed. Day after day he threshed his limited vocabulary to boiling point without ever impressing any of us. We all knew him too well by now to take seriously anything he said about his mistress. For once we underrated him.

Surprisingly it was Blitski who first discovered Bella Herbert. She swept in under the high dome of the Public Library one damp morning, and in a voice which rattled the notices requesting silence, asked for a book on political science which Blitski happened to be reading at that moment. He brought her back to the house in Kemptown not quite sure he had done the right thing. As it happened, Landau was there alone, and the affair was consummated that very morning on the bed so recently consecrated to the pursuit of finer things.

Bella must have been about thirty at that time, although she would never have admitted it. She told us in a stage whisper which cloaked every remark with innuendo that she was a war widow, and continued to wear black so many years after only because it enhanced her sex appeal. Blitski, being Blitski, had hastily formulated a theory that she was searching for some kind of intellectual life, or at least the trappings of its illusion. She owned a small house overhanging the sea a few miles south of the town, and Blitski, immersed at the time in a study of eighteenth century Whig society, was convinced that she saw it as a kind of salon and herself as its benign matriarch. According to him, this dream had been dying of malnutrition, and only when she stumbled across the supine body of his revolutionary intelligence in the library had the old fancies revived. Blitski clung to this fond belief long after the facts had chopped it into shreds, and only finally abandoned her as promising subversive material when she slipped into bed with Landau one afternoon even while Blitski was trying to engage her in a discussion of the psychological implications of the Theory of Surplus Value.

In an old-fashioned, carefully studied, faintly nineteenth century sort of way, Bella was an attractive woman. Because she lacked, or perhaps deliberately shunned, the topical pertness of the girls around us, Landau soon lost interest in her as a mistress, though his admiration for her poise and obvious experience never wavered all summer. Her appearance was melodramatic, at times even absurd. She possessed what Landau liked to describe as a statuesque figure, that being a phrase he had lately acquired from his erratic reading of the poets. The slight droop of her carriage created an illusion of slender grace where there was only height, but she floated prettily, and always about her mouth hovered the hint of an exasperating smile, as though social exchanges were a bore she gently complied with because it would have been uncouth not to, although we had it on Landau's authority that the smile quite disappeared when she was making love. Without actually mentioning money, she gave us to understand that she had a small private income. She disparaged the house she owned as ' a silly little house, darling, a cottage really ', but for Blitski and I, for whom a house, any house, even a cottage, meant something that other people's parents might just conceivably own, she became transformed into the feminine embodiment of Café society. As Landau put it, she had class. Her clothes were stylish, and three or four nights a week she ran a small sports coupé to and from the Arcadia. There were rings on her gloved fingers and a cheque book in her sequinned evening bag. She was an utterly strange species and for a while she fascinated all four of us.

As Bella herself well knew, the fascination lay in the strangeness. So long as we knew of her only what she chose to tell us, she could indulge in any affectation which happened to appeal to her, which is why there was a certain constraint between her and I at first. She guarded the mystery of her own identity most jealously, and at our very first meeting it must have seemed to her for a moment that I might be the one to penetrate all her carefully raised defences. Landau introduced her to me early one evening in our cider bar. Probably I wasn't expecting much. Landau was at the height of his froth about this time, but then this wasn't unusual for him. If it wasn't Bella, it was bound to be someone else, I told myself. Usually when you met them, the gazelles of his inner life turned out to be silly sheep, and I was further irritated by the accident of my absence on the morning of Bella's sensational Kemptown début. Ever since that speedy unveiling ceremony I had been assailed by talk of this wondrous perfumed essence who had flitted like a pagan goddess through our mundane boarding house life, shattered the equipoise of our domestic routine and then disappeared again. I was confused, caught between boredom at Landau's routine eulogies and jealousy inspired by Blitski's unexpected substantiation.

When he introduced us Landau actually stood up, which on any other occasion would have astonished me. But I was too engrossed in the disturbing thrill of recognising Bella to take much notice of him. I identified her instantly as the quiet dark one whose car Maxine had borrowed to drive me home from the party at Lancing, the enigmatic lady who sat sipping gin most evenings at the Arcadia, the amused spectator at my last glorious clash with Crawford. I then made the mistake of telling her all this. The lazy smile flickered uncertainly for a moment, as though her balance was about to be disturbed, but she rallied in the same breath and kept me at a conversational distance for the rest of that meeting and for some days after. Evidently she preferred to be a lone wolf, and in all the time we knew her, never once did we meet a friend of hers or stumble on the trail of any of her social connections. All we did get were a few accidental glimpses which, being accidental, only enhanced her luminosity. Victor caught her emerging one night from the town's largest theatre, escorted by a much older man in evening dress with an unmistakable proprietary air. It was a blustery night. Down on the pier the wind had blown the music all over the timbered floor, and Bella had insured against the night air with copious white furs. Victor, whose powers of observation tended to become blurred on these occasions, said she glittered like a tray of jewellery. It was a revival of *Private Lives*, and I remember going to watch a matinée in the vague hope of finding some clue to Bella's nebulous sensibilities. Perhaps I would have, had I not been hopelessly sidetracked by the scene where the hero has to play ' Some Day I'll Find You ' at the piano. His harmonies were all over the place, which gave me a reassuring sense of superiority. When I mentioned this to Bella she told me not to be so provincial. Blitski, who had always been bored to death by the assumption by jazz musicians of superiority in all fields, thought this very funny, but Landau, casting himself for once in the role of staunch friend, pointed out to Bella that as I had been born in Yorkshire, I had every justification for appearing provincial.

The sole link between her and our tiny world was Maxine, and when we asked her, there was almost nothing she could tell us.

' I don't know really. She just turned up at the Arcadia one night with a few faces I sort of knew. The faces went after a couple of days, but she stayed. It was race week, I think, just before you started to work down there. We all had a few drinks, and after that, I don't know, she just started to come about.'

Blitski persisted in his theory of a *rentier* capitalist whose pangs of social conscience were urging her to subsidise the arts, but as Landau pointed out in one of his rare moments of lucidity on the subject, there were more effective ways of doing that than sitting in the Arcadia bar four nights a week. To me she seemed simply a woman posing as a girl, equipped with time and some money, worldly wisdom and a curiosity about what she took to be the low life. Apart from the fact that she fancied Landau and not me, her taste seemed impeccable in all things. She drifted into our orbit like a body from another world, and as it was a world we knew nothing about, we found it very easy to pass judgement. She seemed in fact to belong to that very group which Blitski loved haranguing from the sanctity of his soapbox, a member of that class which lives on its investments and enjoys a purely parasitic existence. Landau summed it up when he returned one night from the Yacht Club. He had changed after work and jibbed into the annual Fancy Dress Ball, wearing his windcheater and his canvas shoes, describing himself as a gigolo. This crude subterfuge had fooled everyone but Bella, who accused him of being uncouth and childish. There had been a tempestuous row followed by an equally tempestuous reconciliation under the Palace Pier, after which Landau, still drunk with her femininity, had wandered dreamlike into my room and awoken both Maxine and me to inform us that Bella Herbert had finesse. If that wasn't strictly true, at least it was the truth we accepted all that summer. Perhaps the finesse alone might not have conquered us, but it was coupled with a burning sexual curiosity, and the two made a deadly alliance. Landau remembered her for years afterwards as complete mistress of her arts.

To the rest of us it seemed quite clear who was to make the first business overtures. After all it was Landau who had first attracted her, Landau who had won her regard on the ultimate battlefield of crumpled bedlinen, Landau who had seen her to her own disadvantage, naked and unashamed, as Victor put it, Landau alone who seemed able to meet her

178

on her own ground and get away with the pretence of being her worldly equal. But he would have none of it.

'Never mix business with pleasure,' he said with the air of coining an epigram. 'That's always been my motto. Turn your mistress into your broker and you end up broker than you were before you had a mistress.'

It was the best pun Landau made all summer, but it got us no nearer to solving our problem. Landau seemed to think that the approach to Bella should come from somebody who was sexually disinterested but, as Blitski gloomily pointed out, this eliminated all four of us.

'It's my size,' he said. 'She'd never be able to take me seriously.'

To me the next best choice seemed to be Victor, but to him the only suitable ambassador was me. As he sensed that the rest of us were gradually working him into a corner, Victor fought back by questioning the wisdom of approaching Bella at all.

'We ought to keep this thing as tight and close as possible. She's the sort of opportunist who'd get stuck in herself the moment she sensed there was some easy money about.'

Landau scoffed at all this. 'We tell her nothing,' he insisted. 'That's the whole point of going to someone like Bella, someone we already know. All we want from her are a few basic facts. We don't have to mention a word about the actual deal.'

But Victor's attitude hardened. I thought his point was a good one. Indeed, ever since Landau had first suggested going to Bella, I had had the uneasy feeling that we were giving a huge opening to somebody who might easily dance rings round us when it came to moneymaking. But I said nothing. I badly wanted Victor and not me to be our spokesman. But he refused to budge. He confessed several years later that his real reason for being awkward was the fact that within hours of Landau's renunciation of Bella and his return to the delights of less sophisticated partners on the pebbles under the Palace Pier, he, Victor, had slipped into the vacancy for a night and felt guilty about it. In the end we solved this problem as we solved all problems, by pushing it into the background.

179

15

THOSE were apocalyptic days for all of us. We were acutely
conscious that barring some freakish stroke of ill-fortune, the
circumstances of all our lives were soon to be altered radic-
ally by the possession of more money than we had ever been
used to. I am certain that all four of us wandered abroad
in a reverie of private splendours subsidised out of the funds
we hoped would soon be ours. I tried to adjust my wavering
mind to the fact that a phase of my life was drawing to a
close and a fresh one about to begin, that soon my flushed
musical studies would no longer be a desperate race against
time and the dreaded day when all the spare cash would be
exhausted. I tried hard and I failed. The desired mental
transmutation from rags to riches refused to come. I did not
know then that a man's lifelong attitudes to money are
conditioned by his earliest contacts with it, and that no
matter what the speculation in Filox Investments might bring
us, money would remain what it had always been for us,
to Landau something his father produced by the invisible
alchemy of trade, to Victor the forbidden fruit, to Blitski a
rude word and to me a carrot which the donkey of greed
never quite got his teeth into, and never would.

The events of those days are hopelessly confused, as they
were even while they were unfolding. What does remain
clear in all its embarrassing intensity is the tremendous
struggle I embarked on to convince myself that taxis were
not necessarily a disastrous extravagance, that apéritifs and
liqueurs were nothing more than part of the workaday world
to come, that assets need no longer be chained irrevocably
to the number of man hours completed, that the women of
my no doubt dissolute future would love me for my money
instead of for myself. And even while I was being routed in
this struggle, I was aware that except for Landau, my partners were undergoing similar ordeals.

About our reactions during this limbo between penury and plenty there persists an obstinate cloud of confusion. In view of the gravity of our adventure I suppose I should be able to recall every nuance in the subtle gradations of mood during this fight to rearraign ourselves on the battlefield of the class war. But when I try to recall it, all that comes back is a vague sense of dread and irresolution. Unless my memory lies, I saw Victor off on the London train and met him coming back on it not once but several times, paper handkerchief sales in the meantime presumably slumping. Blitski too did what he could to ease the strain by pointless travelling, even selling his collected edition of Henry James, bought with the proceeds of three months' work as a sorter in the post office, to pay for his railway tickets. When occasionally he did decide to spend a night by the sea, he talked with more nervous profusion than ever. Sometimes on fine nights, when the programme Landau had arranged for us seemed too like the last one to be respected, the two of us would embark on one of those rambling, inconsequential discussions which always began with the general and ended with the particular, a predictable drift from Marx and sex to what either of those tired themes had to do with us. We shambled along the broad corridor between the houses and the sea in the small hours, leaving behind the pendant necklace of the corporation coloured lights, our path lit by the concrete lamp-posts bending over the road like malignant serpents, stretching away to Rottingdean and infinity. We would lean on the blistered paint of the promenade rails staring blankly at the shifting tides, wondering why either of us, financially unambitious men, should have placed ourselves in a situation of such pure absurdity.

In the meantime Landau and I were left occupying the rooms we had taken as musicians and were now using as a base for high theft. We continued to live our musicians' routine because it was the only one known to us, taking our meals and regulating our alarm clocks in accordance with ballroom timetables which no longer applied to us, changing our clothes in the early evening as though we had never been pushed across the great divide which separates the performer from his audience. I was perplexed by the fact that to me the days went by quickly and slowly at the same time, although I should have realised that, considering my dual involvements in the future, this was perfectly logical. The truth was that there was something else besides Filox Investments which troubled me, and just as I naturally wanted our shares to soar as soon as possible, so did I want a certain parcel to take as long as possible to reach me. I dearly wanted the parcel to arrive after the shares had soared, but again I was out of luck.

Three days after our discussions about Bella Herbert, the postman knocked on the front door with such violence that Landau awoke and came into the kitchen swathed in the pale blue bathrobe his mother had bought him at the start of the season as an insurance against sea breezes. He scowled across the room, slumped into one of the wooden chairs and scratched his head. He yawned twice and then said, ' What's in the parcel?'

' I told you it was coming,' I answered, staring sadly at the bulky square package before me on the table.

' I still don't believe it. Go on. Open it.'

I tore off the wrapping, and there, as I knew they would be, were a dozen new long-playing gramophone records. Landau sat up.

' Tom, I apologise. I was sure you were having me on,' and he leaned forward to study the titles.

' This is great,' he said. ' You're made. Come on. Let's find out what they sound like.'

But I continued to sit there staring at the brown paper, scattered now all over the breakfast table. It represented a crisis for me of such enormity that for a while even Filox was forgotten. On the afternoon of our raid on Landau's family vault I had gone calling on Ray Knowles, and had been received with such unpredictable warmth that for most of the encounter with Landau's parents I had remained numbed with the horror of the new situation I appeared to have drifted into. For Knowles, without investigating me in even the most superficial way, had appointed me as his record critic. His offices were in a cul-de-sac behind Charing Cross Road, and I had such difficulty finding them that there came a point, when I was marooned on the island in the middle of Cambridge Circus, when I almost turned back. Only the fear of Landau's contempt kept me going till I found the premises of Knowles' paper. The first five minutes of our meeting had been deeply discouraging. Knowles had sat across the desk from me, his tiny eyes beaming behind rimless spectacles, and kept shaking his very large head as he kept repeating, 'So you're the one who wrote the letter.'

I kept nodding in agreement with this question until he said in the same dreamy tones, 'Can you make tea?'

'What?'

'Tea. Can you make tea? I know you can write a letter, but can you make tea?'

'What's that got to do with it?'

'Now there's a good chap,' he went on in an excruciating wheedling tone which I later came to know all too well. 'There's a stove in the other room, by the switchboard. You'll find tea, milk and sugar there. Got any matches?'

He threw a lighter at me. I caught it and walked back down the dim corridor back to the switchboard. The girl who had received me when I entered had gone. As I lit the primus stove, I could just hear Knowles singing away to himself. 'So you're the one who wrote the letter.' He kept it up all the time it took for the kettle to boil, by which time the phrase had ceased to have whatever meaning it might once have had. I poured out only two cups of tea, because there seemed to be nobody else in the building. I carried the cups gingerly back to his office.

'Ah.' He leaned forward and took his cup, tossed in four lumps of sugar, stirred the brew with the chipped end of an old desk ruler and sipped noisily. Then he put the cup down on his desk, looked at me with more interest than he had so far displayed and said approvingly, 'You don't make a bad cup of tea, son. That's a rarer talent than you think. The berks round here can't grasp that " one for the pot " rule. I keep telling them, one more for the pot, but they don't take a blind bit of notice of anything I say. One of these days you'll read in the papers, " Editor poisoned by pissy tea ". It makes you sick the way they won't listen.'

He took another sip of tea, his face grave with the devoted concentration of the gourmet.

'You came up from the coast today?'

'Yes, Brighton.'

'You're working there. How'dya get the time off?'

'I *was* working there.'

He laughed. 'You mean the letter. You know why I asked you to come and see me? I just wanted to see what kind of madman would write a letter like that about his own employers.'

He drained his cup, banging it down on the desk before commencing to take off his glasses and polishing them with his handkerchief. Without the glasses his face was a contradiction, tired yet younger.

'Well, now that you've made me tea, what can I do for you?'

I looked at him in some confusion, but he seemed as serious as he ever would be.

'You said in view of possible repercussions I should come and see you.'

'Obviously you don't like working. If you wanted to work you wouldn't have written a letter like that. You married?'

'No, not yet.'

'Don't bother. I'm older than you. I know what I'm talking about. Don't get married. Ever. You done any writing before?'

'Nothing published, but . . .'

'I know. Six novels, a play in blank verse and a cycle of short stories on a theme not yet decided. What did you have in mind?'

'Me? Nothing. You said to come and see you.'

'That's right, so I did. Look, how much were you thinking of? We work on a tight schedule here, you know.'

'I'm sorry, I don't follow.'

'That's right. He's not started yet, and already he's quibbling about money. To be perfectly frank, we don't pay contributors. The circulation doesn't run to it. What we do is, anything you review you can keep. Now. You write about the new records and after that what you do with them is your own affair, understood? You can get fifteen bob an album with no trouble. Here,' and he produced from the inside pocket of his double-breasted, wide-lapelled, tea-stained blue birdseye suit a small white business card. 'It's my brother-in-law's shop. You tell him he's to give you fifteen bob a time. Tell him I said so.' I gazed dumbly at the card.

'Look, do you want the job or don't you? You fill a page with record reviews each week and you can keep the discs. Most of them are a load of rubbish anyway. And another thing. Flog them while they're still new. You wait till the next issue comes out and my brother-in-law will knock you down to twelve and a tanner. He's a right thief, him.'

'Do you want something every week?'

'What then, every month? This is a weekly paper, and if we don't carry reviews every week, how do you think we'll get advertising space from the record companies? Oh, and that's another thing. Make sure you cover something by each company every week. They're very touchy about that kind of thing. Leave one of them out one week and they start getting a persecution complex. Just keep that in mind.'

'How many words is a page?'

'Depends what words. You use long ones, if I remember your letter. Say two thousand. And none of that popinjay stuff. I don't mind you panning something, but one libel case and we're all out of business.'

'I see. Where do I get your records from?'

'You just write your address here and I'll send them on. It'll probably take a few days. Good-bye,' and he walked out of the office, slammed the front door and pattered away down the stairs. It was not till then that I decided to take out insurance against further literary troubles. I left a note on his desk saying, 'My pen name is Leonard Landau.'

When I told this story to Landau he refused to believe me, and anyway, he probably considered it very small beer indeed after the triumph of the loan from his parents. But the one thing which characteristically did not disturb him was my intention of using his name for my blasphemies against the backscratching conventions of show business. On the contrary, he seemed to regard it as the finest gesture of self-sacrifice I had ever made.

'You'll be doing the work and I'll be winning the reputation,' he said gleefully. 'What a set-up. Every time you want to give yourself a rise, you just squeeze a couple more reviews in on the page.'

'That had occurred to me.'

'And it's all tax-free.'

'That also had occurred to me.'

'I know what's going to happen. I can see it all. You living on your investments from the capital we make out of Filox, a gentleman writer selling review copies at fifteen bob a throw. What a life. You'll be independent of the saxophone, you realise that?'

'That's just it. I don't want to be independent of the saxophone. I like the idea of playing it well enough to make a living.'

'You can still play it, can't you? The only difference will be that you won't have to worry about the Rhodes and the Fields of this world.'

I think it was because of the sheer beauty of this new situation I described to Landau that he changed his mind and refused to accept it as truth, so that when the brown paper parcel eventually arrived he was as overjoyed as I was anguished.

'The first thing is to hear what they sound like. Come on. We can make a few notes and you can get the reviews written in no time.'

'No I can't. This sort of thing takes time. If I don't watch it, I won't have any time left for practising.'

'What do you mean? You can write that sort of crap in your sleep. You know. You get a few phrases, like, let's see, "compellingly personal solo", "astonishingly resourceful contribution", "ferociously spiralling dialogue", you know the kind of thing I mean.'

I looked at him with renewed interest.

'Here, Landau, you sure you wouldn't like to write the stuff yourself?'

'No, that's your job. But I can help if you like. Let's work it out. How many albums he send you? Say twelve. That's what, twelve times forty-five minutes on average. Come on. You know what my sums are like.'

'Nine hours. We can't possibly do it in one day. It'll kill us.'

'Course not. We split the load. You do three hours, I do

three hours and Blitski's due back tomorrow, he can do three hours.'

'Blitski? Review music? He's tone deaf.'

'So are half the faces on these records. Stop worrying about it.'

And so we went to separate rooms to put in our three hours of listening, Landau using his own portable record player while I wrestled with an old radiogram of Mrs Stewart's abandoned in the front passage of the house for some years. As it happened Blitski adamantly refused to have anything to do with a column which would be headed with the words, 'By Leonard Landau', and after only half an hour Landau himself soon grew weary of his new responsibilities. And so I settled down to my chores, earning fifteen hypothetical shillings for roughly three polysyllabic paragraphs on each album. Every time we had a visitor from one of the town bands we would play them an album and pick their brains for ideas. Whenever we went to parties our review albums went with us. Landau called this the first democratic reviewing process ever invented (he had been reading Shelley again), and to my surprise, after a week, I realised that all the albums had been heard, analysed and finally reviewed. Blitski typed out my neat copy, which was sent off to Knowles in an elegant stiff-backed buff envelope.

'You'll probably get the proofs back in a couple of days,' Blitski said airily. 'When you do, you make your annotations in the margin.'

But there never were any annotations, nor any proofs. In all the years I filled out my weekly page for Knowles, I never saw a proof, or recognised an editorial emendation, or received a word of praise or rebuke from my publisher. No record company ever used a good review as an advertisement or a bad one as an excuse for withdrawing their support. I can only conclude that nobody ever read a word of what I wrote. One week the bulky envelope went off to Knowles containing in error a few lines of verse written by Blitski in honour of the view from the West Pier at night. Knowles printed it, and it finally appeared sandwiched between a damning indictment of heavenly choirs and some fulsome praise for a flugelhorn solo of 'Smoke Gets In Your Eyes'.

16

It was on one of those sad autumnal days when dusk seems to fall directly after lunch that we eventually paid our visit to Bella Herbert. I remember looking out of my bedroom window and being suddenly depressed by the view. One broad ray of pellucid sunlight struck through the sullen banks of cloud, dappling the smooth green face of the sea with a flattering white light. Sky and sea merged into a forlorn wash. A few sailboats, oblivious of the approaching storm, bobbed about, defining the horizon. The gulls hovered inland, and over to the east darkness gathered itself for the assault. Only the certainty of the rain tempted us finally to call on Bella. Landau agreed that if it was to be an uncomfortable afternoon we might as well ride it out in the rumoured comfort of Worth House, which turned out to be a creaking Queen Anne relic with three floors and two rooms on each floor. The drawing-room was at the top of the first flight of stairs, and so evidently the nerve-centre of all operations that whatever lay beyond the first-floor landing might have been a cardboard façade nobody took seriously, least of all the owner, who had cluttered the staircase leading to the top floor with packing cases, carrier bags and hatboxes.

The drawing-room surprised us all. It was tiny, over-furnished, and in its personality totally disconnected from the picture of the *femme fatale* which we had all formed in our minds. Had the room been bare I might have spanned it in three or four strides. But the tortuous convolutions of the designs on the Chinese carpet, the carefully deployed wing chairs, the nest of tables, the velvet-covered footstools, the lampshades standing sentry on either flank of the tiny hearth, the writing-desk and the lead-windowed bookcase scattered with clay mice and stylised figurines, all seemed to give the room not so much space as substance. Perhaps it was a trick of the shadows flickering in the firelight, perhaps the pretentious aura of Bella herself, perhaps the sheer density of the atmosphere, but whatever it was, I felt it was I who was too large and not the room that was too small. It was a triumph of affectation over plane geometry.

Bella seemed pleased enough to see us, and was probably as bored with the dull shift of the days as we were. We shuffled about, concentrating on the negative task of not smashing anything. The room disconcerted me from the moment I stepped into it, and I could see that the others were reacting in the same way. Although there was a touch of the archaic about Bella, she looked the sort of woman who would go well with divans in rooms with plenty of space for sprawling and lounging, with the Hollywood modernism of the 1930s. But in this laughable bastion of phoney gentility, our innocent coarsenesses seemed like acts of vandalism. The gestures we made were altogether too expansive and our sensibilities too blunt for the exquisite politeness of the décor. Once, when Victor's custard-pie laugh bounced against the silent walls, the three china plates on the shelf over the door shivered in disapproval. Even the bulbousness of Blitski's nose seemed an affront to the mincing symmetry of that drawing-room. He told me later that one thing which obsessed him throughout our visit was the fear that the stagecoach in the Dickensian painting over the hearth might turn round and disappear for ever up its painted road and over its painted hill rather than suffer our intrusion. He was not the only one prone to illusions that afternoon. Once, in the deceptive light of the flames and the two lampshades, I thought I saw the cameos on the walls wince in well-bred distaste.

Not that the room itself was so unusual. We had all seen several like it before. It was the knowledge that it belonged to Bella which confounded us. None of us, least of all Landau, was able to equate it with Bella's sexual dynamism. I wasn't sure what kind of a room I might have expected her to receive guests in, but I certainly hadn't bargained for *chinoiserie* and Victorian fire-irons. Though I can still see that room, still sniff the musk of dusty unread books and stale perfume, I forget what we talked about most of the time. We must have discussed something, because we were trapped there for more than two hours. At first there was a great deal of giggling, which soon congealed into a constrained silence. It must have been some time later that Bella disappeared to make tea, at which point there were hurried whispered consultations between us. Blitski was all for a stark financial confrontation, brutally approached and relentlessly pursued. When the rest of us hedged he started to brood.

'I thought that's why we came here in the first place.'

'You know very well why we came here,' Victor said gloomily, 'and that's because we all fancy her.'

'Where's she gone?' I asked.

Landau, who had been peering through the glass of the bookcase at the chipped menagerie inside it, said without turning round, 'The girl's at least gone to the trouble of making tea for us. Why can't you all shut up?'

We took his advice and watched him staring at the animals. Finally he came to his conclusions.

'I reckon this kangaroo is pregnant. You can see the baby sticking out.'

Nobody disputed the point. Instead Victor suddenly collapsed in one of the wing chairs and began shaking with silent laughter. Blitski, reclining on the carpet before the fire, squirmed round and said, 'Now what's the matter?'

Victor fought to control himself. 'I was just thinking. Suppose she sends tea in with the butler.'

Landau misheard him and spun round, real concern in his voice.

'Whose this Butler character?'

'No, *her* butler,' Victor explained, sobered by the confusion. Landau now appreciated the joke and screamed with laughter. The sight of his exposed Adam's apple bobbing up and down set me off, and by the time Bella returned with the teatray, the four of us were falling all over the room. She put down the tray on the largest of the nest of tiny tables.

'All right, boys. Let me in on it. Bella wants to laugh too.'

I would gladly have broken her nose for that excruciating affectation of referring to herself as though she were a fictitious character, but all I said was, 'We were wondering what it would be like to have a butler.'

'I had a butler once,' she replied, 'in the pantry of a hotel in Weston-super-Mare. It was very uncomfortable.'

Landau grinned. 'Boasting again, Bella. You only do it to make us feel small.'

Blitski, who seemed embarrassed by the turn the talk was taking, blurted out, 'Ever had any dealings with stock-brokers?'

While she was still searching for an answer, Victor cut in and asked if he could use the bathroom. By the time he had returned, Blitski had suffered his customary tea-time accident of scalding the tip of his nose through immersion in hot tea. His eyes watered so profusely that when Victor came back he thought Blitski had been crying.

'What's the matter with Cyrano de Bergerac?'

'Leave me alone. I'm drinking my tea, that's all.'

While Bella was administering Vaseline with the tip of an elegant little finger, I accidentally chipped the rim of the sugar basin on the coal scuttle. Bella didn't seem to mind. She drifted lazily through the afternoon with an absent smile on her face, as though she were not quite sure what was amusing us, but was quietly savouring a far subtler joke of her own. I think she enjoyed the idea of playing the grande dame to four callow youths. For one thing it established the right mood for any future, more intimate relation-ships. A little respect was what she wanted, which, if it be-came too inhibiting, could soon be dispelled by an invitation to spend a night in the bedroom across the landing. By up-staging us at every turn in the social game, she could always negotiate from strength, spilling us out of her bed and out of her life as soon as she had done with us. That after-noon, watching her move about the congested room with such smug serenity, I even found myself wondering whether after all Landau had been quite truthful about his brief affair with her, and whether it had not been Bella who tired of him. But then I dismissed the idea. The novelty of being spurned would have filled Landau with such delighted admiration that he would never have been able to resist tell-ing us every detail, not caring in the slightest how well or how badly he came out of the account. The real explanation for Bella's affected poise was that she liked to think of herself as a woman of the world, and the pretence of tutoring four big bad bohemians through a formative period of their lives must have gratified her far more than the actual thrill of conquest.

After the incident of the sugar bowl the images refuse to form, except for the recollection that when Bella went back to the kitchen with the teatray Landau went after her, and that neither of them returned for some time. Blitski occupied himself with an attempt to assess Bella's literary tastes. He stood before the bookcase, reviewing its contents with a sneer, announcing that if he hadn't seen it with his own eyes he would never have believed it.

'Believed what?' I said.

'All this tripe.'

'You were the one who said she was a connoisseur, remember?'

'Absolute tripe, the whole lot.'

Victor took a handful of coal from the scuttle, crossed over to the window and lobbed the pieces into the fire. One of them missed and bounced on to the carpet. I picked it up and tossed it into the quiet flames.

'I wonder what they're doing out there?' Victor said.

'Not talking about stocks and shares, count on that,' Blitski answered, turning his back on the offending bookcase. 'I knew if we came here it would end up with sex. With Landau it always does.'

'You're wrong,' I told him. 'Once Landau packs up an affair he never starts it again. He's funny about that.'

'How long are we supposed to sit here waiting then?'

'Oh, stop nagging, Blitski. If your nerves are like this now, what kind of shape are you going to be in when we really go into business?'

I was really addressing the question to myself, having been rudely awakened by this visit to the fact that our escapade in the stock market was likely to be a sore strain on all of us. Adjusting ourselves to the eventual profits was worrying enough, but surviving the ordeal of the actual gamble was something I had quite overlooked. Landau and Bella must have returned from the kitchen soon after this,

and when we left at six o'clock the rain was already spatter-
ing down on the gravel path outside the house, bouncing off
the roof of Bella's car with a metallic tattoo. The journey
to Kemptown was a silent one. Bella smoked and concentrated on the road. And while the windscreen wipers swished
out a languid foxtrot rhythm, the rest of us stared out
of the windows at the deserted road. Throughout the afternoon, not one word had been mentioned about Filox Investments. Unless of course Landau had brought the subject up
in the kitchen. After she had dropped us off at the house I
asked him.

'As a matter of fact, no. I decided it wasn't the proper
time or place. For a thing like this, the circumstances have to
be just right. I couldn't just go into it cold, now could I?'

'You were in there long enough to buy and sell the whole
market ten times over,' Blitski said.

'So can't a man talk over old times with a girl?'

'What do we do next?' I asked. 'Bella was our only
hope. There's nobody else.'

'I've been thinking about it,' Landau said thoughtfully.
'When we were coming back in the car just now. I shall
instruct our bank manager to buy the shares for us. You
look in that booklet the bank gave me when I opened the
account. It says definitely that they advise on investments.'

'Why didn't you think of that before?' I asked him with
some irritation.

'I didn't want to just do it the ordinary way. I thought
we might find a more interesting way of doing things. But
it'll have to do.'

We sat around the room, each of us confused by his own
thoughts.

'There's still time to back out,' Victor said. Nobody
answered him. The drift in our affairs seemed insuperable.

And then two things happened which suddenly changed
everything. Landau went to his bank and gave the manager
the necessary instructions, and Van Rhodes phoned the
house. Unable to face the thought of being in the same town
as our investment fund at the moment it was being committed, Victor and Blitski had left on the noon train. The
phone call came just after lunch, while Landau and I were

sipping lukewarm coffee. I had been asking him questions about the processes he had put in motion at the bank that morning, but he was uncharacteristically reticent for once.

'Look, there's nothing to tell. I just told him what to buy and how much, and he said okay and that was it. What did you expect . . .'

'There's the phone,' I said. 'I'll get it.'

When I came back into the kitchen Landau was picking his teeth with a match. He must have noticed the baffled expression on my face, because he threw down his toothpick and said, 'What's wrong?'

'It's Van Rhodes. For you.'

'Rhodes?'

Landau's face broke into a truculent smile. 'You sure?'

'Sure. There can't be two Van Rhodes. And he definitely asked to speak to you.'

He went into the passage and picked up the phone. I went with him.

'Hello, yes, this is Landau . . . you what? . . . well, I don't know . . . I may be committed . . . tonight? that's out of the question . . . Monday perhaps . . . All right, I'll come and see you. Right. Good-bye, and keep smiling.'

He replaced the receiver on its hook and grinned at me.

'I knew they'd be in trouble without me. Personality, that's what that band lacks. Tom, he wants me to come back. One of his boys has gone down with chickenpox. He says will I fill in the rest of the season.'

'And will you?'

'Why not? Only this time I go back on my own terms. A quid a week more, and at least two featured spots a night. He wanted me to start straight away, but you heard what I said. Let him stew for a bit. But I shall be going back. We have to stay here till this Filox thing's over, so I might . . .'

'Why? We can be in London or anywhere else while the price is rising.'

'No, Tom. Always stay within personal reach of the bank. You never know.'

And so Landau dusted his dinner suit, bought a new box of reeds and found for himself the most valuable property in the world at this moment, a way of passing the time. Indirectly I benefited too, because now it was necessary for him to practise once more, which meant our daily duets began again.

Taking everything into account, Landau let Rhodes down very lightly. He was granted his rise, allowed his two feature spots a night, and for the rest of that season, his last as a musician, he was a model saxophonist—except for his insistence that the chair on which the infected musician had been sitting be thoroughly fumigated. Landau was no hypochondriac, but he was not the sort of man to meet trouble halfway. Or so he said.

17

THERE followed a succession of grey sunless days, when sea and sky merged into a third entity, composed of both but resembling neither, a drab damp bowl under which we seemed to be wandering like punchdrunk fighters. Low clouds scudded across the sea's face, and from them sometimes fell a fine spray of summer rain, although never enough to release Landau from his responsibilities on the pier. But he seemed quite unconcerned. He alone appeared to be indifferent to our prospects. As the days dragged by he allowed himself to become submerged once more in his warm bath of posture and pursuit, moulding events to his own private conception of what a summer season should be, romancing breathless girls on the dry pebbles under the pier, arguing bitterly with his fellow musicians about the finer points of our craft, trying on but rarely buying new clothes, meeting new people and becoming utterly engrossed for a day or two in their remarkable idiosyncrasies, imagined or not.

His behaviour during those faceless days was a fascinating spectacle. I had always known him to be superbly resilient, but this really did seem to be his finest hour. Inevitably I began to wonder whether it might not be a big pretence, the great performance of a master-actor determined not to show his anxiety, the worried man giving the definitive portrait of the hero with a grandiose contempt for circumstances. If it was, then it was a tremendous mental triumph on his part, and I was too dumb with admiration at first to be very disturbed. After all, I told myself, it was just as well that at least one member of the combine was proving able to keep his head. Landau at any rate would never panic. I felt sublimely confident about that. It was the straw I clung to throughout the hours of doubt and delay. If we were to lose every penny overnight, if there were to be another Wall Street crash between now and the announcement of the take-over, if they devalued the pound over the week-end, it would still not mean the end, because there would always be Landau to think of something.

But then, one night on the pier, while talking to a girl who had spent the previous hour winking blatantly at me every time she danced past my seat, it occurred to me that perhaps all this was even more of a performance than I had been assuming. Suppose Landau hadn't invested the money at all? Suppose the whole thing was one of those giant make-believes so vividly stage-managed that Landau had even managed to convince himself? What proof did any of us have that the shares had actually been purchased? We had only Landau's word for it.

'Well, it's done,' he had said when he strode into the kitchen on the morning we became speculators. He looked unusually grave. 'It's done now. All we have to do is sit and wait.'

But for what? He had shown me no papers, no documented proof. How adamant he had been about going to the bank alone. And how vague when asked about the processes of brokerage. Vague, or evasive? At that moment on the pier when these misgivings first flashed into my tired brain, instinctively I looked up at him. He certainly looked nothing like a man about to make a raid on society. He was standing in the spotlight on the tin-roofed bandstand, his long thin body arched in concentration. A hundred couples drifted across the bleached pine boards, the measure of their sliding paces dictated by the warm sloppy sound of Landau's clarinet.

His composure maddened me, implying as it did a lofty superiority over the rest of us. How, I asked myself, can a bigtime investor play 'Charmaine' with that kind of concentration when any minute a few columns of figures in a newspaper can make or break him? There was I, unable to concentrate on music or anything else. There was Victor, more gaunt and guilt-ridden every day, drifting like a madman up and down the Victoria line. There was poor Blitski with his insides practically falling out from the strain. And yet Landau could stand there and worry whether his vibrato was too wide for waltzes. Something must be wrong.

And yet how could I accuse him? My only possible chance of enlightenment might come from the conversations I wheedled him into, hoping he would make some chance remark to confirm or deny once and for all the extent of our commitment, if indeed it existed at all. But when I edged him into the subject the following morning at breakfast, he seemed to have lost interest in the whole affair. I sensed I was boring him, until finally he was goaded into making one last attempt to define our position.

'Look, Tom, there's absolutely nothing we can do about it now. We just have to sit and wait, like I said. You said so yourself last week.'

'So I did. But it's just that . . . oh, I don't know . . you don't seem to be very worried, that's all.'

'Should I be?'

'I suppose so. There's a lot at stake really. Financially, I mean.'

'How do we know that? Look, suppose we make a profit of a farthing a share. Would you call that a lot being at stake? And anyway, it wouldn't make any difference if millions were involved. Life has to go on, Tom.'

Before I could say anything, the echo of his own words wafted back to him in that split second of contemplation he sometimes granted to his more ambitious remarks. He grinned in appreciation of his own wisdom, like a plain girl suddenly confronted with a flattering portrait of herself. Then he made an extravagant gesture with both arms, as though he had stumbled on the secret of existence, which in a crass kind of way I suppose he had.

'Hey, that's wise. That's really very wise. " Life has to go on ". I tell you it's all that poetry and crap I'm reading these days. It's beginning to have an effect.'

My chance was gone. He was already galloping off down some enchanted byway of his own mind, and there was not the slightest prospect of heading him off. I envied him this supreme detachment, this nonchalance in the face of what might turn out to be great events, even though I knew this strength to be born of a certain insensitivity, a blessed lack of vision. One of Blitski's more pompous verdicts came back to me. 'Landau ', he once said, 'will never be stalked by the in-

198

cubus of imagination.' For once Blitski was right. Landau would never be a coward because he was too unsubtle to grasp the consequences of heroism. It was his very failure to perceive what was at stake which enabled him to rise above the whole business. It also explained his genuine bewilderment, gradually darkening to exasperation, at the moral collapse going on all round him. By the fifth day Blitski was no longer able to function at all, and fled without warning for the last time.

'What's got into him? Have we done anything to upset him?'

'Of course we have. We've mentioned money to him. You ought to know by now how being involved personally with real money always makes him feel ashamed.'

'But that's ridiculous.'

'Tell him, don't tell me. Right now he's probably cowering in his mother's kitchen waiting for the law to pick him up. No, that's more Victor's reaction. Blitski would never be able to do anything as constructive as trying to hide. He'll be paralysed at the thought of all these real-life events we've involved him in. Probably he'll never forgive us. You see, as far as he's concerned, we've committed an unpardonable breach of the code, like farting in front of a duchess. You never live that kind of thing down.'

Landau looked at his watch. I was boring him again. He rose from his chair, slapped his stomach, as if to reassure the food he had just eaten that it was in the very best of hands, and probably unaware that his waistline was slightly more pendulous now than it was when he departed earlier that summer from Victoria on the *Brighton Belle*. He looked at me absently and said, 'Gotta dash. Date with a chick at seven. See you.'

He went up to his room. I sat there by the open kitchen window listening to him lumbering about over my head. The water in the bathroom spluttered and gurgled as he whistled in time to his own movements. I could picture him spitting into his towel as he wiped his face, arranging his bow tie under the goitre of his pre-raphaelite Adam's apple, checking up to see whether he really did possess a chin or not, walking to the door and then turning suddenly on the threshold in an attempt to surprise himself and catch a glimpse of his reflection from an unfamiliar angle. He alone was free of the implications of our gamble. It occurred to me that because his father must have found himself in precisely this stiuation a hundred times, there was nothing terrifying about it to Landau. He was insulated with the inherited *savoir-faire* of the petty speculator, and it was proving a far more effective defence than all Blitski's abstruse knowledge of capital and labour . . .

The door upstairs slammed shut and Landau's feet came skittering down the stairs. He poked his head round the door. The smell of after-shave floated in with him.

'What time you coming in?'

'About nine. Maybe a bit later.'

'Right. See you then.'

The head disappeared, the feet clumped away and a few seconds later the front door slammed. Its noise echoed through the empty house. The plates on the table shivered for a moment and then were still. I glanced up at the clock on the wall and went up to my room. Through the window I could see Landau moving swiftly through the early evening crowds, slipping past knots of disenchanted day-trippers who had gambled on the weather and lost. Once he half-turned as a young girl of the required shape and poundage crossed the road. His profile was stained for a moment by the pink glow of westering clouds. Then he turned the corner and disappeared. I went into the bathroom. Landau's dirty shirt lay on the floor, crumpled and forgotten. I turned on the bath taps and slowly undressed. One day closer to whatever it was that Blitski and Victor had fled from, whatever it was that had disrupted my musical routine, whatever it was that Landau resolutely refused to take seriously.

The trouble was, of course, that apart from Victor himself, who had what Blitski would have described as tenuous links with the machinery of commercial brigandage, none of us had any business experience of any kind. More important than our ignorance at making money was our ignorance of how it felt to possess any. This was the deadliest factor against us. To a man who thinks in terms of fifty pounds as the ultimate sum, the sudden prospect of thousands is a vision disturbing enough to carry with it a legacy of ineptitude disguised as ill-fortune. It was noticeable that the four of us worried about our *coup* in inverse proportion to our knowledge of the world outside our tight little mental islands. Landau, who knew least of all, thrived the best. To him the whole affair was reduced by his own intellectual limitations to the dimensions of a daring but minor episode, related in some obscure way to his practice of secreting virgins under the pier. He really seemed to assume that making a raid on the markets was all part of the predictable cycle of events for a dance hall musician, and would clearly expect something similar to happen next summer and the one after that.

For him life had magically opened its arms on the day that Van Rhodes had engaged him for the season. That contract meant far more to him than mere tangible proof of his first professional engagement. It was the official acknowledgement by the world at large that it was after all to be Landau's personal oyster. Not only would he be playing six nights a week to the great British public instead of one, but the public itself would be different, as far above the municipal hall audiences in the evolutionary scale as full-time musicians were above the casual labourers we had always worked with in the past. In Landau's imagination professionalism meant not just a fuller life, but a life different in kind, where every event was melodrama, where all the girls were beautiful nymphomaniacs, all the sunsets first-hand Turners, all the preposterous daydreams the raw material for reality. He had told himself a thousand times that to be a professional musician was to live in wonderland, and what more apposite to the economics of wonderland than a sudden strike of gold? Now I understood perfectly his mood of exalted madness that May evening when I saw him off at Victoria Station. I thought at the time that he was behaving like the parody of an explorer about to discover a new continent. In fact, this was exactly how he saw himself. He had embarked for the coast utterly convinced that in some way, unknown to him for the moment but soon to be revealed, he would undergo experiences which would change him for ever, and that whatever the circumstances of his return home at the end of the season, they would, in some mysterious but irrevocable way, have transformed his personality for all time. Perhaps he would be married, although he doubted it. Perhaps he would be rich, although he doubted that too. Perhaps he would come back handsome, which seemed at least feasible. Or he might be famous, which was much more likely. Possibly down on the coast, jostled by musicians and dancers, boarders and landladies, he would stumble on the secret of maturity. This seemed to him almost certain. But whatever the unknown factor might prove to be, he knew that nothing would ever be quite the same again. I recalled once again the way he had flourished that new diary when we were having tea at the Regent Palace, how he had actually stroked the pages representing the summer months, had been overcome by the sheer rapture of his realisation that very soon now those blank pages would be giving up their secrets.

'Even now,' he had said that afternoon, 'everything and everybody is rushing to keep their appointments with these pages. How about that, eh?'

And we had both sunk into a brooding speculative silence so deep that only the sudden violent Slavonic outburst of the gypsy orchestra had roused us. They struck up a selection from 'White Horse Inn', and Landau, his newly-won status flung about him like a purple cloak, gave all his attention to the music. Most of Landau's dreams were no more than the cheap absurdities of a young man who never read novels but was convinced that life was like one. The maddening thing was that events were proving him right at every turn. No wonder he had spurned Madame Vivienne's offer to read his fortune on that first day of the season. Landau was the one man in that town on that day who knew about his own future, and to have paid Vivienne for corroboration would have been like spending good money on yesterday's newspaper.

This burning faith of Landau in the ever-changing contours of the universe was contradicted with comic intensity by Victor's equally burning faith in its dogged immutability. His behaviour was conditioned by the two dominant tenets of his code, first, that he was a mediocrity, and second, that this mediocrity was so monumental as to withstand anything circumstances might throw against it. He knew perfectly well that the sudden acquisition of money would transform the threadbare carnival of his existence—for Victor was very much a man of outward appearances. His prescription for curing despair had always been a shave and a new suit, and now that the prospect of a hundred new suits was dangling before his eyes, he was too frightened to look. Unlike Landau, who nurtured a thousand dreams and could therefore afford to put any one of them to the test with impunity, Victor possessed only one, opulence, and clung to it like a miser.

I turned off the bathtaps and tested the water with my toe. I drew some more cold, and then stepped into the bath. The one factor which held Victor from panic and despairing flight, I told myself, was his failure to find any flaw in the plan we had almost unwittingly formulated. He admitted we might succeed but only because it wou'd be difficult for even a halfwit not to. Balanced against this nervous confidence was his guilt at the thought that but for him, none of us would ever have heard of Willie Marshall or Filox Investments or any of the other dull forbidding names looming like giant shadows over everything we did. Victor had never met Landau's father, and saw him in his own private fantasies as a kind of Oscar Homolka caricature of the stock nineteenth-century immigrant, a relic with a broken heart and an accent to match. The thought that this pathetic character, pinched and frugal, oppressed and downtrodden, might lose his life savings over this scheme was a constant torment. Perhaps if our enterprise had been born of a solemn committee of ways and means Victor would have felt less uncomfortable. He was always the man to require the crutch of official procedure to prop up his rickety ego. But all this had come about through his seedy amorous pursuits in a second-rate palais-de-danse, which made him terribly ashamed.

Victor's biggest difficulty of all, however, was a literary one. If Landau had not read enough novels, then Victor had read too many. Back in his teens he had thought about it for a while and then cast himself as a cross between Mr

Polly and F. Scott Fitzgerald, an unfortunate creature doomed to suffer the wretched early manhood of the first and the premature death of the second. Now that he was faced with the prospect of being Kipps instead, he was finding it very hard to adjust to a complete reversal of character. His picture of himself was suddenly rendered obsolete, a fact which, added to his burden of guilt over Landau's father, was beginning to make life quite impossible for him. Landau did his best to dispel anxiety about the money, but not even his callous laughter was much help.

'Listen, my old man wouldn't feel the pinch even if we lost every penny. There's always a market for trousers in Turnpike Lane, you know, don't you worry yourself about that.'

But Victor could not help worrying himself about precisely that, and consented to go on only because there appeared to be no effective way of withdrawing. He talked so persistently about what Polly would have done that at first Landau thought he was referring to a girl-friend whose existence he had been keeping secret from us. When Victor explained that Polly only existed in the pages of a novel, Landau scratched his tight curls and wondered aloud what kind of partners he had landed himself with.

As for me, I was in even worse shape than Victor. My own reasons for anticipating catastrophe were typically pseudo-logical and just as typically self-pitying. As I had never had any money in the past, it therefore followed that I would never have any in the future. It also followed that as I was part of the syndicate, then that syndicate was obviously doomed. The lunacy of this syllogism never struck me forcibly enough at the time to make me change my mind, and so while I indulged privately in wild, desperate hopes, I presented to my partners a front of unbroken gloom which was my propitiatory offering to the gods of chance who, I had heard, always laughed at optimists like Landau. I found the long days of waiting hardly tolerable simply because of this irritating confusion inside my own mind. Was I hopeful or not? Vale of tears or silver lining? I kept telling myself that the optimism was my own affair, while the public defeatism might be useful against the day I might have to use it to smother disappointment.

And yet I too could see no good reason why we should not succeed. Had it not been for the crude mechanics of our entry into the game of taking something for nothing without breaking the law, my confidence would surely have been unshakeable, like Landau's. But I was still callow enough in those days to look for subtlety where there was only blatant grabbing. Our escapade seemed altogether too clumsy to be the stuff of which empires are made. Did Morgan and Rockefeller begin like this? It seemed laughable that making a large sum of money should hinge on the chance encounter of a frustrated company director and a randy waitress.

But it was Blitski, theoretically the best-informed of us all, who was hardest hit by events. One of his favourite scenes in literary history was the death of Shelley, so perhaps it was only to be expected that the tiny cockleshell of his ego should be swamped by the great tidal waves bearing down on us all. In some peculiar way he managed to predict catastrophe and remain quite passive as he did so, as though the disaster he could see looming ahead was in no way connected with the happy revolutionary who had dropped in on us a few weeks before. The sudden translation of his theories into hard practice had been a traumatic shock for him, and so instinctively he had retreated far back into adolescence and beyond. He could talk all night like a grown man about the lottery of capitalism, but let chance thrust a ticket into his hand and immediately he reverted back to the undersized schoolboy. Like so many men who walk the world with an invisible soapbox, Blitski was always unnerved by the smell of real as distinct from hypothetical profits. He had never handled more than twenty pounds at any one moment in his life, and here he was awaiting the consequences of a financial landslide. His theories had been nurtured in a climate of pure reason untainted by the smell of hard cash, at lunchtime harangues in Lincoln's Inn Fields, jousting with students from the London School of Economics, in conversations through the night in the smoky bedsitters of the Socialist Party of Great Britain, in half-drunken rambles through Hyde Park on Sunday afternoons, spluttering at the Anarchists, croaking at the Trotskyites, waving ineffectual arms at the Jehovah's Witnesses waiting patiently to get into heaven. His aphorisms might not have been very subtle, but then, as he was always saying, neither was the capitalist system. And at least his thoughts were the product of an uncorrupted mind. We had put a stop to all that. Because of the inconsiderate generosity of his friends, without himself desiring it in the least, the sardonic doctrinaire spectator had been flung into the glare of the open arena.

Two days after his last flight, his hegira as he called it, he returned to Kemptown, further demoralised by the discovery that the old domestic sanctuary had failed him for the first time in his life. He came back resigned to the company of his fellow speculators, a broken man who could no longer hold his food, read his books, or sleep at night. He wou'd sit dumbly on the edge of his bed during our watching brief, rejecting with the dramatic eloquence of his pallor Landau's casual truculence, Victor's haggard sense of guilt and my own nervous hope, trying vainly to disengage himself from the whole business, knowing he had contributed neither thought nor capital nor even enthusiasm and was only involved at all because some Saturday night reactionary had hit him on the nose with a raw potato. Landau diagnosed it as a simple case of the idealistic conscience shying away from the illicit pleasures of unearned income, although he never put it in quite those words. But even this was not true. Blitski's socialism was not remotely connected with any kind of philosophic concern for the inequality of the distribution of wealth, or even with compassion for underdogs like himself. It was a pure abstraction, a harmless intellectual vanity to be paraded before other dilettantes, who saw in the exploitation of their fellow man nothing more inspiriting than an excuse for displaying the tired sophistries of their brains. And now we had spoiled his favourite game. How could he ever speak again with that flushed soapbox enthusiasm about the fundamental insanity of speculation? By his own definition he was now one of the madmen, and it was the three of us who had done it. It suddenly occurred to me as I was sponging my toes that if we should happen to win through, Blitski might turn out to be extremely ethical about accepting his share of the profits.

The bath water was cold, and now I climbed out shivering. Outside the window the sunset was already inked in by advancing darkness. I dressed hurriedly and dashed out of the house as fast as I could, pursued by the conviction that unless I did not soon get among normal people with mundane conversation, my head would explode. That night Landau was in great form, making friends with perfect strangers, inspiring undying devotion in girls who would not be able to remember what he looked like in three days' time, arranging everybody's movements and generally living up to that resolve, still rampant, to take life by the throat. That night he and I met some people who were having a party out at Rottingdean. By the time we got back to Kemptown the grey of sea and sky had joined forces once more and the housewives were nosing out bargains in the fish shop downstairs.

18

EVERY morning after breakfast, as part of our new routine, I went down to the newsagent's shop next door to the lending library, to buy the combine's copy of the *Financial Times*. Not that any of us were able to make much sense of it. Its phraseology was too obscure and its vital backpage statistics too cramped for the uninitiated eye. It took us a whole week-end of dogged research to discover that the reason why we could never find Filox Investments in any of the daily quotations was that the firm's official title was Marine Filox, in the industrial section. It was incidents like this which made me suspicious of Landau. How could he have bought the shares in a company whose name he didn't know? But when I faced him with the question he called me a hairsplitter.

'I just said to the face at the bank, "Buy me Filox". How many firms with a name like that do you think there are? Stop worrying. It's all under control.'

Our ignorance about financial matters was so complete that I even considered the possibility that our shares might rise without any of us realising it. When the only sign that something has happened is on the back page of the *Financial Times*, it is very easy to believe that it hasn't happened at all. This time it was Victor who calmed me down.

'To a newspaper like that, a deal like this one is front page stuff. Don't you worry about the back page. When the time comes, if it ever does come, the front page will tell you all you need to know. Including warrants for our arrest, I shouldn't be surprised.'

But I trusted nobody, least of all myself, and every morning I scanned that back page, limping through the labyrinth of its small print in search of the great news.

One Thursday morning I awoke with the conviction that today was to be our day. I had no logical explanation for this feeling, except perhaps that the sun was shining brightly and

I had managed to go three days without so much as touching a slice of bread or a potato. But this time as I walked the few yards to the newsagent's, I kept telling myself that if I willed it hard enough, those columns of microscopic figures would adjust themselves to the required shape for us this morning. I had always been a great believer in the art of making newsprint change its message by sheer exercise of the will. As a small boy I had had great practice, putting my thumb over the stop press cricket scores and straining every fibre to make Yorkshire 400 for 5 at close of play. And now I was doing the same thing, except that instead of cricket scores it was my own bank balance I was praying for. By the time I stepped out of the shop with the paper under my arm, I was convinced that provided I could resist looking at the day's prices until I arrived back in the kitchen, then the whole thing would be settled at last. I even started considering how best to break the news to Landau, sitting in the kitchen morosely sipping coffee, and to Blitski, still deep in a troubled guilt-ridden sleep. But I wilted and stood there in the street, feet astride. I opened the paper, creasing its pink-tinted pages so that the whole back sheet was under my eye. Eddies of wind puffing up the side streets from the sea crackled the newsprint under my fingers. My mouth felt dry, and under my shirt I could feel my pulse thumping. But before I could focus my eyes on the relevant column, a woman's voice spoke from behind the paper.

'Don't tell me you've turned to high finance in your old age?'

I recognised the insinuating voice even before I dropped the paper to my side. It was Bella Herbert, a shade too immaculate for the high spirits of the morning, in a neat pink costume and a matching pillbox hat.

'It's a bit early for you, isn't it Bella?'

She made no reply, but continued staring at me with a kind of mistrusting curiosity. I felt my cheeks modulate slowly to the colour of the newspaper I was holding.

'Why don't you come back to the house and have some coffee?'

'All right, I will,' she said, without taking her eyes from me.

As we strolled back down the courtyard to the front door she remarked, still looking at me, 'I thought musicians only read the trade papers.'

'Oh, you know me. I like to read anything I can lay my hands on, doesn't matter what. This morning, for instance, I go in the shop and I see this paper on the counter. The colour looks nice, so I try it. I must say it looks a bit dull though.'

'Not if you know what you're reading.'

We went into the kitchen, where Landau was standing over the stove waiting for his second cup of coffee to come to the boil. He glanced round as we came in, saw the confusion on my face and made a brave attempt to rise to the occasion. He crossed over to Bella, put his arm round her waist and gave her an affectionate peck on the cheek. She firmly disengaged herself.

'But in the morning no,' she said. 'And anyway, your breath smells disgusting. You haven't washed your teeth today.'

Landau grinned and said, 'In Milton's day they didn't have toothpaste, so what do you say to that?'

'You and Milton both.'

He grinned and poured an extra cupful of coffee into the pan on the stove. Bella sat down at the table, on the chair next to mine.

'Coffee won't be a minute,' Landau said. 'Take off your hat and make yourself comfortable if you're staying.'

'Mind your own business,' she answered sweetly, and her eye caught the pile of old pink newspapers stacked on the sofa. She turned and focused that quizzical look on me again.

'Actually I came to see Maxine.'

'Still asleep,' I told her.

'Well I suppose you should know.'

Landau turned off the gas and carried the steaming pan over to the table. Then he slopped its contents into three breakfast cups of contrasted design.

'She hardly ever shows her face before twelve o'clock,' I said, taking my cup. 'Was it important? I could give her a shout.'

'It can keep. It was just that I happened to meet a friend

of hers last night. Fellow called Marshall.'

Landau gave me a quick glance and then buried his face in his cup as Bella turned on him.

'Oh,' I said too quickly, 'how are things down at the Arcadia these days? They're managing without me then?'

Without bothering to look at me Bella said to Landau, 'Two out-of-work saxophone players reading the *Financial Times*. What's happened to you two?'

'I might as well tell you the truth,' I said. 'You know I'm always trying to think of plots for stories? Well, I've been working on this idea of the perfect murder. The killer gets a job as typesetter at the *Financial Times*, knowing which shares his victim has been buying. Then he changes just one figure on the day's quotations, knowing that the victim will read the figures, think he's ruined and kill himself.'

'Hey, that's not bad, Tom. When did you think of it?'

'About three seconds ago, I shou'd say.' Bella took off her hat, patted her hair, and carefully dropped four spoonfuls of sugar into her coffee. As she stirred it, she looked at me again and said, 'If you like I'll introduce you to this Marshall fellow, he's a businessman himself. Perhaps he could advise you about your plot.'

'What is all this, Bella? We haven't got any plot. What are you talking about?'

And Landau, glowering at her, went to the door to call Maxine.

'I told you it wasn't important,' Bella said, and lit a cigarette. 'Well, aren't you going to look at your paper?'

'Oh, I shan't actually read it. I just wanted to get the feel of it. For the story.' I tossed the paper on to the pile on the sofa and sat there wondering whether I was after all a rich man. Landau came back and sat down.

'So tell me, Bella, what's been happening? Any good parties?'

'None. I think this town's dying on its feet. The Arcadia's like a morgue and no one ever seems to come down from town.'

'There's always the pier.'

'I wouldn't set foot in that dump if it was the last outpost of civilisation.'

'I didn't tell you, did I? I'm working there again. I knew they couldn't do without me.'

'If you hate this town so much, why do you live here?' I asked.

'As a matter of fact, I've been asking myself that lately. I'm seriously thinking of selling up and going back to London. Three years is more than enough.'

'Stay, Bella,' Landau said gravely. 'Better to be a big fish in a small pool.'

'What is that supposed to mean? That I'm too naïve to go to town?'

'Why do you think we're staying on here? Only because we'd be lost if we went back.'

'I meant to ask you that. Why do you stay here?'

'I told you. I got my job back.'

'What about him then? He's not been forgiven, has he?'

'I'm not waiting to be forgiven.' Her remark irritated me.

'No, we're gathering our strength before the winter campaign. Anyway, we might be leaving any day now, eh, Tom?'

'Any day.'

A door slammed upstairs, and a few moments later Maxine came into the kitchen wrapped in a cotton dressing-gown with red roses on a yellow background.

'Hey, Landau, what's all the shouting about? Hi, Bella.'

'Madame here demanded your presence.'

'Where's my coffee then? If you're going to get me up at the crack of dawn, the least you can do is make me some coffee.'

'I bring you greetings from an old friend,' Bella said. 'A man called Marshall. I met him at that little drinking club. I can never remember the name. Just where Hove starts. He said you and he are old friends.'

'In a way. I didn't know he was in town.'

'Oh, yes. He told me he's got some kind of business deal on.'

As she said this, Bella watched Maxine's face and then glanced at the pink newspapers on the sofa. Maxine took the cup of coffee Landau handed her and said nothing.

'He was very mysterious about the whole thing, of course.

They're so tiresome, these smalltime tycoons. The way they go on, you'd think there were Stock Exchange leaks going on every day.'

'He never talks business to me. When we're together, he has other things on his mind.'

'I'm sure he does. I noticed last night. Bit of a lecher.'

Landau decided to put in a word for youth.

'You're all off your heads, you girls. You hang around with these old faces when there's all these virile young chaps about.'

'Where?' said Bella, trying to freeze him and failing.

'If you can't see it, I'm not going to draw a map.'

'Of course,' Bella said, ' the biggest obstacle to leaving this town is money. One needs a little capital if one is to set up house somewhere.'

'I'm sure one does,' Landau said, aping her intonation. 'Why don't you drop all that " one does " crap. You're among friends.'

'You surprise me.'

Maxine sprinkled a few cornflakes into a bowl, splashed cold milk over them and began munching. Between mouthfuls she asked Bella, 'Did Marshall say how long he was here for?'

'Two, three days. He said his deal will be through by then, but until it is, he has to be on call. Board meetings or something.'

'Two or three days, eh?' Landau said, looking at me.

Bella turned on him innocently. 'Oh, do you know him too?'

'I have never set eyes on Willie Marshall in my life,' he replied, luxuriating in an entirely honest remark for the first time that morning.

'He's an associate of Victor's, not mine.'

'Oh, that rather good-looking boy you brought up to the house the other day? Is he in business too?'

The conversation was now drifting a little too close to the truth for comfort, and I made a despairing attempt to head Bella off and with luck out of the house.

'Victor's a travelling salesman whose weekly wage wouldn't keep you in gin for one night. And although I don't know the man, that probably goes for Marshall too.'

'Oh no it doesn't. Last night he was flinging money around like confetti. Do you ever get the feeling your friends are keeping something from you?'

'As a matter of fact yes,' I said. 'You, for instance. You've been talking in riddles ever since you got here.'

'In that case I'll go,' she said, and replaced her hat. 'And then, as soon as I've gone, you can study the market prices in your little pink paper to your heart's content. Your eyes have been burning a hole in it ever since you threw it down. No, it's all right. I can see myself out. Thanks for the coffee.'

After she had gone, the three of us sat there for two or three minutes without speaking. Then Landau stood up and stretched himself.

'It's amazing how far the smell of money carries.'

'I always thought she had hyper-sensitive nostrils,' and I drained my cup. Maxine finished her cornflakes. 'If Bella needs money, why shouldn't she have it?'

'Because,' said Landau walking over to the back door and gazing out at the garden, 'the more people know about this deal, the less chance there is of there being any money to have. That's why. So don't you go telling her the score.'

'You know me, Landau. I'm stup'd. I don't even know what the score is. Anyway even if I did, there wou!dn't be any need for me to tell Bella.'

'What do you mean?'

'I mean that once Bella Herbert sniffs a trail she eventually gets to the end of it. Look, do you think now she's got her hooks into Willie Marshall that she won't have him telling her his life story in no time? It's down to lambs to the slaughter.'

'She's right, Landau. I told you if you gave Bella half a chance, she'd dance rings round the lot of us.'

'Not round me she won't. Look, you heard what she said. Marshall expects the whole thing to be wrapped up in two to three days. That doesn't give her enough time to find out what the shares are, buy and still make a profit. Two or three days is not enough, not even for her.'

'Two or three nights might be,' Maxine said. 'I lay you

odds that about two o'clock tomorow morning she'll have it all out of him, whatever it is, right down to the last detail. Any takers?'

'Well that's up to her,' Landau said. 'If she can make it her way, good luck to her. She'll have earned it. All I'm saying is, we don't hand anything to her on a plate.'

The phone started ringing.

'I'll go,' I said. I was glad of the chance to break off a conversation so speculative about a situation so nebulous that I was in danger of losing my frame of reference entirely. If the money was disrupting our routine before we had so much as seen it, what effect might it not have when it was spendable? Neither Landau nor I had so much as thought of practising for three days. Not since I started learning at thirteen had I neglected my studies for so long. I had made the cardinal error of failing to keep my life as simple as possible. I was . . .

The voice on the other end of the wire was Victor's, telling me he would be arriving some time this evening, in case anything broke tomorrow morning. I thought it best not to mention Bella's predatory visit or Marshall's expectations of two to three days. When I returned to the kitchen Landau and Maxine were sitting silently at the table.

'It was Victor. He's coming down tonight.'

'What's the point? That's what I want to know. He keeps going up and down for no reason. It's making me nervous.'

'He's like us I suppose. Trying to kill time till it's over.'

'Well I just wish he'd pick his spot and stay there, that's all.'

Maxine's eyes lit up with a rare glint of perception.

'Here, you lot are not in trouble, are you?'

'No, not trouble. Just a small problem, that's all.'

'That's right,' Landau added. 'A small problem. It's nothing. Don't worry.'

'Who's worried?'

'Listen, Maxine, will you be seeing Marshall?' I asked.

She shrugged her shoulders. The dressing-gown slid down to reveal one tanned shoulder.

'Maybe, but never go running after them, that's my golden rule.'

'You ran after me.'

'I'm talking about business, not pleasure. Anyway, it wouldn't do any good. He'll probably be all dazzled by Bella for a bit. I'm not entering any contests just to choke Bella off for you.'

There then occurred one of those violent metamorphoses of which Landau was the pastmaster. His face broke into a smile, he jumped up, visibly throwing off the anxieties of his business career and began being very hearty. 'I don't know about you lot, but I'm going out to get some of that sun. Might as well, while it's still here. While *we're* still here. Tom, how about the beach? Or a bit of . . . Hey, I know. Why don't we do some practice? Haven't done much work this week, you know.'

'You go on. I'll follow on later. Say the cider bar at two?'

'The cider bar at two it is,' he said, and strode out of the room, whistling happily as he went.

'I don't know how he does it,' I said.

'Does what?'

'You know. Pushes things out of his mind like that. How can he think of sunbathing at a time like this?'

'Actually there is one thing guaranteed to push everything out of your mind for a bit. I've never known it to fail yet.'

I looked at her but she avoided my eye and concentrated on flicking fragments of cornflake across the tablecloth at me.

'Of course,' she said, 'if you don't believe in that kind of thing . . .'

But I did, and it was not till an hour later that I suddenly remembered I had still not checked today's prices. But by then I was in no position to go and look. It was Blitski, emerging from his martyr's bed at three o'clock that afternoon, who arrived in the kitchen, found nobody had waited breakfast for him, and saw from the morning paper what we had all feared. Marine Filox still stood obstinately at eleven-and-threepence a share.

19

More than a week had now gone by since Bella's breakfast visit, and still the price of Marine Filox stood immovable at eleven-and-threepence. I began to get the feeling that there must exist some cosmic law precluding the possibility of that price ever rising. There was one terrible morning when it actually fell to eleven shillings and even Landau's composure was dented. But the fall in Marine Filox turned out to be the end result of some specialist's finding that hay fever was an imaginary disease easily routed by the application of a little will power on the part of the sufferer. Within twenty-four hours the theory had been consigned to limbo with all the other specialists' theories and Marine Filox rallied to eleven-and-three, where it seemed fated to remain for ever.

I would liked to have known whether Marshall was still around, but Maxine denied having caught so much as a glimpse of him since the scene in the Arcadia. As for Bella, she seemed to have gone to ground. Landau sneaked into the Arcadia once or twice in the hope of finding her at the bar, but nobody there had seen her. We were so bemused by this time that in an attempt to occupy ourselves we took once more to our instruments. Our duets in the long room with the glass walls occasionally became so frenzied that we managed to clear our minds, if only for an hour or two, of the financial junk that had been cluttering them for what seemed like years.

At about four o'clock one afternoon, when the windows of our practice room were registering the first streaks of the rain that was to fall for the rest of that day, I stopped blowing in mid-cliché and said to Landau, 'Something must have gone wrong.'

He pulled his clarinet from his mouth, a look of extreme exasperation on his face, and said, 'Sure something's gone wrong and I'll tell you what it is. You stopped playing in the middle of a chorus. If you're going to do things like that all the time, how do you expect to improve. It's not professional, Tom.'

'I'm sorry. It's eight days now since Bella to'd us what Marshall said. Two or three days at the outside, remember? I tell you, something must have gone wrong.'

I could see he was trying very hard to be patient. He placed his clarinet on the table between us and thought carefully before speaking.

'Now look. Maybe you're right. Maybe something has gone wrong. But how do we know? All we can do is sit tight and wait. I told you that when we first went into this thing, that's how speculators earn their money, by waiting. Just try not to let it get you down.'

'How can you say don't let it get you down? Three thousand quid.'

'Two seven fifty. We paid back a discount to my old lady, remember?'

'All right. Two seven fifty. I still say something's gone wrong. I bet you we lose the lot.'

'In that case we send a message of condolence to my old man. But I still say it won't come to that. The shares are still at eleven-and-three, aren't they? That's the price we bought at isn't it? So that means we're breaking even doesn't it? Well, doesn't it?'

'I suppose so.'

'What's all this " I suppose so "? Of course it does. We're not a penny worse off than we were before we went into this thing, and on top of that we stand to win much more than we can possibly lose. Come on, let's go and get some tea before you bring me right down.'

I remember that this was the day Blitski finally cracked. We found him stretched out on the kitchen sofa with a handkerchief over his face. The lines of his nose made a hillock on the bumpy plain of his features. Faint groans were coming from underneath the handkerchief. Landau strode over to the sofa, uncovered Blitski's face with the flourish of a stage magician and said, ' What's wrong now? You going coy on us?'

Blitski grabbed the handkerchief, replaced it and resumed

his groaning, but not so quickly that I did not have time to notice that his usually flushed complexion had faded dramatically to ashen grey.

'Hold it, Landau. He really looks ill.'

'Course I'm ill,' came a voice from under the handkerchief. 'It's my bowels. They've fallen out, I tell you. This business will be the death of me yet, you see.'

'There's nothing wrong with your bowels,' Landau told him. 'What you've got is acute inflammation of the bankroll. Look, Blitski, you have a good fry-up for tea and you'll feel much better. You've been starving yourself, that's the trouble with you. I tell you what my prescription is. Bacon-eggs and beans. You get a panload of that down you and you'll be swinging in no time.'

This time Blitski pulled the handkerchief from his face himself.

'Do me a favour, both of you. Don't mention food. Cook what you like, eat what you like, but just don't talk about it.' Then he slumped back on the sofa, re-covered his face and was silent.

Landau cracked six eggs and slopped them into the frying pan.

'The game is to get the eggs well on their way before you bung the bacon in. Otherwise you burn the bacon to a frazzle before the eggs are ready.'

His resilience seemed unconquerable. He smiled to himself as he manipulated the fat around the frying pan, prodding wayward rashers of bacon with a wooden fork.

'Well, chaps, another day nearer to the jackpot, eh? It won't be long now.'

'Do you think Bella might have said something to Marshall that queered the whole deal? I mean, it's possible.'

'Now why would she want to go and do a thing like that? She could stand to gain as much as we do. Actually I've been thinking quite a bit about that the last few days, and I look at it this way. If Bella is shrewd enough to make out with Marshall, well, I'm all for it. I hope she does row herself in somewhere. She's a good girl, Bella.'

The eggs chuckled happily to themselves in the pan. Blitski suddenly bounded from the sofa and dashed from the room.

'Where's he gone?' asked Landau as he flipped three plates on the table.

'Lavatory, I think. He wasn't kidding about his bowels.'

Landau tipped up the frying pan and scooped its contents into the three plates. Then he returned to the dresser and began to rummage for the tin opener.

'Here,' he said, tossing the breadknife at me, 'you cut the bread while I open the beans. I'm starving hungry.'

We had just begun to eat when Blitski returned, at greatly reduced speed, resumed his position on the couch and replaced the handkerchief over his face. Landau glanced at him for a moment with clinical curiosity before returning to his food. For the next minute or two the only noise in the room was the clatter of cutlery, the champing of jaws and the occasional muted abdominal rumbling from the sofa, but after Landau had deftly cut his way through half of his meal, he leaned back reflectively and said through the food in his mouth. 'Come on, Blitski. Your lovely fried egg and bacon and beans are all getting cold. If you don't eat it soon the fat will all start congealing.'

Blitski leapt up again, this time holding the handkerchief to his mouth and rushed from the room. Landau seemed genuinely astonished.

'Where's he gone this time?'

'Same place, I think.'

'What, again? There'll be nothing left of him at this rate. Still, never mind, more for us,' and he laughed hysterically. Small particles of half-chewed egg and bacon shot across the table and landed with unerring accuracy in the centre of the breadboard.

'You know what?' he said reflectively. 'I've decided what to do with my share of the profits.'

This was a fresh perspective that Landau had hit on. We had all been so preoccupied with the prospect of getting the money that none of us had given much thought to what we might do with it when we did get it. Once more Landau was showing the way.

'I have decided,' he announced, 'that after all the trouble we've had, it would be complete madness not to use the loot to make sure of security from here on.'

The remark surprised me. I had always imagined that Landau, if ever he found himself in possession of a sizeable sum of money, would run berserk till it was all gone and then revert back to the family bankroll. Yet here he was talking about security. This escapade was changing us more than I had realised.

' Yes, security, that's what I want. You know what I'm going to do with the loot? I'm going to invest it.'

' With luck you might be able to get as much as five per cent,' I said, encouraging this sudden fit of sanity. But he glared at me.

' Five per cent? I don't mean that kind of investment. I mean something that will give me a real return. Forty, fifty per cent.'

' What are you going to do, print money?'

' Tom, I'm going to sink this whole bundle into something cast-iron. Look, what is the one thing London hasn't got even one of? I'll tell you what, an all-night jazz club. The first man to open one will be made for life. What's the matter?'

He must have noticed the horrified look on my face and become genuinely concerned for me. However, I knew it would be pointless arguing with him. That much at least this summer had taught me.

' Oh, nothing. It's a very good idea. But I wasn't thinking of that. What do we do if the money does go down the pan?'

' It can't do, Tom. How can it?'

' I know, but just suppose it does.'

He thought about it for a moment, pursuing the last rebellious fragments of bacon round his plate with an upturned fork.

' Well, I suppose in that case we knock my old man. He can stand it.'

' But won't you feel guilty?'

' Course I will, but feeling guilty doesn't cost anything.'

He considered what he had just said and laughed again.

' How about that? Conning your own father.'

' Yes, but we'd have to pay him back somehow.'

' Don't be ridiculous. How long do you think it would take us to raise that kind of money? It might take years.

We'd be in hock for the rest of our lives. And anyway, there's another point about the money that none of you has thought of yet. My old man's too much of a coward to ask for it back. Bloody spineless, that's what he is. Any more bacon in the fridge?'

'You can have Blitski's. Something tells me he won't be needing his share.'

Landau leaned across the table, speared one of Blitski's rashers on the end of his fork, held it aloft and stared up happily at the dangling food.

'I wonder what caviar is like?' he said.

'I had some. Last winter. I was playing this wedding at Shoreditch Town Hall. Remember that place? Domed ceiling and terrible acoustics. Well, they let the band loose in the buffet—the couple couldn't have been married before—and we cleaned it out in one hit. A bit like chopped herring, only not so good.'

Landau dropped the bacon into his mouth, let the fork clatter on to his plate and leaned back, munching meditatively, a bastion of inviolable complacency.

'Listen, what you were saying just now about Blitski. He's not really ill, is he? I mean this business of the money's not going to send him round the bend or anything?'

'How do I know? Perhaps it's driving him sane.'

'Well he's your friend. As far as I can see, he's bone idle, and good luck to him. But what's he got against making money?'

'I don't know really. I think its something to do with his upbringing.'

'Don't you start all that analysis crap. I just asked a simple question, that's all.'

But it was anything but a simple question. It was hard to think of anyone less suited than Blitski to the drudgery of a respectable position. The anarchist in him—for that is what Blitski really was—might yield to the temptation from time to time to ridicule the money system, but he had no real desire to change it, any more than he wanted to alter the calendar or the colours of the rainbow. He just wanted to confirm his inborn suspicion that the whole thing was ridiculous. The true Blitski, the quintessential soul hiding behind the cardboard armour of polysyllables and the pseudo-science of economic theory, did not so much reject the system as refuse to admit it was there.

' The thing is,' I told Landau, ' that he thinks money's got nothing to do with him personally.'

' But that's mad, Ben. How does everyone let him get away with it? I mean his family and stuff like that?'

' It's difficult to explain.'

' No it's not. He's just lazy.'

Landau was wrong. Being congenitally idle had nothing to do with it. I knew that under differing circumstances the idler could be galvanised into the most strenuous activity. What had really saved Blitski from the indignity of coming to terms with the same life that Landau kept taking by the throat, was the all-enveloping ignorance of his parents. Although English by adoption for the past forty years, neither of them could read or write the language. Their empirical philosophy of following their instincts was probably very wise, except that the instincts in question were those of a feudal Polish village and not those of a small flat in twentieth century London. Blitski's father rose at six-fifteen every morning, compiled his towering encyclopaedia of beetroot sandwiches and went off to sew stitches in suits and overcoats which eventually found their way on to the backs of the selfsame film stars at whom Mrs Blitski gazed in idolatrous incomprehension every Monday and Thursday at the local Classic cinema. When she was not confusing herself by trying to follow Louis B. Mayer's contributions to modern art, Mrs Blitski pottered about the flat, encircling the grease-clotted gas cooker with the circumspection of a cowardly hunter stalking a tiger. And that was all. Both parents followed their entirely honourable instincts because nobody had ever managed to convince them that those instincts were misplaced. They believed only in birth, marriage, childbirth and death. Their cerebral muscles continued to twitch just as though the cars and motor-cycles parked outside in the street were sheep and pigs. If you had told them that Cossack steeds were prancing down Regent Street, they would have shot the bolt on the front door and continued to go about their modest business. Blitski, whose imagery was sometimes unfortunate, used to compare them to the chicken who keeps on running after its head has been chopped off.

All this was bad for Blitski's prospects as a useful citizen. What did his peasant parents know of the petty aspirations of that lower middle class to which they were supposed to belong? What did they know of the stigma of unemployment, or of the scandalising effect of an unkempt beard and sandals without socks? The only Bohemia they had ever heard of was the one in Czechoslovakia, and so their only son remained an inscrutable mystery to them. Did he refuse to work? Then that must be the accepted way in this peculiar, half-mad country populated entirely by foreigners. Did he sleep all day and read all night? Then the English must have taught him such strange habits. Did he disappear for weeks at a time, returning home much thinner and very much quieter? Then it was the English who must have been ill-treating him. Did he lock himself in his room and make funny marks on bits of paper with an iron machine which made clacking noises when you struck it? Then it must be some obscure tribal rite of the natives.

And so Blitski sidestepped the treadmill because his parents were too naïve to know that without the treadmill there could be no respectability. They were too old to learn new tricks and too tired to argue. Besides, they knew their son was some kind of genius, so how could he possibly be lazy? Of his genius they were sure, because of his phenomenal conquest of that senseless language the English used. Only he could tell them at a glance in the newspapers what was showing at the Classic. Only he could compile their laundry lists for them. Mr and Mrs Blitski could not read or write Polish, let alone English, so how could they possibly criticise?

But all I said to Landau was, ' You must understand. He's led a sheltered life.'

' I thought you said his folks were poor?'

' They are, but what's that got to do with it?'

' According to Blitski, everything. Don't you remember? That first day you brought him here. He said the trouble with rich families was that they smothered their children with luxury. If that's the scene, how come I'm better at doing things than he is?'

'Because you're thick skinned. He thinks making a lot of loot is like thieving. And you know how honest he is.'

The lavatory cistern flushed again, and a few moments later Blitski came staggering back into the kitchen, taking up his former position on the couch.

'Listen, Blitski, we've been talking about you. There's something we ought to clear up. What I mean is, getting money out of shares isn't against the law or anything like that. You don't have to worry about the police.'

The voice from under the handkerchief sounded more enfeebled than ever.

'Do you mind opening the window a bit? The smell of that bacon fat's choking me.'

'He's got no stomach for anything,' Landau grumbled as he opened the window not more than half an inch. 'He can't talk about money. Bacon fat makes him sick. What kind of a man is that?'

I could not answer him so I did not try. Landau took up his seat at the table and began working his way through the sweet biscuits.

'Looked in the pink paper today?'

I nodded. 'Filox is still at eleven-and-three. If something doesn't happen soon we won't have enough to pay the rent.'

'What about Maxine? She'll put you in it.'

'I can't go on taking money from her indefinitely.'

'Anyway, there's always the bank. Any customer holding the shares we do can get a small overdraft any time.'

'So it's overdrafts now, is it? I'm telling you, Landau, this whole thing is getting all out of hand.'

'You didn't think making money was simple, did you?'

'No, but I never realised what a strain it was going to be.'

He gave me what I think was supposed to be a penetrating look and began lecturing me.

'You know your trouble? You want something for nothing. There's profits coming? All right, you have to work for profits.'

'That's really rich coming from you. Who cooked up this whole idea to get rich without working? If it wasn't for you none of us would be trying to get something for nothing.'

'Ah, but it isn't for nothing. Just now you were complaining about the strain. Worrying like that is the hardest work of all. By the time we get our hands on the loot we'll all have earned it, you mark my words.'

It appeared that Blitski was not quite so supine as the handkerchief over his face suggested. Now he sat up, uncovered his face and said:

'He's right. Whatever we've got coming to us, I've earned my share. I never felt worse in my life.'

'See?' Landau said. 'Every day we have to go on waiting is another day of hard graft, so don't start getting pangs of conscience when it comes to the share-out.'

I was sure there was a loophole in his argument, but as I had no particular desire to find it, I closed the conversation by going up to my room and preparing myself for one of those outings which Landau was so good at organising. Tonight, the rain having released Landau from showing up at the pier, we were to visit a local holiday camp packed, according to him, with frustrated women hungry for fresh men. Landau only visited holiday camps on Friday nights, when the possibilities of the male regulars who had arrived the previous Saturday were exhausted. The fact that this time he turned out to be wrong was beside the point. We had contrived to fritter away one more day.

20

THERE was a wood where bluebells grew. Landau stumbled on to it one afternoon in the company of a Mrs Ellsworthy, a sporting type he picked up one morning at the local dry cleaners. I don't think he knew the flowers were bluebells, but one evening he returned from the wood so convinced of its romantic properties that he insisted on placing a small sprig of blossom in the drinking glass on his washstand.

'Hello,' I said. 'Where did you cop for the bluebell?'

'What?'

I could tell from the slightly petulant look on his face that he was about to make further use of his perversely ingenuous act, and the prospect did not appeal to me. I didn't feel like playing the whiting scene all over again, so before he could elaborate I went on.

'That flower. There, in the glass. It's a bluebell. I didn't know you went in for that sort of thing.'

'Ah, yes,' he replied. 'Reading all that poetry has definitely changed me. As a matter of fact, there's quite a story behind that bluebell.'

'I believe you.'

'Listen, there's this wood, see. You take a chick in this wood, any chick, and you lie down on the bluebells and you must score.'

'I just don't know about you Landau.'

'What's wrong now?'

'You must be the only man in the world who finds bluebells an aphrodisiac.'

'Look, it's all in the books. Back to nature, Shelley and all that crap. We're too civilised. We have to go back to the earth, and that's what I do in the wood.'

'Shelley said that?'

'It amounts to the same thing. I go in the wood with this Olive and . . .'

'With who?'

'Olive. Olive Ellsworthy. She's the greatest thing.'

'Christ,' I said. 'Olive Ellsworthy. What do you call her for short, Ollie? For a man who once swallowed a chick because her name was Flora, you certainly live freely.'

'What's in a name? It's the woman who counts.'

'Yes,' I said.

'Anyway. This wood. It's absolutely a hundred per cent foolproof. I can definitely recommend it.'

I could see he believed what he was saying about the wood, but whether it was Landau or the marijuana speaking I could not be sure. Looking back on it, I am half-convinced that everything he said and did that summer was the fruit of his communion with his home-made cigarettes, but then, even unsullied, Landau was such an original spirit that I may be doing him an injustice. Whatever the true reason for his attachment to the bluebells, he believed enough in their powers to play out the last sexual comedy of the season surrounded by them.

Ever since the eclipse of the beloved Bella, Landau had hungered for another woman cast in the same flattering mould. But it did not take long for even him to realise that girls of Bella's calibre were at a premium in our social circles. Gradually he came round to the expedient view that maturity was all. If he could not acquire a mistress as accomplished as Bella, then at least he could find one who was as old. Mrs Ellsworthy was a well-preserved lady of about thirty-five whose husband appeared to have been mislaid some years before and never been heard of again. To ease her marital conscience, Mrs Ellsworthy persisted in the fiction of a lovelorn amnesiac wandering the world, slowly dying of a broken heart. The truth, I thought, was probably a little more prosaic, especially when I discovered that Mrs Ellsworthy survived on fairly large and very regular sums of money drawn from the expense account of a company of which her errant husband just happened to be a substantial shareholder.

But the most vital fact about Mrs Ellsworthy was her religion. She was without any question the most fanatical observer of religious ritual I ever met. Nothing was allowed to stand in the way of her beliefs. No matter how demanding her scrupulous observance of ritual ceremony might prove to be, no matter what difficulties they might cause or how much money they might cost, Mrs Ellsworthy remained staunchly devout, and I remember Landau saying to me that if everyone who professed a faith was half as conscientious in respecting its spirit, the world would be a much better place. I suppose the truth of this remark was not diminished by the fact that the religion which Mrs Ellsworthy followed so pietistically was Hedonism.

I had an idea that for her bluebells were not nearly so essential to the good life as they suddenly appeared to have become for Landau, and that in a horticultural crisis a bed of thorns or a mud flat would have proved just as serviceable. I noticed also that her methods of holding on to a man once she had grappled him to her were beautifully simple. To prevent the quarry from running away she simply weighed it down with jewellery. Landau had not paid more than three visits to the bluebell wood before he was festooned with a gold watch, a signet ring, a tiepin, an initialled cigarette case, a fountain pen and one of those identification discs he had sneered at not so long ago.

'You can't go on taking all this junk from her, you know. You'll send her bankrupt.'

'It is more blessed to give,' Landau said, 'than to receive. I read that only last night. If you could see how it knocks her out to give me presents, you wouldn't talk like that. I just haven't got the heart to refuse her.'

'I'm surprised. I always thought you liked to stay independent of your women.'

'And so I do. There's no strings attached to this one.'

'How can you be sure?'

'Course I'm sure. Look, in a few days we'll be getting out of here. We'll be away before she knows what's happening.'

'It's only fifty-eight minutes to London, which is a fact you've tended to overlook ever since you got here.'

'All right, so before I go I give her back the whole collection, and that will be that.'

He twiddled the ring on the little finger of his right hand. Illogically it looked to me like the vague prelude to a knuckleduster, and I saw that he was embarrassed by Mrs Ellsworthy's calculated liberality.

'I tell you what,' he said. 'I'm meeting her at seven o'clock. I'm not sure what we're doing, but why don't you and Maxine make up a foursome?'

'No thanks. I can just see me and Maxine rolling about in the bluebells. Anyway, she's funny about going out with strange women.'

'Ask her. See what she says.'

'All right. But I don't promise anything.'

The truth of it was that Maxine and I hardly ever saw each other these days. I suppose the fact that she was still living in the house meant that she retained some vague kind of proprietary interest in me, and there had been that interlude on the afternoon of Bella's visit. But our unspoken pact never to ask questions of each other had by this time evolved into a relationship so loose as to be virtually non-existent. Landau, with his excessive involvement in his own affairs, had noticed none of this, and if I told him now, he might start getting righteous on my behalf and try throwing Maxine either into my arms or out of the house. Of course the fact that she had been the one to put the finger on Marshall still counted for something, and even Landau must still remember that but for her we would never have had the chance to rifle the till of Marine Filox. But Landau took sexual morality very seriously, even other people's, and might take it upon himself to see that I was well done by. I wanted none of this. It was not that I was in love with Maxine, but simply that the possibilities of her presence was spice in the lumpy pudding of our life in Kemptown.

Later that day I went up to Maxine's room to see what she thought of Landau's foursome idea. She was not there. Her bed was unmade and looked cold enough not to have been slept in for some days. The morning newspaper rumpled among the bedclothes was three days old, and the half-empty coffee cup on the dressing-table was rimmed with crusted liquid. I glanced in the wardrobe. Her dresses still hung there. Several pairs of court shoes were scattered on its floor. This was still her official residence then, even though she was away on some prolonged state visit. I went downstairs again and wrote a few letters, including one to Ray Knowles enclosing some reviews, and another to Victor telling him that so far there was no change in the situation. There was still just time to catch the five-thirty post, so I went down to the post office on the corner and found myself standing behind a familiar torso in the stamp queue.

'Hello stranger. We were getting worried about you.'

Maxine half-turned and smiled at me.

'I was just coming back to get changed. How's things?'

'So so. Nothing's changed. You doing anything tonight? Landau's got some grass widow in tow. He wants us to make up a foursome.'

'No thanks. He's a bit too frantic for me. I'll tell you what though. Why don't you look into the Regent tonight? I'll tell you why. I might need rescuing.'

'What's that supposed to mean?'

'It means, come into the Regent about nine o'clock and take me away. If I argue, take no notice. Don't matter what the company is.'

'What shall I say?'

'Ask Landau. He'll think of something.'

'No he won't. He's preoccupied with bluebells at the moment.'

'What?'

We walked slowly back to the house together, not saying anything. I was surprised to find myself feeling possessive, making elaborate plans to be dynamic that night at the Regent.

But when I walked in there at ten minutes past nine it was to find Maxine sitting alone at one of those little tables whose lampshades are embossed with the piano scores of old hit songs. She was sitting staring at the notation of 'Tuxedo Junction' when she spotted me, and before I had reached her, she had gathered up her handbag, fished out her lipstick and started beautifying herself in preparation for departure.

'So who needs rescuing?'

'I only said I might need help. Willie Marshall phoned me today. He said his business was finished here and he wanted to see me before he went back. He never showed, that's all. Bella must be hanging on like grim death.'

'Marshall said that? He said his business was finished?'

'That's what he told me. Come on. Let's get out of here.'

'Where to?'

'It's amazing how little you know about this town. There's parties going on all over the place. I haven't slept in my own bed for three nights.'

'I know. I looked in your room this afternoon.'

'That's sweet,' she said. 'Come on.'

We jumped into the two-seater she had hired and drifted around the town for a couple of hours, calling in at different houses, gauging the heat of the celebrations and testing the wine before moving on to the next venue, and all the time we moved I kept thinking about Marshall having finished his business. It must have been past midnight when she stopped the car a mile or so outside the town and said, 'Why don't we go back to the house and pick up your horn? I remember how fed up you were last time we went to a party without it.'

'Where are we going then?'

'Private party. At one of the hotels. Some people I know. It'll probably go on all night.'

'You sure we'll get in?'

'If you bring your horn we will. You'll be free cabaret, see? When people take a room for a party, they count on people like you who like showing off so much that they do it for nothing.'

She saw the concerned expression on my face and laughed.

'Come on. I was only taking the rise.'

The 'room' she had referred to turned out to be a medium-sized banqueting hall whose mirrored walls magnified it into a vast arena and whose six grotesque chandeliers were linked by an intricate network of multi-coloured streamers and wires, from which depended at irregular intervals the precarious Chinese lanterns which gave the room its only light. Large as the hall was, it was not large enough to contain the festivities, and sounds of celebration spilled out into the corridor leading to it. At the far end of the room, facing the doors, was a crudely improvised bandstand serving as a platform for crudely improvised music. The Latin-American group in occupation appeared to be miming with a distinctly amateur-

232

ish touch. The musicians blew and scraped and the dancers flung themselves about, but apart from the occasional clang of a cowbell, I could hear no evidence to suggest that the band was actually playing. This was due to the fact that most of the dancers, anxious to convince each other they were enjoying themselves, were screaming at each other and stamping their heels on the wooden floor, which I could feel vibrating under my shoes.

Maxine immediately beat a strategic retreat to the ladies' room, so I fought my way over to the long trestle tables against the wall, crammed with chicken legs, bowls of salad, cheeses, French loaves and crates of bottled beer. While I was steadily munching my way through the remains of a cheese, a short plump boy, sweating from all pores, crashed into me and started to apologise. Then he thought he recognised me and slapped me a little too heartily on the back.

'I know you. You're Herman's friend. Did he come with you? Anyway, nice of you to drop in.'

I cou'd see he was drunk, and before I could inquire about the mysterious Herman he almost stumbled into me again.

'What's in that case you're carrying?'

'Only my dirty washing.'

Maxine came barging through the crowd to rescue me.

'Willie, you're drunk again,' she said to my new friend. 'Go on. Get out of it.'

She gave him the lightest of shoves in the chest and Willie disappeared very slowly, under the wreckage of one of the tables, sinking into a pile of cardboard boxes, beer crates and discarded chicken legs. This new location must have been more comfortable than it looked, because when I made my way back to the table hours later, he was still there, propped up in one of the cardboard boxes, happily sleeping, his head lolling on one side and an empty beer bottle dangling from his hand.

'Willie's our host,' Maxine said. 'He always gets like this at his own parties.'

'What's it in aid of?'

'Nothing special. Willie gets a kick out of this sort of thing. I bet you he doesn't even know who half these people are.'

This was not difficult to believe. At least three hundred

guests and gatecrashers in various stages of undress and drunkenness clamoured about us. The band struggled on, but only the nervous tics of the dancers' bodies suggested that anyone could hear anything. To cross from one side of the room to the other demanded ruthless techniques of pathfinding through knots of people apparently stuck together with some powerful fixative. Before long I had lost contact with Maxine, and all I saw of her for the next hour or so was her flushed laughing face as it flitted by under the pink and yellow glow of the lanterns. Once or twice the mad pattern of the dancing swept us to within a few feet of each other, but the floor by this time was so crowded and the noise so deafening that it was all I could do to wave a single arm and scream ' Hello.'

At half past two a further ingredient was tipped into an already impossible brew when six of Willie's friends entered staggering under the weight of twelve cases of champagne. In the stampede that followed I found myself carried forward like a front row forward in a rugby scrum, ending up at the small improvised bar in the far corner of the room next to the bandstand. Just as I was raising a glass of champagne to my lips, a posse of young bloods came galloping past and dashed the glass from my hand. Most of its contents flew into the face of the girl standing next to me. I turned and saw it was Maxine. She was laughing and catching the drops with her tongue as they trickled down her nostrils.

' Great party, eh?' she yelled, by this time all of six inches away from me.

' What?'

' The party. Good.'

' Oh yes.'

' Why aren't you playing?'

' Eh?'

She wriggled forward until her lips were pressed against my ear and shouted, ' When are you going to play?'

' Oh, yes. Soon.'

The Latin-American musicians had by now been swallowed up in the jaws of the monster writhing about the room, and now the music, still barely audible, was coming from a quintet none of whose members I had ever seen before. By crouching behind the champagne crates with my back between the wall and the outside world I was able to assemble my instrument. As I clambered on to the stand I realised the futility of trying to introduce myself to the other musicians. The shouting and stamping was so deafening that only by pressing my ear to the piano strings was I able to recognise the tune. There was nothing to do but play for my own amusement and try to ignore everything else.

The champagne and the beer had blunted my judgement, and I cannot remember how well or for how long I played. At any rate I experienced none of that dead weight of depression which usually assaulted me when my critical faculties came into head-on collision with my creative ability. Perhaps it was just the alcohol, but when a long time later somebody clutched my arm while I was playing 'Lady Be Good' I felt sure that the bourgeoise had disturbed the composition of a masterpiece. I stopped blowing, opened my eyes and glared down at the offending hand tugging at my shirtsleeve. It belonged to Maxine. In her free hand she clutched an unopened magnum of champagne. She must have been sitting on it for hours. I secreted my instrument in a comparatively safe place under the piano and jumped off the stand, almost falling on my face. She nodded towards a small side door and led me down a short passage into an anteroom lit by a single lamp and furnished with a sofa and two armchairs.

'Phew,' she exclaimed, and crashed into the deep cushions of the sofa. 'I thought it was time for a breather. You mind drinking out of the bottle? Most of the glasses seem to be broken.'

'Course not.'

She prised the cork from the bottle, threw back her head and gulped down great draughts of the champagne. I sat next to her and observed the strict-tempo undulation of her Adam's apple. It seemed excruciatingly funny. She wiped her lips and passed the bottle to me. While I was drinking she started laughing.

I pulled the bottle away. 'What's wrong?'

'Your Adam's apple. It's going up and down like a yo-yo.'

'So was yours.'

She snatched the bottle back and began drinking again.

After two more gulps she returned it to me but before releasing it she scrutinised my face.

'What's the matter now?'

'I think you're drunk.'

'Course I'm not. Givvus.'

I drank some more.

'You do like me, don't you?' she asked with some anxiety.

'Who's drunk now?'

'What if I am. Do you?'

'What?'

'Like me.'

'Course I do.'

She seemed greatly relieved. 'That's all right then.'

'I'm going home soon.'

'It's a bit early yet. Only quarter to four. Wait a bit and we'll go together.'

'No, I mean London. Going home properly. I'm going back.'

'Oh.' The imbecile smile vanished.

'When?'

'Any day now. I'm not sure. Soon though.'

'Oh.'

'I thought I ought to tell you.'

'Why me?'

'I don't know really.'

She laughed a ribald, most unfeminine laugh.

'Shall I tell you what's wrong with you? You take everything too seriously.'

'I know.'

'If you know, why do you do it?'

'I don't know.'

'You just said you did.'

'Come on. Let's get back. The boys in the band will be wondering what's happened to me.'

'Let them wait,' she said, and returned her attentions to the bottle. When she had drained its contents she looked at me for a long moment, twiddling the empty bottle in her two hands.

'I'll miss you when you've gone.'

She nestled against me and said in a wheedling voice, 'Why

can't you stay down here? With me. You don't have to go back do you? Not really. Stay with me.'

'All right,' I said. 'You've talked me into it. I'll stay down here with you.'

She recoiled from me as if I had punched her in the face.

'For God's sake, you're not serious?'

'Not really,' I told her, laughing despite myself. 'I really do have to go back.'

'Anyway, I'll miss you when you've gone.'

'No you won't, not really.'

'No, I know, but it's nice to pretend.'

We sat there silent for a few minutes, staring at the opposite wall, and then I rose from the sofa.

'I'm going back. I feel like playing.'

'You're too drunk to play. Sit here till your head clears.'

'No. Come on.'

But she was right. I got as far as the bandstand, but for a long time I was not quite able to raise my instrument high enough to get my lips round the mouthpiece. Eventually I gave it up and sat on the wooden chair listening half-dazed to the music and the noise of the dancers. I have a vague recollection of Maxine sitting there next to me for a while, and then a disturbance on the floor connected somehow with a Chinese lantern which fell on to the screaming dancers and exploded with a loud pop. Some time after that I must have started playing again, vaguely aware that Maxine had gone and that the crowd in the room had thinned appreciably. The Chinese lanterns flung their yellow and orange suns at me. Laughing braying faces thrust themselves up and then dropped away to be replaced by more faces. Confetti fluttered in my face. Great looping parabolas of flung paper streamers cut wonderful turquoise and purple and cerise patterns in the air and I tried to play in sympathy with their slow undulations to the ground. Then there was a general all-enveloping sense of pinkness. The paper was so close to my face that I could hear it crackling as a disembodied hand waved it before me.

'I must be playing especially well now,' I thought to myself, 'otherwise why would they be shouting my name? I can't stop now, not in the middle of this great solo.'

But the pink paper and the shouting voices refused to melt away as the coloured streamers had done. Each time I opened my eyes, each time I took a great gasping breath of air, there was the pink paper, shouting my name.

'Tom! Tom! Stop a minute.'

Finally I gave up. No peace in this world for the dedicated artist. I focused my eyes on the figure before me. It was Landau. As he waved the pink sheet the tears streamed down his face. He was very drunk.

'Tom. It's happened. They went to fifty-one-and-nine-pence. Look. It's in the paper.'

I stared at him and then at the edition of the *Financial Times* with which he had been trying to catch my attention.

'There must be some mistake,' I said, sobering up now with every word. 'I looked myself this morning. They were still at eleven-and-three.'

'No, it's here, in black and white.'

'You mean black and pink. I looked myself this morning. You were with me in the kitchen, remember?'

'That was yesterday you fool. It's half past seven in the morning.'

I climbed down from the stage and sat in the nearest chair, my body trembling in every limb. A vague feminine presence at Landau's shoulder smiled glassily at me. Landau was still crying, and evidently oblivious of everyone in the room except the feminine presence and me.

'We've been looking for you all night. We've been over this town with a tooth-comb. It broke in the evening papers last night, but when we went to the Arcadia they said you'd been and gone. What happened to you? And why are you playing jazz this early in the morning? I've heard of keenness but this is ridiculous.'

'I'll explain later. Show me the paper.'

I took the newspaper from him and screwed my eyes up in an attempt to read the tiny print of the market quotations. Landau was absolutely right. 'Marine Filox,' it said, 'Fifty-one-and-ninepence', followed by a small plus sign and 'Forty-shillings-and-sixpence,' the amount by which each share had risen.

'What do we do now?' I asked, bewildered.

'I don't know about you but Olive and me are going to celebrate.'

The glassy smile grabbed his arm even tighter.

'We're going back to the bluebell wood. See you later—partner.'

Before I could protest he and Olive were half-running, half-staggering down the hall and through the door. I looked for Maxine after that, but she must finally have tired of waiting for me and gone her own way. Quite sober now, I packed my instrument in its case and walked down the hall, side-stepping the last few dancers, and taking care to avoid the débris of broken lanterns and champagne glasses littering the floor. The last thing I saw as I passed through the door was Willie, still asleep in his cardboard bed. I walked slowly through the morning crowds back to the house on the hill, drank several cups of black coffee and then fell into a dreamless sleep which ended with the local church bells at six o'clock that evening. I made more black coffee, and then took a stroll through the town, wondering why Landau and Maxine had left me to an empty house. As I passed the Town Hall, I saw that the bluebells on its front lawn were crushed, almost as though somebody had been rolling about in them.

21

THE OTHERS had all gone back to London. Landau, the last
to leave, had asked me to go with him but, without quite
knowing why, I had turned his offer down, which surprised
me as much as it did anybody. After nearly five months in
this town I had grown heartily sick of it, able to associate it
now only with the disturbing confusion of my experiences at
the Arcadia and the nervous ordeal of watching the market
prices. Now that it was all over I was eager for release. On
the other hand I was troubled by my own depressed mood,
no doubt a reaction against all the weeks of worry, and told
myself that perhaps a day or two alone in the town might
restore something of my equilibrium. In a way it was pleasant
to exercise my freedom by not taking it, but on the other
hand there was no practical reason for staying.

All around me were hints that I ought to be moving on. As
yet another season drew to its dying fall, the town's tempo was
noticeably slowing down. On my last morning I noticed the
ice-cream stands already putting up their shutters against the
coming winter squalls. Soon the proprietors would be off to
count their profits in suburban villas, planning an even bigger
turnover next year, pondering whether an increase in their
flavour range would justify itself with their accountants. On
the promenade were still a few would-be straggling celebrants.
Three young girls in paper hats wandered past me looking for
the parade which had melted away. They giggled as they
caught my eye. I felt like telling them they were too late, but
then I wondered, too late for what?

Out beyond the promenade rails the distant breakers were
still riding in on to the shingle under a sun which obstinately
refused to stop shining. I leaned over those rails for perhaps
the hundredth time that summer and contemplated the sadly
deserted beach and the indeterminate skyline. The bandstand
was closed, the Punch-and-Judy men had gone home to rest

up for the rigours of the Christmas season, and far out where the retreating breakers met the shoreline two young boys with orange faces were scraping the barnacles from the hull of a converted landing craft called *The Vulgar Boatman*. The sea threw back the blinding rays of the sun, just as it had that morning on the pier when we had hunted for chords in the glass-walled room and been driven by rain into the cool twilight of the darkened theatre. Then the season had been new and promised everything. Today only the sun and the sea were the same. I stood there considering the ritual of a last swim. Many times that summer I had galloped across the pebbles to meet surf that was too spent a force to do more than bathe my sweating limbs and slop a few mouthfuls of brine at me, leaving me magically refreshed and somehow revitalised against the monumental stillness of the world awaiting me up beyond the strand of the toffee apples and pin-tables. But then I remembered that my swimming trunks had already gone up to London in Landau's luggage, so instead I waved a casual farewell to the sea.

I went back to the house, made fair copies of some reviews for Knowles, and then took myself and my bags in a taxi to the station. For the first time that summer the left luggage office looked half-empty. On the day I arrived my saxophone case had been packed in among thousands of portmanteaux and carrier bags. Now, as I watched my one suitcase and that same saxophone case placed in the void between a bundle of fishing rods and a tartan dinner suit, I kept trying to convince myself that my departure was not the intensely dramatic action I felt it to be. All the way up in the taxi, a short but symbolic journey, I had gazed out at the buildings as if determined to memorise their shape and location. Now, as I stood in the station forecourt and told myself that this was all absurd, that I would be back in this town a hundred times, I thought of the still non-existent orchestras whose coaches would bring me here. But it was no use. My arrival at the station persisted in presenting itself as the entry of a funeral cortège at the cemetery. So the corpse left the station and took a slow, lingering walk down the hill back to the sea, past the café owners sweeping out their forecourts and putting up their deflationary winter tariffs, past coffee bars still open but deserted, past fish-and-chip emporiums of gilt and marble and neon still hoping to tempt late-comers to the carnival. And there, waiting at the bottom of the hill as if a concrete manifestation of my new status was Wheeler's. So I went inside for lunch, leaving my astonished waiter a fifteen-shilling tip just to show him how little money meant to me now.

It was as I came out of the restaurant, already regretting my rash act of patronage, as I stared out at that sea which was just as much a promise of enchantment now as it ever had been in childhood, that I admitted to myself why I had stayed on. Bella Herbert. There must be something I could say to her, some word or gesture that would consummate so unsatisfactory a relationship, although I had no idea what shape it might take. A man cannot simply walk out of some-body else's life like this, I told myself. It wasn't done. It wasn't sophisticated. On the other hand, what could she pos-sibly want with me? With some relief I dismissed the idea of calling on her and walked resolutely in the opposite direc-tion, towards Hove, and for a while the disturbing theme of Bella Herbert was banished from my thoughts. Landau and I had hardly explored this end of town, a subtle tribal instinct telling us to keep away from territory where strangers might turn out not to be strangers after all.

A generation before, my own relatives had sported on these same beaches, forming and breaking adolescent alliances, revelling in salt-water friendships that would surely never die, stimulated by the sea and the surf into a kind of tem-porary sanity. A few of their shadowy deeds were embalmed in the blurred snapshots I had gazed upon with a profound sense of mystery and pastness in my childhood, staring at the pathetic figures in the hope that they might give up secrets I knew now to be non-existent, except for the most baffling secret of all, the passage of time. I stopped to lean against a low wall enclosing a small flowering green, and recognised it as the same wall that one of my aunts had leaned against in a vanished youth of thirty years before, smiling hopefully at posterity in clothes that posterity would quickly learn to laugh at. In the photograph, the white walls, betrayed by the box Brownies of the 1930s, had been sepia, like Ronald Colman in 'The Prisoner of Zenda', and I remembered thinking when I first gazed at that photograph that the seaside must truly be a wonderful place if even the walls were suntanned. Perhaps these same aunts and uncles had shuffled round the floor at the Arcadia. Certainly the place looked ancient enough. I felt embarrassed, as though the laughing shades of my own past were watching me. Five minutes later I was sitting on the top deck of one of those open buses which ran along the road to Bella Herbert's house.

We wheezed past the pitch-and-putt course whose innocent deceptions Landau had never mastered, empty now except for the irrelevance of two distant figures on the rise walking to the next hole. On the downs outside St Dunstan's a blind man followed his dog across the grass. Landau's pier fell behind and out of sight, and before I was prepared for action I found myself obliged to jump off the bus, which had stopped a few yards from Bella's house. All my misgivings returned. What would I say when she opened the door? I told myself that I was a rich man now and that rich men never have to bother about such things. *Savoir faire*, as Blitski always used to say, was simply a question of your bank balance. Yet I knew it was not quite the bravado of money which impelled me to walk up the drive and ring the bell.

Its tinkle echoed through the house but no footsteps responded. I rang again and waited, half-hoping now that Bella's absence would reprieve me. Still no sign of life from inside the house. I walked over to the side gate and looked into the garden. Under the single apple tree, its crabbed fruit still pendulous, a man stood with his back to me, peering up at the windows for any sign of life, as I had. I recognised him even before he turned. I called out and he came running along the side path and through the gate. When he saw it was only me he looked crushed.

'Oh, it's you,' he said in tones of bitter disenchantment. 'I thought . . .'

'Bertie? What are you doing here?'

On his face was the saddest and yet the most comical expression I had seen all summer, as though he were numbed by the force of a tragedy so absurd that even he, its victim, could not help seeing the humour of it. He ignored my question and looked again at the house in disbelief. I spoke this time more in an attempt to shake him out of his trance than from any hope of getting any sense out of him.

'What a surprise finding you here.'

'Why shouldn't I be here? After all, it's my house.'

'This is Bella Herbert's place. You know, the one who . . .'

'I know. I know.'

He walked slowly past me, hands deep in the pockets of his unbuttoned camel's hair overcoat. I strode after him.

'Where is she? Where's Bella? Do you know?'

'Gone.'

'Gone? Where? How do you know?'

'Gone. Hopped it. Cleared off. Without a word. Not even a note. I looked.'

'Maybe she just slipped out for ten minutes. Let's wait around.'

'She's gone for good, I tell you. She's cleaned half the place out.'

'Were you a friend of hers?'

He gave me a pained look not entirely untinged with pride.

'I mean, did you know her well?'

'Not well enough, son, not well enough. I knew I shouldn't have let it go this far. Eleven weeks' rent. I knew that was too much.'

I could see he was beginning to enjoy playing the role of the betrayed sugar daddy.

'Bella told me it was her house.'

'Well, I'm telling you it's mine. You can take your choice, me or her. She took a lease for the rest of this year. Still, I suppose she paid me in a way. Oh, Bella.'

'Bertie, I'm shocked,' and I was.

'That's funny. That you should be shocked, I mean. I thought the whole town knew. Coming into the Arcadia practically every night like that. And all those stupid decoys she left with after the last dance. I thought everyone knew. It just shows you how much you can get away with when your luck's in.'

Something occurred to him for the first time. He turned sharply on me.

'Don't tell me you were . . .'

'Not me,' I said hastily. 'We were just acquaintances.' After all, Bertie was still a bandleader, and you never knew when you might be in need of a bandleader.

'What were you doing here anyway?'

'Just saying good-bye. I'm going home this afternoon. I just wanted to pay my respects, that's all.'

'Mind you,' he said, pushing through the front gate into the road. 'I've had the feeling there was something funny going on for a couple of weeks now. Nothing I could put my finger on, mind you.'

'How do you mean?'

'I'm not sure. But I've got an instinct about these things. There was definitely something brewing. She was different somehow.'

'You mean another man?'

'Could be, although I happen to know that Bella's been faithful to me the whole time she's been here.'

'I'm sure you're right,' I murmured.

'I think she might have met somebody with money. It would have to be someone with money if it was anybody.'

'You reckon she was one of those, a gold-digger?'

'Bella was much too broke to run off like this. To get away she must have come into some money, God knows how. She could run through cash like nobody I ever saw. She must have made a quick killing somehow. I don't know. I wouldn't put anything past that girl.'

'Well, I wouldn't worry too much. There'll be another batch of them coming down next season.'

'What about my eleven weeks' rent? Tell me that. How do I get that back? And my tea service and my fire-irons and that Georgian mirror on the drawing-room wall, the cameos, those two paintings . . .'

'Christ, she must have left town in a pantechnicon.'

'Never mind,' he said, 'teach me a lesson. I don't think. Come on. I've got the car. Want a lift back into town?'

We drove slowly along the coast road, Bertie preoccupied at the wheel while I smoked and looked out at the sea. Just once, as we glided round a bend in the road which put the house out of our vision, he looked round, in case Bella might be standing on the roof. But then the sight of more familiar streets seemed to lift his spirits and he turned his attention from his troubles to mine, switching roles to become the wise old professional.

'You know, if you'd have played your cards right, you could still be with me at the Arcadia. You should have behaved yourself, you know.'

'I know. Only things just kind of happened.'

'In this business you don't do those kind of things. You shouldn't have done it, not to me.'

'Yes, I'm sorry about that.'

He glanced at me again. 'Anything to go back to?'

'Not exactly. Only I'm not particularly . . .'

We drew up outside the back entrance to the Arcadia. As I jumped out Bertie said, 'Do me a favour will you? Just don't come back here next year, that's all. I couldn't face all that again.'

We shook hands and I thanked him once again for employing me. He put his free hand deep in his trouser pocket and drew out two five-pound notes.

'What's this for?'

'It's in lieu of notice. Go on, take it.'

'But I got the sack. I'm not entitled to it.'

'What are you, a moralist or something? Don't be a fool, take it. Look, the firm will never know. I'll put it down to expenses. Me, I wouldn't give you a penny. But as it's the firm's money, you might as well have it.'

He thrust the notes into my hand and disappeared inside the Arcadia. A policeman gave me a suspicious look as I stood there in the street clutching the notes and laughing wildly.

I walked slowly up the hill to the house for the last time, trying to remember with every step what it was at the back of my mind which kept trying to tell me there was something I ought to do before I caught my train, something I had forgotten about but which would need to be done before the season was quite over. But I couldn't think what it might be, and finally when I was standing in my room I gave up trying. I glanced around me to make sure I had not left anything behind, silently bidding farewell to this little cell that had housed me through the tumultuous days of the summer. If

I had possessed a camera I think I might have photographed it just for old times' sake, so that in twenty years' time I could point to it and say to my plutocratic friends, 'That is the bed and that is the dresser on which my present vast fortunes were founded.' I closed the window and tightened the dripping tap. Then I made the bed and stepped back, making sure there was no sign of my tenancy except for the note of thanks addressed to Mrs Stewart, who had disappeared to Suffolk to stay with friends days ago.

I made my way down the shadowed passage to Landau's room. The snapshot was still stuck in the dressing-table mirror, but knowing Landau I guessed that the oversight must be intentional. While I was peering at the indistinct features of this anonymous brunette I noticed a small black object which must have slipped down behind the dressing-table and become wedged against the wall. I squatted down and dragged it out. It was Landau's diary, the one he had acquired cut price on the day he had become a professional. I flipped through its pages. The entry for 30 April read, ' I must practise more and chase girls more.' On the last September page there was still that £90 ringed round. The rest of the pages were blank. I threw the diary down on the bed, and then, as I was about to close the door behind me, had second thoughts and went back for it. I shoved it into my jacket pocket, making a vague resolution to return it to its owner the next time I saw him. But I never did.

I went downstairs, glanced into the back garden to take a last look at Landau's arm-chairs, and then passed through the little courtyard for the last time into the street. As I walked towards the station I suddenly remembered what it was that had been nagging at my mind, that one last rite to close the proceedings. I turned and walked rapidly back to the pier, passed through the turnstiles, free this time, and tapped on the closed door of Vivienne's booth. From inside came the clanging of a bucket and the scrape of a scrubbing brush on the deal floor. After a moment the brush plonked into the pail and the top half of the door opened. Vivienne looked out belligerently, her hair tied up in a kerchief and a broad smut of soot across her pinafore.

' Well, if it isn't the future tycoon. Haven't you gone yet?'

'Just going. My train leaves in half an hour. Here,' and I gave her Bertie's two five-pound notes.

'What's this for?'

'Next time your grandfather shows up, give him a night on the town for me, will you?'

Then I went and caught my train.

PART THREE

Epilogue

I was lying in bed one afternoon looking for work when the phone rang. It was Landau, and his voice, once so integral a part of my own life, sounded now almost like a call from the dead. More than two years had passed since the episode of Marine Filox, and although nothing had been said between us to tilt the subtle balance of our relationship, both of us knew it was over. At first, of course, we had both insisted on behaving as though nothing had changed, and even spent a couple of evenings at his house under the pretence of trying to write songs together. But the atmosphere in the household was even more strained than before, possibly due to the fact that every time Landau's father asked for his money back, Landau kept telling him it was 'tied up', which made me feel so guilty that I could hardly swallow Mrs Landau's tea and cake. But it made no difference. After a few weeks Landau tired of our pointless little charade and began to drift further and further afield in pursuit of his own hare-brained schemes to enlarge his capital, festering rapidly in a current account at a local bank. When I heard his voice over the phone again that afternoon I realised that it was already more than a year since we last met. Could it have been that long ago? Yes, I remembered now, the last morning of the court case, when after the verdict had been delivered he had stood feet astride the Strand pavements and laughed insanely while I watched him and tried vainly to re-main sober. Now that he was on the other end of the wire I found it difficult to equate him with the questing corsair of Brighton beach.

'Hello, Landau. What's happening?'

'Listen, this is important. No, don't interrupt. Big deal coming up. You want to be involved?'

I considered for a moment. It was the middle of March, and all I had in the book was a factory dance on Easter Saturday, a wedding in May, and a short tour with a Latin-American group later in the summer.

'All right,' I said. 'I'm game. What's the deal?'

'Good. I knew I could rely on you. Only I can't talk about it over the phone. Top secret. Look, I'll ring you back.'

But he never did, although I have not the slightest doubt he intended to. Whatever you said about Landau, his intentions were always of the best. And perhaps it was just as well that he never phoned back. I was by no means sure I was capable of sustaining any more burdens as heavy as the one he had humped on our backs in Brighton. Besides, probably all he wanted from me this time was capital, although he knew perfectly well what had happened to my cut of the Filox profits. After giving Maxine £500 to buy a third share in the restaurant next to the Arcadia, there had been just enough left to pay the costs and damages in the libel suit Happiness eventually brought against me for the letter in Knowles' paper. Landau blamed Blitski for the whole thing, and although he was right, I was inclined not to feel too badly about it. After all, Blitski had dreamed all his life of crashing the market, and suddenly to find himself in sole possession of an improbable but entirely true story about jazz musicians on the Stock Exchange, must have put too great a strain on his sense of loyalty. Primly rejecting his rightful share of the profits, Blitski had gone instead to Fleet Street, where, after hawking his story around for a few days, he had finally sold it to the highest bidder. It was only two days after the news broke in the *Daily Mirror*, complete with a reproduction of that same photograph which had once done duty at the entrance to the pier ballroom, that the writ for libel arrived from Happiness's solicitors. Why it was me being sued alone and not Landau too I never discovered, although it may have had something to do with the fact that on the day the story broke Landau had turned himself into a limited liability company and transferred all his holdings into an organisation called 'Lease-Len'. In any case it turned out to be a return to sanity for me and the start of an erratic but not entirely unsuccessful career for Blitski, who drifted in his own chaotic way from writing news stories to concocting three-act plays which I am sure he thought were profound but which the London critics hailed as the most scintillating social comedies since the early Noël Coward.

As for Victor, he was still embarked on his crusade in pursuit of the holy paper handkerchief, secure in the knowledge that his share of the spoils was earning him 4 per cent in the Co-operative Building Society. Nobody ever needed respectability more than Victor, and what is there in the world more respectable than 4 per cent? As to the price he had paid for this nest-egg, it was small really when you came to think of it. The decision to dissociate himself from his three partners was not the end of the world, for him or the partners, and who knows, the excruciating sense of guilt might pass one day. But for the moment the three of us were like strangers accidentally encountered in the corridors of a particularly notorious brothel, and just about as desirable as companions. Never mind. I was still doing what I could for that vicarious ambition of Victor's, still struggling to find out what it was that transformed a limping amateur into a glib professional.

I slid out of bed and opened a large black leather case lying on its side under the window. Its newness still made me itch, after two weeks, to handle its contents. As I snapped open the gleaming silver locks, I thought how curious it was that Landau should have phoned this afternoon of all afternoons, less than twelve hours after the last of the ripples from the Filox whirlpool had started its outward journey. Last night I had been playing with a society orchestra in a West End hotel. It was one of those boring affairs where the slightest deviation from the written text would have induced an acute spasm of palsy on the part of the bandleader. When the interval came I spurned the free coffee and chicken sandwiches, descending instead to the hotel foyer, where I chose an arm-chair in the corner from which to watch the parade passing by. I had not given a thought to Filox since the court case, but now, as I lounged back, virtually invisible, I was conscious of a sudden wild wave of exultation that I was still the beggar at the feast, still the outsider uncommitted by the baffling money-splashing complexities of the charade being enacted before me. A commissionaire in the uniform of an Afghanistan field marshal manipulated the swing doors.

A supervisory entity in black jacket and striped trousers hovered solicitously around nothing. Lift boys dumped genuine pigskin suit-cases on to the muted carpets, and flustered girls feverishly jammed plugs into switchboards as though injecting vital fluid into the veins of those on the unseen end of the line. It was almost like the opening of one of Blitski's masterpieces, except that Blitski would never have thought of the subtle symbolism of the dwarf who now came marching through the foyer disguised as the boy on the biscuit tin, and shouting something I was unable to distinguish. As the dwarf came closer, people near me stopped in mid-sentence, hoping the name he was calling might be theirs, but it was not until he had walked briskly to within three feet of me that I heard what name he was calling.

'William Marshall, please. Mr William Marshall.'

The boy marched on, and soon his voice was drowned in the murmurous sea of small talk. I watched, but nobody ran after him. In a few minutes he was back again.

'Mr Marshall, please. Mr William Marshall.'

Then he vanished into the restaurant.

I sat there, tensed now, with my eye on the reception desk. After two or three minutes the dwarf re-emerged from the restaurant with two people in tow, the woman first, holding her long skirts clear of the dusty carpeted floor, then the man, in an evening dress a size too small for him. He was of medium height but the liberality of his waistline gave him a stumpy, overbalanced appearance. He was flushed and out of breath. As he navigated the desert between the restaurant doors and the reception desk, I heard Maxine's voice again, speaking in a kitchen fifty miles and a million light years away. ' . . . as a matter of fact, he's got a pot chest . . . sort of blotchy face, with those funny little purple veins round his bugle . . . about five feet eight.'

So this was the great business brain so hopelessly out-manoeuvred by a dumb waitress and a half-mad saxophonist. He looked even more hopelessly out-manoeuvred now, with Bella Herbert's arm threaded firmly through his. I suppose I could have gone up to her and said, 'Bertie Fields says where's the money you owe him?' or something like that, but that would have been uncharitable. It would also have been tactless, because the brunette who was singing with the orchestra that night, and who had talked the bandleader into booking me in the first place, had been standing at my shoulder for the past three minutes watching me studying the couple at the reception desk.

'At it again, I see,' she said, sitting on the arm of my chair. 'It's my fault for letting you out of my sight, I suppose.'

'Don't know what you're talking about.'

'You sneak away and in two minutes you're ogling every bird in the hotel. Come on. They're waiting to start.'

As we walked upstairs to the ballroom, my fellow-worker said to me, 'You look worried. Anything on your mind?'

'As a matter of fact,' I said, being perfectly truthful as always, 'I was wondering where I'm going to raise the loot to pay the next instalment on my new horn.'

'You musicians,' she said. 'You're all mad, the whole bloody lot of you.'